Uncle Sweet Uncle

A Novel

By

Dominick Tartamella

Uncle Sweet Uncle   Dominick Tartamella

This book is a work of fiction. Names, characters, places, and incidents are
the product of the authors imagination. Any resemblance to actual
persons,living or dead or events are entirely coincidental.

SalDom Publications

ISBN:0615567630
ISBN 13:978-0615567631

For Mom and Dad.

1

Business As Usual

It was ten pm on a December night in the small town of Mesapeena,
New Hampshire. The way the snow flurries fell to the ground was
reminiscent to something out of a Norman Rockwell painting. Deep past the
tree filled woods lied a large abandoned warehouse that sat silently in the
snowy wonderland. The peacefulness of the night was broken by the sound
of Elvis Presley singing "Blue Christmas" through a big black Cadillac's
radio speakers. As the car pulled up to the warehouse it swerved slightly
before parking, the head lights dimmed. Two shady looking men (in their late
twenties, early thirties the oldest) sat in the car looking a bit eager. The man
sitting shotgun abruptly shut the radio off and shot a dirty look at the driver.
The driver sighed. "What a scrooge you are, huh?" The man sitting shotgun
looked at the driver dumbfounded. "We have to get into character dick.
There's nothing intimidating about Christmas music." The driver nodded in
agreement. "Why the fuck did we have to take my car anyway? Your truck
would've been better in this weather." The man sitting shotgun rolled his
eyes. "We can't let this guy think we don't have the stuff. What big time drug

dealers drive around in a beat up, piece of shit pick up truck?" The driver giggled ever so lightly. "I don't know man, I've got a bad feeling about this." A certain seriousness took over the driver's face as he spoke.

There were more than enough reasons for the driver to be having second thoughts about what he and his old bud were about to do. For starters they weren't drug dealers, not in the least. The guy sitting shotgun, Mike, was a high school drop out who worked at the local Burger King and though he was head manager and was probably making pretty good dough, it wasn't quite good enough. You see Mike always wanted to live like the Scarface or Cagney type (Cagney in his gangster pictures of course, not Yankee Doodle Dandy). He didn't want to be the nine to five schmoe who had to actually work for his money. At a young age he did pretty petty crimes here and there but deep down he wanted more, eventually he got arrested for a little harmless grand theft auto. After doing a reasonably light sentence and gaining a record, he applied for a job at the home of the whopper. Lately he's been looking for a big change to help break away and tonight he has that chance.

The driver on the other hand is a different story all together. His name's Billy and his strength and weakness is that he's one hell of a stand up guy. At any given moment he would be willing to do anything for his friends, which is exactly how he got himself into this little predicament. Billy went to college for a few years and took some business courses like many undecided college students do. He met the girl of his dreams there and after a little accident he became a father. He dropped out of school and got a job at TD bank and each day he does what he has to, to provide for his family. One hell of a guy indeed, it really is a shame he had to get mixed up in this mess. Just another instance of being in the wrong place at the wrong time.

Billy was now beginning to look concerned, he was thinking about the fact that neither him or his bud had any idea who this guy they were meeting really was. If they're pretending to be big time drug dealers, how do they know this guy wasn't pretending himself. What if he's a god damn cop? Jesus Christ that would be something, Billy began to ponder. Then your wife and two year old could be greeted by officers later tonight, officers with the bad news that your husband was arrested. Shit, they'd probably even think they were really big time drug dealers and rip apart the house looking for some of the nonexistent stash. Mike turned to Billy and seemed to read his mind with one glance of his now sweaty face. "This guy's just some fuckin' loser junkie, desperate for some shit. What could possibly go wrong?" Billy was slightly reassured by his friends words. No way he's a cop, he can't be, he said he met

6

the guy ripping lines in the bathroom of a shanty night club, Billy told himself. What cop does that? Not even an undercover cop would do that, would they? Before Billy could think about it any further an even older, dark blue Cadillac became visible as it came slowly down the road facing the warehouse. Mike turned to Billy with a slick grin. "This is it, let's go." Billy turned the car off, both men stepped out into the snow and made their way into the warehouse.

The blue Cadillac pulled up and parked about twenty feet away from the other caddy. A shadowy figure stepped out of the car, an average sized man, about five ten. He wasn't the biggest man on campus but that made no difference. The man walked slowly toward the warehouse. Actually it was more of a monstrous strut, his arms were extended slightly and swinging at his sides. His bearded face began to form in the moonlight and his blackish gray hair was brushed back in the neatest way. His eyes were dark and they went well with a face that was cold and grim. He walked toward the warehouse and clinched his snug brown jacket collar to shield his bare skin from the winds unwanted chill. For a moment he looked like any ordinary man going about his ordinary business, but he was hardly that. This man is Paulie Aldo, he is fifty five and he is what some would refer to as a homicidal maniac.

7

Inside the warehouse Billy sat on a crate smoking a cigarette while Mike unzipped a large duffel bag. Inside was one small bag full of cocaine, underneath the drugs were five towels which gave the bag a bulky look. Suddenly there were two knocks at the door and the two men could see the blurry silhouette of their visitor. They gave each other a cautious glance before Mike zipped up the duffel bag and made his way to the door. Billy stood up from the crate and placed the bag on it before assuming an intimidating position next to the crate. Mike opened the door and Paulie peeked in like a curious child. "Hey there pal." Paulie spoke like an old friend. Relief came over Mike as he let the man in. There was no way this guy was a cop, he was too much of a character, Mike thought to himself. Paulie grinned as he entered the warehouse, Billy stared and thoughts similar to the ones Mike had just had eased his mind. Paulie turned to Billy "What are you trying to do, intimidate me?" Billy swallowed his throat but tried his best to keep looking tough. What's this guy's deal?, Billy wondered. Paulie's deal? It had always been the same, business as usual. To Billy and especially to Mike, Paulie seemed like an easy target for what they had planned. They'd give the junkie loser a taste of the blow, get the money and right when he's feeling comfortable and happy to have his stuff, bust the guns out on him. What will he do? He can't do anything, he'll probably crap his pants.

8

Ten thousand was a lot of money, it was worth the risk, wait what risk? There was none. This guy was going to get his ass robbed and that was all there was to it. For the amount of coke he wanted he had it coming to him, he should have known better. One thing that had definitely crossed both Billy and Mike's minds was that if this guy was such a junkie loser, where the hell did he get the ten beans? Paulie had told Mike a few days earlier that he had some people who owed him favors and he'd get the money one way or another and this had ended their financial curiosities. But all that coke for one guy? That's a hell of an addiction. However, when the men went over it in there heads it was really not that much of a problem, they were strapped and he wasn't, well he at least didn't look like he was. So even if worst case scenario he didn't have the money they could just beat him to a pulp, leave him for dead and be on their way. If he was a cop... well they already ruled that one out, there was no way he was. As for the whole leaving him for dead thing, that was another problem entirely. The guy's still hadn't figured out what they were going to do after the whole deal was through. I mean they weren't killers, though Mike had already decided he would do it if he had to. Should they just let him go? Maybe the beating within seconds of his life was the best choice. When it came down to it, maybe they should have planned ahead, gave this thing a little more thought. Maybe they could have even

9

picked up a copy of "Drug Dealing For Dummies".

Mike quickly explained to Paulie that Billy was just his partner looking out for his best interest. Paulie had a look on his face that seemed to be saying maybe I should have brought someone for that myself. But overall Paulie didn't seem to care all that much and he turned his attention to the duffel bag on top of the crate. "That the stuff?" Mike smirked as he began to think, this was going to be easier than he expected. "Billy, give him a taste." Billy wiped some excess sweat from his forehead and slowly unzipped the duffel bag. Sitting right on top of the abundance of towels was the lone bag of coke, Billy threw it to Paulie and he caught it effortlessly. Something about that catch, Billy thought. A junkie would have probably missed that or at least caught it a little more sloppy, Billy realized he was being ridiculously paranoid and dismissed the thought. Paulie raised the bag of coke to Mike and gave him sort of salute, similar to something one might do while toasting a drink. Paulie ripped a hole in the small plastic bag, held it to his nose and proceeded to take a giant, aggressive snort. Billy and Mike watched in awe and slight disgust as Paulie snorted the hell out of the bag.

After Paulie finished the bag, he rubbed his nose viciously with his index finger and thumb. "What a fuckin' rush!" Mike smiled and thought about how much of a fucking mess this guy was, just another stupid junkie with no idea of what kind of shit storm was about to hit him. As soon as they had sight of the money, it would be go time. Paulie finished rubbing his nostrils and regained whatever composure he had in the first place. "That's some heavy fucking shit guys." Neither man looked all that amused but they gave their casual pitiful smirks anyway. "Glad you like it." Mike said while he looked around curiously. "Now as for the money." Paulie pulled a handkerchief out of his jacket pocket and began to wipe his nose, he remained silent as if Mike hadn't said a thing. After another moment he folded the handkerchief and put it back into his pocket, a light sprinkle of coke was still smeared on his nose but he didn't seem to notice. The two men stared at Paulie bewildered by the fact that he still hadn't replied, they glanced at each other in disbelief. Finally, Mike turned back to Paulie and spoke loud and sternly. "The Money! Where is it?" Billy seemed a bit surprised by the anger in his friends voice but remembered they had to be intimidating. Paulie rubbed his nose a few more times before answering. "Yea I got it." Paulie looked at both men as if expecting them to take his word for it. Billy was now staring at Paulie with a very serious look. "Do you have it on you?". The light smirk that had been on Paulie's face the whole time had now faded. "I told you I got it." Billy sighed and Mike burst into the conversation. "Let's see it then!"

11

Billy began to feel uneasy about the situation and Paulie's calmness was making him even more nervous. He was getting so worried that he thought about pulling his gun on Paulie just to be safe, the man was so calm, almost too calm and there was something not quite right about that. Billy quickly remembered what Mike had said, no guns until the cash was shown and fought off the urge. He took a deep breath and tried to calm his nerves. Mike was also starting to become a bit nervous, although his anger outweighed it significantly. Paulie still hadn't shown the money and for the last minute or so he'd been having a stare down with Mike. If Paulie was going to try something, Mike was ready to blow him into oblivion. Paulie's foolish smirk returned to his face. "How about this, you show me the rest of the stuff and then I'll show you the money." Paulie spoke like he was trying to finagle a car salesmen into throwing new mats into the deal, he seemed to hardly even be phased by this potentially dangerous situation.

Both Billy and Mike were beginning to feel threatened by Paulie's lack of fear or stupidity. So Mike decided to come back with a counteroffer in the most plausible of tones. "Get the fucking money man! Or we're going to have problems!" Billy swallowed his throat expecting the worst, Paulie stared and seemed to completely ignore the relevance of Mike's previous statement. "You know, I really do get the feeling you guy's are trying to intimidate me." Mike picked up a small crate that sat on the floor and smashed it, sending the room into an uproar. Just as Billy was thinking of pulling his gun, he noticed his friends was already pointed at Paulie. "You want to be intimidated? How's this for intimidation?" Mike was now as stern as he could be. Paulie flinched ever so slightly as Billy's barrel came pointing at his stomach. Both their guns were identical and resembled the PPK's from the old James Bond movies (they got a good two for one deal off a guy Mike did some time with).

With two guns now pointing at him, Paulie's calmness seemed to fade away and spots of sweat began to form on his forehead. "Ok...Alright...Calm down." Paulie stuttered nervously as he spoke. Mike began to move closer and rested the top of his barrel against Paulie's warm skull, Paulie closed his eyes and took a deep breath. "If you don't tell me where the money is I'm going to blow your fucking head off, got it?" Billy watched in awe as his friend changed into someone he had never seen before, he looked down at the gun in his own hand and felt sick to his stomach. What was he doing here? He had a wife and kid at home, a family that relied on him and here he was risking his life for some bull shit drug deal. That was it, he wanted this to be over, he couldn't wait to tell Mike he was never doing anything like this

13

again. Another thing he couldn't wait for was the sound of his wife's voice, once he walked through that doorway and heard that voice it would all be better. He began to fantasize about the relief of walking into his house but his mind came crashing back to reality as Paulie begged. "I got it, I got it, it's in my trunk. I don't wanna' die, ok? Just calm down." Mike looked as pissed as ever and hoped Paulie was telling the truth for his own sake. Billy on the other hand had actually began to feel bad for Paulie, he was just some addict who was probably trying to pull a fast one on Mike. When he realized Mike had brought a friend his plans were ruined and he didn't know what to do. Now he was helpless.

"We're going for a little walk to get that money." Mike said as he pushed Paulie toward the door. Paulie moved towards the door and the three men headed outside. Mike and Billy began to follow Paulie to his car. Mike's gun barrel was now pointed right to the back of Paulie's neck. At this point Billy had just about stopped worrying and just wanted to be done, he trailed behind the two men and carried his gun at his side ever so carelessly. There was really nothing to be worried about now, Paulie was caught and he either had the money or didn't. Mike was fed up and if he didn't get the cash Billy was pretty sure he'd beat Paulie until the snow on the ground looked like a cherry slushee. The snow was really coming down now and the wind blew

14

the flakes all around making all three men squint as they continued to the car. Paulie put his hands in his pockets (probably for warmth) and Mike snapped at him immediately. "Put your fucking hands up!" Paulie threw his arms up over his head instantly. "I wasn't... I wasn't doing anything."

As the three men came up to the snow covered car Paulie began to whine to himself. "Oh my god, how the hell did I get myself into this situation...These fucking drugs really got a hold on me." Billy stared at Paulie with a look of pity as Mike interrupted the one sided conversation. "Shut the fuck up junkie!" Paulie sighed and pleaded nervously. "I'm sorry, please don't hurt me." "If the money's in there, nobody's gonna' get hurt, ok?" Billy said compassionately and Mike glanced at him with a look of disappointment. "It better be in there, or your dead." Paulie swallowed his throat at Mike's words. "It is, it is... I promise." Paulie stopped walking as he came up to the trunk of his blue Cadillac. His hands were still surrendered to the air and the pistol that Mike held was still close to his neck. All three men stood silent for a moment in the snowfall. Mike gave Paulie a forceful shove toward the trunk and he stumbled before landing on the top of it. His bare freezing fingers dipped into the thick layer of snow that sat on the car as he caught his fall. "Open it!" Mike said. Paulie frantically searched his pocket for the keys, and when he finally did find them he was jittering so much he

15

nearly dropped them in the snow.

"Let's go!" Mike shouted as he felt his patience in the man beginning to fade. Paulie was now trembling, mostly from fright and partly from the cold weather. His hands continued to shake as he bent down to stick the key in the slot. Paulie squinted his eyes trying to block off the flakes of snow that were partially blinding him and pushed the key forward. His jittery hand missed the hole completely and he dropped the keys on the white ground. Paulie picked them up just as quickly and heard a sigh of annoyance come from behind him. "Get out of the way!" Mike screamed before ripping the cold,wet keys out of Paulie's hands. When Mike had the keys safely clinched in his fist, he lifted the butt of his gun and smashed it into the back of Paulie's skull. Paulie moaned   and fell down to the ground with a thump. It was obvious from Billy's dismayed expression that he was disturbed by this. "Jesus." Billy cried. Mike smirked and moved towards the trunk. Paulie was now rolling over in the snow holding the back of his head, grunting to himself. Billy moved towards the injured man as if to help him. "Leave him there, screw him!" Mike commanded and Billy followed. "What the hell was that for...come on." Paulie said from the ground. "Shut up before I do you anymore damage." Mike said as he stuck the key into the trunks slot and tried to turn it.

16

As Mike continued to struggle with the key he realized that it must have either been jammed or frozen from the weather. "This God damn thing is frozen shut, Billy give me a hand." Billy rolled his eyes, the last thing he wanted to do was help Mike anymore than he already had, he sighed and reluctantly walked over to the trunk. Paulie began to crawl slowly away from the car, Billy and Mike who were now both facing the trunk took no notice to this. Mike gave the key one last attempt before Billy nudged him out of the way. "Let me give it a shot." Billy said as Mike moved out of the way. Paulie was now about five feet away from the men and the car, he looked back toward them cautiously as he continued further through the snow. Billy began to play around with the key, shaking it back in forth with hopes to trigger something. Finally after a minute of fiddling Billy felt something click and the key turned slightly. A relieved smile crossed his face. "I think I got It." "Thank God." Mike said with a sigh of relief. Billy attempted to lift the trunk open but could feel some friction coming from it. "I think this is a little frozen too, give me a hand." Billy said and Mike came right to his friends aid.

Billy and Mike lifted the trunk and the moment they did, two massive rottweilers jumped into their arms. Both men screamed out in terror and utter

17

disbelief as they fell to the ground, instantly dropping their guns. The two behemoth's began going to work on the men. They chomped and devoured chunks of flesh from the men like two sharks eating a couple of seals. Both men continued to shriek, their loud screams now full of agony. Paulie began to laugh as he picked himself off the ground. "Sorry about that boys, these puppies haven't eaten in a while." Paulie's tone was now as calm as it ever was, he was no longer trembling nor sobbing. Paulie reached down towards the bloody, snowy chaos that was happening before his eyes and grabbed the two guns. The two dogs were a bit too busy to be bothered by Paulie and continued their feast without so much as a glance. Paulie casually tossed one gun into the trunk and closed it, he continued to hold the other tightly at his side.

Judging from the fact that one of the rottweilers was now biting down on Mike's throat and blood was gushing onto the animals furry snout, (not to mention that Mike had stopped moving completely) Paulie decided the man was dead. Billy, whose legs were still being gnawed was alive and sobbing. Paulie gently brushed some snow out of his hair and moved towards the beaten man. "Alright boys, that's enough." Paulie raised his gun and put a bullet into each of the dogs, they howled as they died. He crouched down to Billy who was now battered, bloody, and barely breathing. Paulie spoke

18

softly to him, in almost a whisper. "There are no other drugs in that bag, are there?" His voice was confident and steady, nothing like it was earlier. Before Billy could reply something crossed his mind, something that he and Mike had thought earlier. You see they were right about Paulie, he wasn't a cop, as a matter of fact he was the furthest thing from a cop, he was a killer. As it seemed he was not just any killer, he was a real deal psychopath. Billy shook his head as best as he could at the question and Paulie didn't look too surprised. "I didn't think so, but that wouldn't of saved your life anyway." Paulie grimaced in a very disturbing way and Billy felt his stomach turn over.

Paulie put his gun down in the snow just out of Billy's reach. For a moment Billy was confused and he began to feel hope that he would get to see his family again. Paulie moved his face closer to Billy's, close enough to be intimate and when he did Billy's face was full of bemusement. There was a silence as Paulie stared at the younger man like   hunter to prey, all that could be heard was the gust of the chilly wind blowing around the night. And then just before the silence was broken, as Paulie stared at Billy with his emotionless eyes, Billy knew his hopes were pointless. "Tell the Devil I'll see him soon kid." Paulie said in a soothing kind of tone. At that moment Paulie pulled a knife from his back and cut Billy's throat with ease and carelessness.

19

It was a vicious way to kill someone but as the blood squirted onto Paulie's face he smiled in disturbing enjoyment. For Paulie this was a normality, this was business as usual. Sure he loved drugs, especially coke and if he was able to score some in bulk tonight that would have been a plus. That wasn't what his business was, he was in the business of killing people and not for money or for the sake of others, but for himself. He did it to fill his own sick desires. If Billy and Mike would have thought outside the box a little and been more cautious, they might still be around.

A short time later Paulie began to drag Billy's lifeless carcass through the snow leaving a streak of blood next to another he had formed with Mike's body. Paulie came up to Billy's Cadillac, stopped and began to search Billy's pockets for cash, he found about sixty bucks and jammed it into his pocket. Paulie then proceeded to drag the cold stiff into the back seat, placing him on top of what was now a pile consisting of Mike and the two dogs. After he loaded the last of the bodies in, Paulie walked back over to his car. He went to the back door, opened it and pulled out a large container of gasoline. When Paulie got back over to Billy's car he proceeded to cover the bodies inside with the gasoline, he whistled casually as he did this. After the interior of the car was saturated he moved onto the outside. When he was finished, Paulie took a few steps back and gave the car one final glance before lighting

up an entire book of matches. He threw the book into the backseat before it
was fully engulfed and kicked the back door shut. He watched for a moment
as the backseat turned into a crematorium. Flames began to spread to each
body and any trace of life that might have been left in the dead faces began to
blacken. The flames spread to the rest of the car quickly and as Paulie walked
back to his Cadillac the car was fully ignited.

Paulie wiped the gun that he used on the dogs with a towel from his
trunk and tossed it into the woods. He then placed the container of gasoline
in the trunk before shutting it. As Paulie got into the car and drove away the
burning car exploded in it's wooded surroundings. When he got back on a
main road twenty minutes later, Paulie noticed a familiar looking woman
standing on the dark shoulder alone. She was shivering and her hair was
covered in snow flakes. The woman was also in quite revealing clothing (a
little too revealing for December weather) and Paulie recognized who she
was as he got closer. She was a hooker that Paulie had seen quite a few times
and though he was able to tell she was never too fond   of him on each
occasion, a lay was a lay. He pulled his car over to the shoulder and rolled
down the window. "How are you tonight sweetie?" The woman's face
dropped at the sight of Paulie's, she recognized him immediately and
remembered his violence. After the damage Paulie had done a few months

ago, she had to lie to her doctor and tell him that she had fallen on a fence post at the park. Why she would be anywhere near a fence post was questionable and the story ended up making her doctor very suspicious of the whole situation. The doctor had the idea that maybe she was raped and didn't want to come out with it, he even gave her the whole "You can tell me" spiel. But she advised him otherwise and the doc eventually dropped the subject, though rape couldn't have been that different from what Paulie had actually done.

Paulie was now staring at her with a deep, hungry sort of look and she began to look around nervously. Paulie smiled in a very creepy way. "Come on get in." The woman sighed "No, you were too rough last time, you hurt me bad." Paulie looked at her with as much sympathy as he could bare. "I promise I won't hurt you this time, I'll go easy." The woman continued to stare at Paulie. It was freezing out there and she did need the money, times were slow. Believe it or not when Christmas is around the corner, hooking is slow. Everyone's trying to save their money for their real loved ones in their lives, what a magical time of year. Before the woman could reply, Paulie reached across and opened his passenger door. The woman took one last look around before regretfully getting in the car. Paulie smiled, touched the woman's leg and drove off into the darkness of the winter's night.

2

Home For The Holidays

Far away in the town of Darnite, New Jersey (a town slightly more populated than Mesapeena) sat a large white country style home. The house sat on a vast suburban like street with many other homes, ones that looked almost exact in detail with the exception of maybe a different roof or garage color. Inside the house, Daniel Lawson sat on his couch reading a book and taking in the warmth of a crackling fire. Beside him, his wife Michelle was decorating their home with symbols of Christmas and holiday cheer. Daniel is forty eight years old, he is the younger half brother of Paulie. But in this instance, maniacs don't run in the family. Daniel is an average Joe, a construction foreman who spends most of his nights at home with his wife and daughter. There was a soft look to him, it wasn't that he was particularly weak but just that he was too trusting, too nice. Earlier in his life when he and Paulie had last seen each other, he had been something of a hot head, especially to his wife. But now after many marriage counseling sessions and a will to not be bothered by the little things anymore, Daniel was a changed man.

Paulie's father had died of lung cancer before Paulie was born, his mother remarried years later and had Daniel. Even at an early age, the two boys had a sort of love hate relationship. It was most likely because Paulie was envious of his younger brother who had gotten the better end of the deal, still having his real father and all. It also didn't help very much that Daniel's father favored the boy over Paulie. It was the little things that dug into Paulie and bothered him the most. Like when Mr. Lawson had brought home a pack of baseball cards for Daniel and had completely forgotten to get one for the other child. When he realized what he had done, he told the boys they had to share them and   could split the cards up amongst themselves (Daniel being the cruel child that most are, took all the good players). By then however it was too late, the damage was done. It wasn't that things were done voluntarily, it was just that when Mr. Lawson thought of his children, he thought of Daniel and he thought of him alone. Years later when Michael Lawson died of a heart attack, Paulie couldn't have been more thrilled. He would often fantasize about the day when the old bastard would croak, hell he even fantasized about killing the man himself. If Paulie had been the man he was today, he just might have done it.

As the years went on and they grew into adults, both brothers got along reasonably well. But after their mothers passing and a few unfortunate events, things fell apart. Paulie and Daniel had not spoken nor seen each other in roughly ten years. This didn't seem to bother Paulie much, with his severely eccentric life style, he was better off being left alone. Daniel on the other hand was very dismayed by this, sure he and his brother had their share of problems but as the years went on he couldn't help but remember the good times and he missed Paulie dearly. His wife Michelle played the role of the perfect spouse to a t. She took care of things at home when he was at work and to top it, she was one hell of a cook. They lived their peaceful lives in a small and quiet town and that's the way she liked it. Although she could tell Daniel missed his brother, Michelle knew with assurance that Paulie was better off far away from Daniel and especially herself.

Michelle finished hanging up three stockings on the fire place and walked towards the kitchen. "I'm gonna' go put   coffee up, you want some?" she asked. Daniel smiled in gratitude as he continued to read. "I'm fine." Michelle gently brushed his shoulder with her hand as she passed by. She was a very beautiful woman, Daniel never doubted he was lucky to have her as his own. Daniel stared at the fireplace for a moment, taking in the relaxing sight of flames burning away the blackened logs. As he continued to stare, one of the newly hung stockings fell from its hook and landed without a sound onto the wooden floor. Daniel closed his book and got up from the couch. As he hung the stocking back onto it's hook, a picture on the top of the mantle caught his eye. The picture was of Paulie and himself, it was probably about ten years old and he was almost positive it was the last picture they had taken together. In the picture the two men had their arms around each other and were laughing hysterically at something, Daniel smiled to himself and picked up the picture for a closer look. As he stood there staring at the photo Michelle walked back into the room, she immediately realized what picture he was holding judging from his pain filled smile. "Daniel, are you ok?" Daniel was hesitant to respond. "Ah... yea. I was just looking at this, I don't know what the hell we were laughing about here." Daniel said as he put the picture back onto the mantle. There was a silence and Michelle didn't know what to say, Daniel spoke again. "Maybe I should call him." Daniel was still staring at the picture with his back towards Michelle, he couldn't see how unenthusiastic she looked. "I don't know, I..." She was about to continue and tell him that he shouldn't call Paulie but something stopped her. If she told Daniel not to call him, would that be weird? Michelle wondered, too insistent? Suspicious maybe?

Daniel continued to stare at the picture before finally looking back at his wife. "What do you think?" he asked without any acknowledgment of the abrupt halt she'd come to in the midst of her thought process. "What ever you think is best." Michelle responded quickly and thought that it came off natural enough. "I know we've had our share of problems and he's had some tough times, but I'm sure he's past all that now." Daniel said sympathetically. Michelle nodded in reluctant agreement but couldn't help herself. "Do you think maybe it would be best left alone?" Daniel did not look too impressed by his wife's words and for a second he even looked a bit angry, he sighed before continuing. "It's Christmas time, I should call him and see if he has any plans. Maybe he could come down here." Michelle was not to keen to the idea but didn't show it, instead she found herself saying things in her head. What if he doesn't want to come here, did you even think about the fact that he might not want to see you? Daniel unaware of the one sided argument that was going on inside Michelle's head stared curiously waiting for some kind of reply. Michelle noticed her husband and instead of bringing her thoughts into reality she catered to the idea in a nonchalant manner. "He's your brother, if you want him here, tell him to come." Nicole, the couples seventeen year old daughter then walked into the room. "Tell who to come?"

Daniel gave Michelle a casual glance before turning to his daughter. "Your uncle Paulie, you remember him don't you?" Nicole did remember him, well at least somewhat remembered him. He was the weird uncle to her, kind of like the one everyone has who is a little too touchy. Except Paulie

27

never did touch her, nor did he talk to her very much. All the memories Nicole had of her uncle were quiet ones. When it came to kids Paulie really didn't get them, so he would stay as far away as he could when they were around. It was probably because he could never really connect with them, sort of like how nowadays he could barely connect with anyone. As Nicole got older she would eavesdrop as her parents talked about Paulie, this is where she heard of some of the bad things that he had done. Back when she was younger Paulie wasn't quite the monster he was today, he was merely a petty thief. Almost along the lines of somebody like Mike the drug dealer. But over time people sometimes evolve and it's not always for the best. "I really don't remember him much." Nicole said before adding. "Wait didn't he go to jail?" Michelle smirked innocently and turned to Daniel who had a surprised and somewhat disappointed look on his face. Daniel turned to his daughter. "He had a little bit of a past but everybody makes mistakes...I'm sure he's doing just fine now."

Inside of Paulie's beat up old apartment he was in fact doing just fine. He was in his bed, on top of his female guest, giving it to her full force. The woman laid with her legs spread looking anything but amused, she almost looked sad at the thought of what she was doing. He could have been going a lot rougher, she thought to herself and was grateful he wasn't. The apartment was dimly lit and smoky, the paint on the wall was a yellowish color that was probably once white and there was a thick hotness in the air that was increasing with each passing moment. As Paulie continued to go even faster, the Woman began to sigh softly to herself. Paulie might have heard her murmur but if he did he ignored it and began to moan and thrust even more aggressively. Sweat poured down his bearded face. His hook nose and messed up hair projected a horrifying sight for the woman as she began to feel the familiar pain. "You like that! You fucking whore!" Paulie chanted. The woman looked disgusted, not just with Paulie but also with herself. "You Bitch,I'll fucking...kill you" At this point the woman looked straight up at Paulie and stared at him with a disturbed glare.

As he continued to repeat obscenities, he thrust harder and harder until finally reaching his climax. He let out a great moan and an even greater sigh of relief before climbing off of the woman. Paulie sat back onto the bed, brushed his hair back with his hand and lit up a cigarette. The woman pulled the sheet over herself and propped her body against the headboard, making sure to keep a temperate distance from the man. "Is that it?" The woman asked without even looking toward him. Paulie glanced at her with a look of contempt. "Yea for now, hang tight. I'm gonna' go make some coffee...you want some?" "No." The woman replied immediately without a second of

29

contemplation. Paulie lifted himself from the bed, put on a pair of shorts and walked to the kitchen.

Paulie walked into the tiny kitchen and turned the out dated coffee machine on. He opened the cabinet that hung over his head and pulled out a sugar bowl. The bowl was close to empty and there was a small metal tube sticking out of it. He stuck his pinky into the bowl and licked it before passing his tongue around the inside of his mouth sloppily, like a child trying to get the remains of a candy bar out of their teeth. Paulie pulled out the metal tube and turned the bowl upside down letting whatever was left fall onto the kitchen counter. He then placed the metal tube into his nostril and began to snort the sprinkles of white off of the surface. After Paulie was done he threw the tube into the bowl and placed it back into the cabinet, he rubbed his nostrils vigorously as he did. Paulie reached into the cabinet again, this time pulling out a second sugar bowl. This bowl was fuller than the other and the substance inside had the grainy look that the first one was lacking.

When Paulie got back into the bedroom with his coffee mug in hand, his female guest was almost fully clothed and ready to leave. The woman's back was towards him and he watched silently as she pulled her wrinkled shirt over her head. She wasn't wasting any time, all she could think about was getting her money and getting the hell out. Paulie continued to stare at her back and when she finally turned around she was startled by the sight of him. Paulie was silent for a moment and took a sip of his coffee as he stared deep into her eyes. "Where are you going? What's the rush?" Paulie asked innocently. She finished putting on her leather boots and turned back to him. "I have to go, I have a call." Paulie stared at her silently again before taking another sip of his coffee. "Well I'm paying for my time." This time Paulie's tone had some annoyance in it. "I have to go, could I please have my money." The woman's words were desperate and   fearful. Paulie continued to stare and the woman began to feel uncomfortable. After another moment of tension, Paulie nodded in agreement and walked over to his dresser, the woman sighed in relief as he did.

Paulie pulled out a wad of bills that probably accumulated to a couple thousand or so and began to count out some of them. Paulie was by no means a rich man, but he was good at holding onto any money he made from his job doing construction and the cash he ripped off here and there. The woman grabbed her purse, walked to the front door and awaited her payment. He counted the money over again to make sure it was correct, picked up his coffee mug and walked over to where the woman was standing. Paulie opened the front door and glanced through the measly two hundred and fifty

Uncle Sweet Uncle   Dominick Tartamella

dollars one last time. As he did, the woman stared out the screen door
watching the light snow flurries fall onto the four concrete steps that lead to
the sidewalk. "It's all here." Paulie said softly. The woman turned around, put
her hand out in an assertive manner and waited for it to be filled. Paulie
grinned something frightening before he spoke. "Well here's your money..."
The woman snatched the bills and quickly looked them over as Paulie pushed
the screen door open. Before she could put the money away or look up,
Paulie abruptly continued. "And here's hot coffee in the face, you ugly
bitch!" Paulie whipped his piping hot coffee into the woman's face and she
let out a heinous scream before tumbling down the small flight of concrete
steps. Coffee splashed and money flew through the air as the woman's body
came down onto the cold concrete. Her head smashed hard against the
sidewalk and she cried out in pain as blood and a tooth burst out of her
mouth. "Hope that doesn't scar you, smelly cunt!" The woman screamed and
sobbed as she began to pick herself and the scattered money up from the
ground. "You bastard!" She cried. Paulie smiled. "Yea have a merry
Christmas." He slammed the door shut leaving the shattered woman to
herself.

    Paulie walked back into the bedroom, placed the empty coffee mug
onto his night stand and laid down in his bed. He looked around for a

32

moment before spotting his television remote on the floor, he reached down to pick it up. Paulie pushed the power button and the glow from the screen lit the dark room. He flipped through the channels before stopping on his favorite show, Fear Tactics. Fear Tactics was a show in which people would set up their friends to be pranked by a television crew. However, these weren't your every day innocent pranks, they were very well planned and thought out. Sometimes they'd prank people into thinking some kind of monster was in the woods and other times they would pretend there was a murderer on the loose who was coming after them. Paulie got a kick out of the whole thing and thought it was hilarious that these people would run around scared to death. Then at the end of the show the actor playing the killer or the monster would ask the victim of the prank if they were afraid. Most of the time the person wouldn't know what the hell to say but sometimes they said yes and then the actor would say "Well you're on Fear Tactics" and point to the camera. Then everyone would laugh and the victims friend would come out and everything would end nice. But that wasn't the part Paulie liked, what he liked was seeing the pure fear in the faces of the people. It gave him a thrill that was similar   but barely up to par with the one he got when he killed.

Paulie watched for a minute but realized the show was ending, he sighed and reluctantly continued to browse through the channels. He was feeling exhausted from the day's work and began to doze off as he clicked the remote repeatedly. Suddenly just as his eyes shut and his dead hand dropped the remote onto the bed, the sound of a special news report pierced into his ears. Paulie's eyes shot open as a stern looking male reporter spoke. "Tonight we take a closer look into the Bloomingdale Slasher..." Paulie was now wide awake and there was no trace in his eyes of the tiredness that had crept up on him a minute ago. The reporter continued. "The evading serial killer who continues to prey on these New Hampshire streets." The screen began to show several different murder scenes, some in homes and some outdoors. Ambulances and police were shown surrounding each murder site as the reporter's narration continued. "With fourteen victims and counting, this blood thirsty maniac shows no remorse or signs of stopping." A satisfied smirk sat on Paulie's face, stopping had never even crossed his mind. More grizzly photos were shown and Paulie continued to stare in a sort of admiring awe.

As Paulie watched the report, he had a flash in his mind of the murders he had committed. One by one, all fourteen victims violent ends went through his mind. He remembered their pain and their fearful screams that had vanished forever into silence. He thought of number's fifteen and sixteen, which he had done not two hours ago and wondered when they would be found and added to the list. His disturbing smirk turned into a grotesque smile as he stared at the television. Paulie may have not always been like this but the murderous psychopath that he would eventually become wasn't born in a day. It was always there, it had to be, dormant maybe, and just waiting for a day to break out. Perhaps that was why he always felt so disconnected from the rest of the happy go lucky people who filled the rest of the world. It wasn't until jail and the solitary confinement that comes with it, that Paulie realized his true calling. Many sleepless nights he'd lay in that cell and wonder how the hell he got himself into it. Even before he'd gotten himself caught and was still out successfully pulling off robberies. He would often find himself having an empty unfulfilled feeling after a job was through. The money was good and at the time that's what he thought he wanted but laying there in that cell night after night, he began to realize that money was the furthest thing from his needs.

It wasn't until Paulie's first confrontation in prison that he started feeling fulfillment for his actions. His life was threatened, three gang members from a white supremacist group cornered him in the prison's library. They wanted his ass or his blood. One man toted a small knife and for the first time in a long time, Paulie was scared. To this day whenever

Dominick Tartamella

Paulie replayed the moment in his head, he always felt that luck might have been the only reason he survived. When the three men approached, he refused the gang bang and they charged at him immediately. The two unarmed men grabbed him and started beating him to a pulp as the other man egged them on. Paulie was in a dream like state as the two men continued to beat on him, he looked up and saw the other man clinching the knife tightly and laughing hysterically. Whether or not Paulie liked it, they were going to rape him. They would continue to beat on him for a few, get him nice and weak and then, one by one, they'd go to work on his rectum. As they continued to pummel him, the knifed man began to unzip his pants. Since he was the leader and he had the knife, he got first dibs. Paulie was thrown down on the floor and rolled underneath a table where days earlier he had sat reading a book. A million thoughts ran through his head as he was under that table but one stuck that was probable, he was a dead man. Even if they didn't kill him, when it was all done he'd be dead inside anyway, he could never live with himself afterward. As the three man chanted for him to get up, Paulie's scarlet covered face looked up and noticed a piece of duck tape stuck to the flip side of the table. Underneath the tape was a brand new, handmade shank. The first thought that crossed Paulie's disoriented mind was, how convenient.

Even in the franticness of his current situation, Paulie couldn't help but see some humor. He had sat at this table everyday reading for the two weeks he'd been confined and never once did it cross his mind that other inmates were using the library to transfer weapons to each other. The irony left his mind just as quickly as it had entered it and Paulie snapped back into reality. He reached for the shank and pulled it from underneath the tape. The blade was small and Paulie was able to hide it in his clinched fist as one of the two unarmed men reached down to pick him up. The man grabbed him by the hair while the other two waited patiently for him to get to his feet. The leader was still clinching his knife tightly with his left hand, his pants were now around his ankles and his penis hung exposed. Paulie caught a glimpse of the man's nude bottom as he was pulled to his feet and knew it was now or never. Paulie stabbed the man who was picking him up in the thigh and he let out an excruciating scream as blood poured out of an artery. Paulie then pulled the shank from the man's leg and he fell to the ground with another cry. Before the second unarmed man could realize what had happened, Paulie swayed his blade up into the man's stomach like a lethal uppercut. The man coughed blood from his mouth and fell to the ground, on top of his fellow gang member.

When Paulie finally stood up he was greeted with a sight of the leader charging at him. The man had managed to pull his pants back up amongst all of the chaos and he held his knife out madly like a happy infant running around with a new toy. The man whipped his knife through the air and Paulie dodged it with a jolt to the left. Before the man could make a second attempt, Paulie swiped his blade across the man's throat, sending blood spraying up and the man smashing down. As Paulie watched the man hit the floor dead, a sudden rush came over him. At first he thought the rush came to him because he had just survived a life threatening situation. But later in his cell he would come up with a theory about himself that would eventually prove true, he liked to kill. Luck, part of Paulie always knew it was luck that got him out of that situation. The other part thought that maybe it was fate, destiny, or something more. If Paulie had not been in that situation, he may have never known the thrill it was to kill a man. Prison is meant to change a man and one things for sure, when Paulie was done serving his time, he was a changed man.

Paulie continued to lay watching the television, thinking about the murders he had committed. He fantasized about the lives he had taken so effortlessly and none of them with a single ounce of regret. His attention went back to the screen as the reporter began to interview another suited man. A stone faced, gray haired man in his fifties with a thick dark mustache

38

sat across from the reporter. There was a fire deep in the man's eyes, the reporter continued his voice over. "Two of the victims to be killed in the last year were Victoria Atkins and her daughter Elana. A picture of the beautiful deceased woman and her twenty two year old daughter accompanied the narration. The reporter continued "The husband and father of these two victims, Mesapeena's own Detective Robert Atkins is here with us tonight."

Paulie remembered killing the women as he did all his victims, but finding out they were related to this detective was news to him. He stared at the screen, curious at what this Detective Atkins had to say. The detective sat in a dimly lit room across from the reporter, there wasn't a single emotion visible on his face. "Detective this man, this monster, has taken the lives of many and destroyed the lives of even more. With you, he was taken away two of the most important people in your life. What are your feelings?" The reporter asked somberly. Detective Atkins nodded in a relatively normal manner considering the topic. "My feelings? I have none, this man took away whatever feelings I had left, now there's just a hole, a chunk that's missing." The reporter nodded in a sort of sick amusement. "Does it make you angrier that you, of all people, are on the police force and still nothing? Not a trace, not a clue and the murders continue."

Paulie watched in mesmerized awe as the detective thought of how to reply. "I've grown to realize over the course of this last year, as the victims grow, that I am not alone. It's not just about me, it's about the other families too, he's hurt far too many and it would be selfish for me to say I'm a police officer, I should have my justice. We're all in the same boat." "Does it bother you that he's out there?" The reporter asked the detective stupidly. "Oh it bothers me, it makes me distraught. The fact that right now he's free, hell he could even be watching this program right now. Going about his day with ease, as more and more of his victims pop up." "If he was watching, what would you tell him?" The reporter asked. At this moment Detective Atkins turned to face directly to the camera. Paulie stared deep into the screen as if the two men were sitting in the same room, inches away from each other. "Your days are numbered. Whether it's today or it's five years from now, you're going to slip up and when you do, we're going to come down on you hard. It's only a matter of time, mark my words, it's only a matter of time!" The detective spoke intensely and as he stared at the camera his face began to turn red with rage. An awkward silence came over the reporter as he could feel the tension building.

Paulie was smirking when the interview came to an abrupt end, The reporter was now back on the screen alone facing the camera. "With the gruesome ways that he has murdered, psychologists had this to say." A professional looking woman sat in a very upscale looking room. "Anyone who kills like this, in these horrific ways, will not stop. The individual is obviously passionate about what he does, and these heinous acts probably help to fulfill something that is missing inside of him." The woman spoke urgently. Paulie stared at the screen with a lost look as if he didn't understand what was being said. Suddenly Paulie's phone rang out through the silent apartment, for a second he was almost startled but not quite. He looked down at the phone curiously and wondered who might be calling. After another couple of rings, Paulie reached for the phone, assuming it was probably one of those annoying telemarketing companies.

"Hello?" Paulie answered with a bit of an attitude. "Paulie, is that you?" The voice on the other line asked in a friendly tone. At first Paulie did not recognize the voice but as it sank into his brain he realized it was his brother. The same brother who had pretty much abandoned him to rot in a jail cell all those years ago. Paulie pretended to be clueless to who he was talking to. "Who's this?" Paulie asked. Daniel hesitated and swallowed his throat, he was nervous to say. "Paulie, it's Daniel, your brother." Half brother. Paulie thought. He was perplexed, why the hell would his brother be calling him after all these years. For a moment Paulie wondered if perhaps his brother was calling him in regards to the murders. That thought was immediately discarded when Paulie realized there was no way Daniel could have heard about them. Mesapeena was a small town located on the outskirts of New Hampshire. The town was split into two parts, South Arden and Bloomingdale.

If Daniel was still living in their hometown of Darnite New Jersey (which Paulie thought he was) they could have dropped a bomb on Mesapeena and Paulie was sure the people of Darnite wouldn't hear the news. Darnite was also a small town, but it wasn't as secluded as Mesapeena was. The people of Darnite might as well have been the only people in the entire world though. All they cared about was themselves and their town, selfish pricks, Paulie thought. Something else that shot down the idea that Daniel knew something about the murders also came to Paulie's mind. To his brother, Paulie might have been a quasi criminal or what not, but he was no murderer. Daniel had no idea that in the last ten years, his brother had grown into a ruthless killer.

Paulie smiled at his self-assurance. "Danny Boy...How are you?" Daniel was immediately relieved that his brother hadn't hung up on him. "I'm good, God it's been a long time Paul." "Yep time flies." Paulie said tediously.

"Listen Paul, let me cut to the chase. I hate that we don't see each other anymore. I just had to look you up in the yellow book on the internet to find you, I mean we're brothers, it shouldn't be like that." Paulie smirked and continued to stare at the television screen which was still showing the same nonsense about the murders. Daniel began to speak hesitantly and with a bit of nervousness in his voice. "So I was wondering, would you like to come here for Christmas?" "There for Christmas?" Paulie was unsure how to react, he was very surprised by the question. Daniel continued. "It'll be fun, we'll catch up. It'll be like a little get away for you, see how the old town's doing."

Fuck the old town, Paulie thought. After what Daniel had done to him, he should just be grateful he didn't go there and kill him. Before Paulie could think any further on the subject, he was distracted by a picture being shown on the TV. It was a sketch, a composite of the Bloomingdale slasher, a face that was almost a spitting image of Paulie's, beard and all. As Daniel continued to ramble on, Paulie stared at the TV silently. Daniel's words were now gibberish in Paulie's ears. The reporter clarified that the composite was from a witness who had come forward a few nights earlier, it was the first real piece of evidence they had on him. Paulie's mind immediately went back to the woman he had seen outside of the seven eleven three nights ago. She was in her thirties and wasn't quite as good looking up close as she was from afar. She seemed to be somewhat distressed and as Paulie walked out of the store, he couldn't help but overhear her telling the person on the other side of the pay phone that she had a flat and needed a ride. Paulie had then heard the woman become very hostile with whoever she was talking to before slamming the phone onto the hook. It was almost midnight and Paulie presumed that whoever it was, they didn't want to come pick her up. So like the gentleman he was, Paulie offered the woman a ride. To Paulie's surprise, she didn't object or think about the question any further, she was probably too furious to think. She simply accepted Paulie's offer and that was the last time she was seen alive. Paulie instantly realized the clerk from the store must have remembered his face, hell he might have even seen the girl leaving with him. Paulie suddenly felt a hatred for himself brewing, he had screwed up. He had killed too many people, he had gotten cocky and now he had finally screwed up. He wondered for a moment if he was getting like every other stupid criminal. Just as that detective on TV had said earlier, like some other-worldly prediction, he would slip up and they would find him. God damn it, Paulie thought. What was he to do? He had to lay low. And as if by some divine working, Paulie realized his brother was still on the phone. "Paul, what do you say, are you going to come?" Daniel asked.

Paulie shook himself out of his worrisome trance and smiled

44

sinisterly. "Yea, yea sure, I'll come, I could use a little getaway." Daniel laughed lightly, he was excited. "That's just great, Michelle and Nicole will be thrilled." Paulie, wanting to cut to the chase continued. "When should I come down there?" Daniel was silent for a moment,thinking. "You could come whenever you want." Paulie nodded. "Good, how about tomorrow?" Paulie asked. Daniel smiled. "Tomorrow, well if you think you could do the drive that quick, why not?" Paulie smirked knowing that he would be on the road within the hour. He had to get out before copies of those sketches were posted all over town. "I'll see you tomorrow little brother." Paulie added. Daniel could not have been happier at the calls outcome and neither could Paulie. "I'll see you then and drive careful." Daniel added. "I will." Paulie said before hanging up the phone.

In the Lawson home, Daniel walked into the living room where Michelle and Nicole were sitting. He had a large grin stretched across his face. "He's coming tomorrow!" For a moment Michelle's face was emotionless before smiling painfully. "Good honey." "Great we have a criminal coming for the holiday's." Nicole added in a very conniving and bitchy tone. Michelle turned to her daughter with a stern look. "Nicole!" Daniel shook his head disappointed by his daughters comment. "He's not a criminal, he got involved with some bad people a long time ago and he went away, but he did his time." Daniel said. "What did he do anyway?" Nicole asked curiously. "Petty things, robbery, car theft. But that was the past, your uncle is a good person. He'd never hurt a soul." Nicole laughed at her father's words. "Yea he sounds like a real saint."

Daniel stared at Nicole with an unpleasant look. "How long is he going to stay?" Michelle asked. "Who knows, he could stay till New years, if he'd like." Daniel said and Michelle could feel some unease in her stomach. "Daniel, I don't know..." Michelle began but Daniel interrupted her quickly. "We have the room. I haven't seen him in ten years. It'll be great, we'll catch up, he could come to the Christmas party." Daniel was ecstatic at the thought, Michelle was sickened by it. "We could maybe even make the party a sort of welcome home thing for him. Wouldn't that be nice?" Michelle gave her husband a fake smile, "It would." It would be just dandy, she thought sarcastically.

3

The Lonely Detective

Detective Atkins woke in his bright bedroom and stared at the extremely sunny morning coming in through his window. What a day, he thought to himself. Downstairs his wife Victoria was cooking a very elaborate and enormous breakfast. Atkins followed the aroma of sizzling bacon and headed into the kitchen. "Robert honey, good morning." Victoria chirped cheerfully as she kissed her husband on his lips. The kitchen was very well lit and Detective Atkins noticed the same unreal sunlight coming in from a window behind his wife. The detective smiled, his eyes wandered around the kitchen taking in the feast like set up of pancakes, eggs and bacon. "Good morning darling, what is all this?" Victoria smiled innocently. "For your birthday silly, you do remember it's your birthday, don't you?" Detective Atkins had a moment of disbelief toward the fact that he had forgotten his own birthday. Suddenly his teenage daughter Elana came trotting down the steps. "Daddy! Happy birthday!" she said excitedly before jumping into her father's arms and hugging him grandly. The detective couldn't quite grasp the disoriented feeling he was having but ignored it anyway without another thought. "If it wasn't for you girls, I wouldn't even know how old I was." Atkins said. The two women smiled and began to laugh hysterically. Atkins felt that strange something in his stomach again but covered it up with some laughter of his own.

As if out of nowhere, a faceless shadowy figure burst through the window directly behind Victoria and pulled on her long brown hair. She let out a heinous scream as her head went back and her thin neck arched into the open. The overly bright sunshine that was shining in through the window moments ago was now replaced by a dark dead glow. The smile ran from Detective Atkins face as immediate horror emerged around him. Elana began to scream as the shadowy figure pulled out a large kitchen knife. Detective Atkins reached for his gun but found only an empty holster around his chest. The shadowy figure slid his knife across   Victoria's throat slowly and blood began to squirt upward as she let out her last dying gasp. Her eyelids came down fast like broken window curtains and her body fell to the floor before decomposing completely in a matter of seconds. The detective stared in shock for a moment before turning back to his daughter. Just as he was about to tell her to run, there was suddenly a large kitchen knife sticking out of her forehead. Her eyes shut quickly just as her mothers had and her body keeled over onto the kitchen table before rotting into a decrepit skeleton. Detective Atkins stared mortified and then let out a pain filled howl.

Detective Atkins opened his eyes and all he could see was the thick blackness of his dark bedroom. He felt himself soaked in sweat and completely alone. His breathing was heavy and off-kilter as he reached to the night stand for his prescription Valume. He popped two pills into his mouth and even without the aid of a liquid, swallowed them with ease. Atkins rubbed his right temple as if trying to decrease the lingering hold of the nightmare. Atkins couldn't shake the fact that other than a few exaggerated details, it had all been true. His wife and his daughter were dead and that was a nightmare he would never be able to wake up from. Moments later Detective Atkins rose from his bed, slipped into a worn robe and headed into his living room. He flicked on the lights and stared at himself in a large mirror that hung behind his couch. The detective's face was the opposite of what it looked like in his dream, he had dark bags under his eyes and a messy looking scruff on his face. He stared at himself in disgust for another second before walking over to a small oak cabinet. Atkins opened the cabinet and searched through a few bottles of liquor, most of which were almost empty. He reached to the back and pulled out a half full bottle of Johnny Walker Blue Label. A smirk came across the detective's face as he stared down at the dusty bottle. It had been a gift from his partner for his birthday the year before. A year that seemed like twenty years ago, a year when everything

49

was still alright. He poured himself a tall glass   and took a seat on his black leather sofa.

The murders that were coming on a year now, still haunted the detective in every aspect of his life. The house which had always been clean began to take on a sloppy look. Clothes were thrown around and cigarette butts were left everywhere, Victoria would have never approved of smoking in the house but she wasn't around to stop it. Cleaning up after himself wasn't a top priority as Atkins had lost the will to do almost everything. He had just recently began to get back into his normal eating routine, for the first eight months he was pretty much starving himself, dropping close to thirty pounds. Drinking was the only thing that he found himself doing on a daily basis, that and continuing the hunt. The drinking may have killed some of the pain but it had no effect on the burning deep down inside, a yearning for closure, for satisfaction, for revenge. He would often blame himself for what had happened. Why had he let them go alone? Like his wife had always said, he let the job get in the way. The irony was now all he had left was the job. They were all supposed to go away that weekend, some type of bed and breakfast on the country side, it would have been so sweet too, a nice getaway. At the last minute the detective had gotten caught up in some stupid case, all so insignificant now. There was no way he could have known what

50

was going to happen, at that time there was no reason to be worried that his wife and daughter would have to pass through Bloomingdale to reach their destination. They were two of the slashers first victims, at first Atkins thought he had made an enemy in his years of law enforcement until more and more bodies started popping up. It wasn't long before the papers first called him the Bloomingdale Slasher.

Victoria and Elana left on a Thursday morning, they should have been there by around midnight but there was dangerous, torrential rain coming down (something they should have perhaps took their chances with). They decided to stop for the night in a little ramshackle known as the moon motel. The place could have been the setting of a horror movie and as a matter of fact, that night it ended up being just that. The bastard must of spotted them, alone and vulnerable. He waited till it was real late, three am, four, based on what the coroners said. He busted in their room real quiet, tied them up to the bed and did his worst. He rapped Elana first right in front of her mother before sticking a knife in her head. Then he had his way with Victoria while her daughter lied dead on the floor. Victoria's throat was slit so deep that her head was almost severed, the cops knew they had some kind of sick fuck on their hands. When Detective Atkins was notified he flew off the coop, darted down to the moon motel and boy was that a mistake. Stepping into that crime

51

scene was the worst thing he could have done. He sometimes wondered if he hadn't of gone in, would he have spared himself the nightmares? He always assumed he would have them regardless of going there or not. He had read the papers, seen the news, he knew in detail how it happened.

As he sat on his sofa drinking his expensive whiskey, Detective Atkins wondered if he would ever have peace of mind again. Sure he would never have his wife or daughter back, that he had somewhat come to grips with, but when was this son of a bitch going to get nailed. As he took another sip of his drink, he stared at the clock that read two am and realized he couldn't even remember falling asleep earlier that night. With the pills sometimes it was like that, he would take so many to ease the pain that he'd just come home and pass out. A couple times he hadn't even made it home. Once at the station he found himself out cold with his face on the desk. Another time he fell asleep in the car ride home, he could have been killed if he wasn't so lucky. The way he looked at it is if he had any luck left, he would have been killed. The chief knew something was up after that and gave him some tough love and some unwanted time off. The chief was a prick but Atkins knew he was right. He spent the two weeks off drinking and thinking, it ended up being a punishment for Atkins. He learned his lesson then, he would never slip up and show his hurting again.

The detective was smarter now, he didn't show his emotions at the office anymore, he was dead to them and joked a lot to cover it up. As the detective sat fantasying about what he'd like to do to the Bloomingdale slasher he noticed something. The fax machine which he had installed months ago so that anytime there was a new murder or any clues (though they were hardly any of the latter) he would know first, was blinking. From the distance he noticed a piece of paper and immediately got up and walked toward the fax machine. He picked up the piece of paper and stared at it for a moment, the received time was ten pm. There was a hand scribbled title across the top reading OUR FIRST BLOOMINGDALE SLASHER COMPOSITE. Below was a sketch of the unholy bearded face of Paulie, Detective Atkins smiled grimly to himself.

4

A Stop Along The Way

Paulie was showered and shaved by around two thirty in the am.
Other than a few nicks and some fuzz he had missed around his upper lip, his
face was now clean cut. With the fresh shave, Paulie looked ten years
younger and if you didn't know his hidden darkness (which no one did), he
looked almost sane. Paulie knew shaving wasn't going to change his face
much, but at least people wouldn't recognize him right away. If anything it
would give him some time to run. But then again who even saw that report?
Paulie reassured himself. He just had to watch out for cops on the way out of
town, as long as he didn't bump into any, he'd be fine. As for the people in
Darnite, he knew nobody would recognize him there. If they did they would
only be old acquaintances that knew him from before he was a killer.

Paulie walked back into his bedroom with a damp towel wrapped
around his stocky body. He searched around through his drawers for
something to wear while water from his still wet torso dripped onto the hard
wood floor. After putting on a brown pair of slacks and a tee shirt, Paulie
began to search his closet and pack up clothes into a large duffel bag. He

54

shuffled through the mess that was his closet hastily, throwing just about anything he came across into the bag. Suddenly the touch of an old familiar fabric stopped Paulie dead in his tracks. He pulled the piece of clothing from out of the disarray and was immediately taken back by the sight of the wrinkled sweater. The sweater was dark red and had a large green Christmas tree in it's center. It was hardly the type of clothing Paulie would have picked out in a store but the cheesy design wasn't what made it so special to him. Paulie held the sweater tightly in his hands and stared at it for a moment with a crooked smile.

It was about eleven years earlier from what Paulie could remember, a while before he had gone away. Paulie was over his brother's house for Christmas, they were opening gifts. Daniel was distracted by some toy he was trying to put together for a younger Nicole. Michelle and Paulie sat by the tree, sipping coffee and enjoying the warmth of the fireplace. Michelle pulled a box from underneath the tree and handed it to Paulie. She smiled shyly and Paulie returned one of his own. The box was wrapped in shiny green paper and topped with an oversized white bow. "You didn't have to get me anything." Paulie said as Michelle blushed with excitement. "Open it." Paulie did as he was told and was surprised to find the hand made red sweater. "Do you like it?" Michelle asked with some anxiousness. Paulie might of normally laughed at the fact that the sweater was quite ridiculous but something inside had stopped him. And somewhere deep where he should have found some humor, he felt a certain adoration. Paulie looked back up at Michelle with loving eyes. "I love it." He smiled and touched her hand very sensually and slow. Michelle smiled with just the same loving gaze but pulled her hand away quickly and walked away, Paulie felt anger and desire building as she did.

Paulie felt that same anger and desire building in him now as he continued to stare at the raggedy sweater. He wondered what life could have been had things not turned out the way they did. He thought of Daniel and a feeling of contempt filled inside of him. Paulie then began to think about Michelle and he felt a sudden calming come over his bones. The past was the past, there was no point of dwelling in it. Paulie pushed away his feelings and began to shake the sweater through the air, clearing the particles of dust from the fabric's surface. When he was finished, he pulled the sweater over his head and took a quick look at himself in the mirror. Paulie then grabbed a navy blue baseball cap, threw on a brown work jacket and walked to his dresser. Inside he grabbed his wallet and a bunch of mixed bills. He zipped his duffel bag, threw it around his shoulder and headed for the door. Moments later he was behind the wheel of his Cadillac and on the road to salvation

Meanwhile back in Darnite, Nicole and her boyfriend Jake were partying with some other teens in an unfinished house. There were about fifteen of them, some were smoking pot, some were drinking, and others were dancing to the loud rap music that was blasting through the otherwise empty house. The house had no electricity and was lit by several sporadically placed candles. Jake grabbed a couple of beers from a loaded cooler that sat in the middle of what could have been a living room and he and Nicole made their way up the stairs to seclude themselves from the other guests. They entered what would soon be the master bedroom, other than some paint cans that were left, the room was bare. Jake and Nicole moved to a corner of the room and sat on the fresh new green carpet. Nicole was shivering a bit and they moved closer together. "It's so cold in here." she said. "I know, there's no heat." Jake took off his wool jacket and put it around Nicole's shoulders. She smiled and Jake began to kiss her lovingly. As they continued, Jake wrapped his hands around her body. He then began to sneak his right hand down her thighs and onto her plump butt.

Nicole quickly pushed Jake's hand away and stopped kissing him. "We're definitely not doing this here." she said sternly. Daniel smirked and let out an annoyed sigh. The story of my life, Jake thought to himself. He'd been going out with Nicole for the last two months and she just wouldn't budge. Jake knew Nicole was a great girl and it wasn't all that he cared about but like any teenager, he was beginning to get frustrated. "Then when Nicole?" Jake asked a bit nettled. "Soon babe, it has to be the right time and place, and being around our drunk friends on this carpet isn't quite it." Nicole said with a smile, Jake rolled his eyes. "Well I guess we could use your house to be at least semi-intimate when your parents go away for New Years." Jake said and laid a soft kiss on Nicole's cheek. "Actually, I don't think they're going anymore." Nicole said. "What why?" "My uncle is coming over for Christmas and he might be staying for new years too, maybe even longer." Jake's new found anger was visible on his face. "You gotta' be kidding me." Jake shook his head in disbelief.

"I know you were looking forward to time alone, I'm sorry." Nicole added sympathetically. "It's alright I guess." Jake said regretfully. "Do you want to know the worst part though? My uncle, he's like an ex-con or something." Jake's eyes lit up in interest. "Really? Wow, he's probably an interesting guy." Jake said. "Yea right, he's probably a weirdo." Nicole quipped. "You never met him?" "I did but I haven't seen him in years, I barely remember what the man looks like." "Well everybody's a little weird, I'm sure he's got some cool stories at least." Jake said and Nicole smirked.

Jake began kissing Nicole again and just as he attempted to slide his hand to her left breast they were interrupted by a giggle coming from the other side of the room. Jake looked over toward the door and saw their friends Eric and Cindy standing in the shadows. "How long have you been there dick?" Jake asked annoyed. "Long enough to know this isn't the right time or place." Eric said before he and Cindy let out another few giggles. "Jerk." Nicole said under her breath as she began to blush. "Are you guy's gonna' come party or what?" Eric asked. Jake and Nicole shared a look of disappointment before unwillingly rising to their feet. Eric and Cindy smiled at Jake and Nicole and they smiled back. The four teenagers headed back to the party.

An hour later, Paulie was well into his drive, the snow that had showed signs of stopping earlier was now coming down heavily. The repetitiveness of the dark empty road had began to bore Paulie and he could feel his eyes getting heavier with each passing street light. It was also no help that he was beginning to come down from the coke he had snorted. Slowly his eyes began to close and then he felt his muscles relax. Paulie was dead to the world for only ten seconds but when his eyes shot open and he swerved away from another honking car, he could have sworn he was asleep for days. "Jesus fuck!" Paulie yelled to himself as he gasped for air and straightened his steering wheel. He hadn't even remembered falling asleep let alone being in the car. When he opened his eyes he expected to see nothing but the blackness of his bedroom, instead he saw two head lights coming right toward him. The heat was blasting in the car and sweat began to pour down his face. As Paulie continued down the road he felt the drowsiness begin again and he knew he would have to stop. In this distance Paulie could see a red neon sign over a building that read Sports Bar, underneath it was a smaller green sign that read "Billiards and Beer". Paulie smirked to himself and pulled into the partially filled parking lot.

When Paulie entered the bar some snow flurries blew in with him. The bar was filled with about fifteen or twenty people, pretty busy for this hour Paulie thought. Most of the people in the bar turned to look at him when he walked in   but no one stared for too long. The crowd was made up of mostly biker types, though there was hardly a real biker in sight. They may have had their vests and long hair but they were posers and Paulie knew it. Real bikers rode their hogs in rain, sleet and snow. Paulie didn't remember passing one bike in the parking lot, just a few shit kicking pick up trucks. Some pairs of people were playing pool at a few different tables, others sat at the bar and the rest were scattered around the floor talking in groups of twos and threes. Some folks were even dancing to the loud blues music that was playing. Paulie took his jacket off and hung it on the coat rack, he straightened his baseball cap and waved a hand through the messy hair that stuck out the sides before heading over to the bar. As Paulie took a seat, some people next to him began to laugh at the sweater he was wearing. Paulie either didn't hear them or didn't care because his face was expressionless.

The overweight bartender walked over to Paulie and took a glance at his sweater before speaking. "What could I get you?" Paulie thought for a moment before answering in a humorous tone. "How about a bud...bud." Paulie smirked but the bartender had no reaction, he nodded without amusement and proceeded to get Paulie's beer. A large bearded man probably about six three, two hundred fifty pounds, sat down next to Paulie. He turned to Paulie and stared for a moment. "Nice fucking sweater!" The man's deep voice was full of sarcasm. Paulie turned slowly toward the man, he had a fake smile across his face and was imagining how nice it would be to cut the man's tongue out. "Why thank you." Paulie spoke in the nicest tone he could pull off. The bartender walked back over and handed Paulie his Bud. "That'll be five." Paulie reached into his pocket,pulled out a ten and handed it to the bartender. "Keep the change" Paulie said. The bartender didn't say thank you but instead nodded in a very selfish manner, like he had the generous tip coming to him. Paulie sighed, took a sip of his beer and tried to ignore his building anger. Suddenly a skinny man with a pale face walked over from across the room and handed the bearded man that sat next to Paulie a fifty dollar bill. Paulie watched casually as the bearded man handed him a small bag with what appeared to be heroin. The skinny man mumbled something that sounded like thanks and walked away, Paulie took another sip of his beer.

Paulie never touched heroin, but the possibility of the bearded man having blow almost made Paulie's mouth water. If he got some coke in him, enough of it, he would probably be able to finish the ride down to Darnite without another stop (unless of course he got the shits, coke sometimes did that to him). Paulie sat for a moment drinking his beer, thinking of a subtle way to ask the man. Before Paulie could contemplate the thought any further he heard his voice shout through the bar. "Anyone know where I could get some blow around here?" So much for subtle, Paulie thought. A few drunks sitting at the bar and some others playing pool looked around but couldn't quite tell where the ridiculous question had come from. The bearded man whose face was getting redder by the second knew exactly where it had come from. The man grabbed Paulie by the collar and pulled him close to his face. "You got a fucking problem man! What the hell's the matter with you?" The man's voice was authoritative but nervous sounding. Paulie stared back him with a crazed look, his eyes were bugged and creepy. Something about that look bothered the bearded man but he didn't show it. "You a cop?" The man said as he pulled Paulie even closer. Paulie began shaking his head frantically, his eyes were now flaring with seriousness. "No I'm not a cop." The bearded man stared at Paulie closely for another moment before letting go of his collar and taking a deep breath. "Follow me then." The man got up, took a precautionary look around and walked away from the bar. Paulie stood up, fixed his sweater collar, and followed the large man.

The bearded man and Paulie entered a shabby looking bathroom. The walls inside were painted dark blue but most of the color had been chipped off over the years. The stall doors were some sort of dark mustard color that reminded Paulie of the prison cafeteria he had dined in so many times. Other than a few curious looking blank spots, the walls and stall doors were covered with graffiti. A filthy faucet sat in the corner and a partially shattered mirror hung over it. As soon as they walked into the bathroom the smell of dried piss was tangible and Paulie could feel his stomach turn. The bearded man locked the door behind them. "You probably don't do this a whole lot but for future reference, try and be a little more subtle next time." The man said arrogantly and Paulie cleared his throat with an accompanied smirk. "So what do you got?" Paulie asked and the man rolled his eyes in annoyance.

"What do you got to spend?" The man pointed his finger at Paulie as he spoke. Paulie looked down at the finger bemused, he then pulled three crisp hundred dollar bills from out of his pocket and held them up to the man's face. "What could I get for this?" The bearded man grinned before grabbing the bills forcefully out of Paulie's hand. "This, well let me see." The man stuffed the hundreds into his left pocket before proceeding to search through his others for the contraband. After a few seconds of fiddling around the man pulled a relatively small bag of coke from out of his pocket. "Here you go." Paulie grabbed the coke from the man's hand quickly, similar to the way the man had grabbed the money from him. Paulie stared at the bag for a moment examining it, he was stupefied by how small it was. "That's it." Paulie said and the bearded man smiled. "That's it, take it or leave it."

Paulie knew he was getting ripped off but instead of objecting he merely shook his head in acceptance. "I guess I'll take it." The man smiled and nodded approvingly. "Great doing business with you." The bearded man said as he began to unlock the bathroom door. "Wait, you know I am kind of new at this. You mind sticking around and keeping an eye out for me while I do it?" Paulie had an uneasy look on his face, the bearded man let out a loud, angry sigh. "I don't got time for this." The man spoke without compassion. "Come on pal, I don't want to get busted." Paulie whined. The man was about to tell Paulie to fuck off when a thought hit him. If Paulie did by some chance get caught by the cops there was no chance he wouldn't tell them where he got the stuff. The large man rolled his eyes. "Alright, hurry up, I'll be out here." Paulie smiled excitedly. "Thanks a million, Jacko." Paulie gave the bearded man a pat on the shoulder and headed into one of the bathroom stalls.

Paulie shut the door behind himself and looked around the inside of the dirty stall. There were feces all around the rim of the toilet as if someone had missed their target. Paulie felt his stomach turn but tried to ignore the disgusting smell as he ripped open the small powder filled bag. Once the bag was open he pulled the metal tube that normally sat in his "sugar bowl" from his back pocket and began to snort viciously. After a moment of indulging he called to the bearded man. "Oh this is real good stuff bud!". The bearded man shook his head in disgust before answering. "Great, I'm very happy for you, could you hurry up?" "No problem bud, sorry." After another minute Paulie finished the bag completely. Instead of leaving the stall he continued making snorting sounds with his nose, Paulie then reached into his left pocket and pulled out a long piece of piano wire. The bearded man listened to the continuous snorts for another moment before heading over to the faucet. The man turned the handle to the right and began rinsing his face with some cool water. He then began to rub some of the water through his greasy hair, brushing it back with his hands. Since the man was too busy lathering himself, he could not see or hear that Paulie had began to creep out of the bathroom stall, with the piano wire wrapped tightly around his hands. The bearded man splashed some more water on his face before shutting off the sink and drying his face.

The man moved his face close to one side of the broken mirror and stared at some lines that had formed over the years. On the other side of the mirror (where the man was not looking) Paulie's face was beginning to become visible. The bearded man was clueless to the fact that Paulie who was tip toeing ever so quietly, was about to strike. Paulie was now about six inches from the mans back, his piano wire was stretched and ready to go. Suddenly just as Paulie began to lift the wire into the air, the man called out to where he thought Paulie was. "Are you done yet or what?" Paulie couldn't help but grin as he continued to lift the wire over the man's head. "Oh yea, I'm done." The words whimpered out of Paulie's mouth and the bearded man's eyes shot open in a jolt of horror. Before he could process the thought of Paulie being right behind him, the thin steel wire wrapped around his thick neck and tightened. As Paulie pulled the wire back the large man's head flew back in a convulsion like jerk. The man may have been large and though he was strong, Paulie was stronger. The man moaned and grunted as he tried to somehow shake Paulie off. Paulie answered back with violent thrusts of the wire and the mans face began to turn a deathly violet. Paulie was pulling so hard that there was now a large vein bulging out of his forehead. Paulie then felt a warm wetness on his fingers, he looked down expecting to see sweat and instead saw blood dripping out of the dying mans neck. The steel wire had began to rip through the soft flesh on the mans throat and formed a scarlet crevice. Finally the bearded man's eyes rolled back into his skull and one last choking phlegmy sound left his throat. Paulie dropped the large lifeless body to the ground. The dead weight hit the floor with a loud thud and Paulie stuck his face to the dead mans. "That fucking coke sucked you fat fuck!" Paulie screamed before kicking the fresh corpse in the head.

Paulie reached down towards the dead man's pants and began going through his pockets. He first went for the one where the man had stuffed the three hundreds. Including his own money, Paulie found seven hundred dollars in the pocket. In another he found two more small bags of coke and even though it wasn't the best stuff he'd had, Paulie decided to take it anyway. "Look at that, two for one." Paulie said with a laugh. He got back to his feet and slowly began to open the bathroom door. Paulie peeked his head out through the crack of the door and noticed that the bar was still pretty full.

67

He looked around and saw that most of the people were now standing at the bar drinking or waiting for drinks. Though the bar was closer than the pool tables were, it was still a good fifteen feet away from the bathroom. Plenty of distance to blend in with their peripheral vision, Paulie thought. He looked to his right and at the end of the hall,about ten feet away sat a door with a red exit sign hanging over it. Paulie pulled his head back into the bathroom, closed the door and stared at the large carcass solemnly.

The people at the bar continued to drink and talk amongst themselves. The bartender hustled around as quick as he could, grabbing drinks for whoever had managed to get his attention. In the far distance, Paulie began to drag the lifeless body down through the back hall and no one seemed to notice. Paulie could not believe how heavy the man was as he struggled to pull him toward the door. The same vein from earlier bulged out of Paulie's forehead as he continued to pull the man by his arms vigorously. When Paulie finally got to the door, he was breathing heavily and sweat was pouring down his face. He took a deep breath and gave the body one more giant tug through the door. Snow flurries began to land on Paulie and his deceased company as he made his way outside the door. When the body was completely through the threshold, the door slammed shut and Paulie fell to his knees in exhaustion. Paulie stayed kneeleddown for a moment, looking around the snow covered back alley. If Paulie would have known the man was as heavy as he was, he would have left the body on the bathroom tile to rot.

Paulie spotted a dumpster and knew his work here was far from over. He jumped back to his feet and once again began to drag the large carcass. When Paulie reached the dumpster he let out a discomforting sigh and began to prop the dead man up into a sitting position. Paulie then wrapped his arms around the cold torso and began to pull the man up as best as he could. From a distance it might have looked like the two men were practicing wrestling moves on each other. "Come on, let's go." Paulie said with a grunt as he brought the body to it's feet. He then lifted the body carefully and placed it on his shoulders. When the dead man's feet were completely off the ground Paulie began to wobble "I got ya, I got ya." He reassured the corpse. Paulie regained his balance and painfully tossed the body into the dumpster. As the body left his shoulders, a zipper from the dead mans jacket got caught onto Paulie's sweater and teared a small hole into the fabric. There was a loud echoing thump when the body hit the metal floor of the dumpster. Paulie felt the tear in his sweater and glanced at it. "Son of a bitch!" He looked down into the dumpster where the body was laying motionless. "Look at what you did to my sweater!" Paulie stared at the body for another moment as if he was waiting for a reply. Finally Paulie closed the lid and began to walk away, as he did he stretched his back with hopes of easing the strain he had just caused. Paulie slipped quietly back into the bar, grabbed his jacket and headed out the front door without catching the attention of a single soul.

5

New Leads

At around eight o'clock the next morning, Detective Atkins burst
through the police station doors holding his new favorite drawing. With all
the excitement from the new evidence, the detective had barely slept and the
black bags he carried under his eyes showed that. He had spent the night
eating a few more of his pills and polishing off the bottle of Johnny Blue.
Atkins had then sat on his couch fantasizing about finding the son of a bitch
slasher and slitting his throat. Before finally giving in to sleep at around six.
Detective Atkins said hello to the usual bunch of officers and then came to
the desk of his closest friend and partner Detective Martin Brodie. Brodie
was thirty six but had a young face that could have made him pass for twenty
five. He was a black man and resembled a young Sidney Poitier, particularly
when he wore nice suits like the gray one he had on now. "Good morning."
Detective Atkins said as he pulled off his trench coat and laid it on the chair
at the desk across from Brodie's.

Atkins coughed as he took a seat and Brodie could smell the alcohol
on the detective's breath. It only proved his suspicion when a second later the

still drunk detective burped up. "Rough night Atkins?" Brodie said jokingly.
He cared for his partner but his drinking was old news, he understood the
situation and who was he to tell Atkins he couldn't drink to kill the pain. The
one time Brodie had tried to talk Atkins out of drinking like a fish, it had
almost gotten them into a fight. As a matter a fact the only thing that had
stopped them from fighting was what Atkins had said to him after things
were heated. "Put yourself in my shoes Marty." And when Atkins said that, it
all clicked in Brodie's head as it should have before. He imagined if it had
been his wife or his two boys that were murdered, he would have lost it,
maybe even ended it all. When Brodie put it in perspective, drinking was the
least the guy could do. Atkins didn't say it a lot but he really appreciated his
partner. He knew Brodie was his balance and he was always there if Atkins
needed him. He was one of the only people that was as dedicated as Atkins
was to finding the Bloomingdale slasher. The detective knew without Brodie
he would have flew off the handle months ago.

Atkins had a giant grin on his face when he held up the sketch
composite of the slasher, it was the first time since before the murders that
Detective Brodie had seen that kind of enthusiasm. "This is it Brodie, the
beginning of the end for this scumbag. He's finally starting to slip up." Atkins
said and Brodie nodded. "We'll get 'em, I've been telling you for months, his

days are numbered." Atkins nodded in agreement and suddenly Brodie's eyes lit up as he remembered something. "Oh wow I can't believe I almost forgot." Detective Brodie reached down into one of his drawers and pulled out a blue box with a matching blue bow on it. Detective Atkins knew what it was before even seeing the gold letters that read Blue Label. "A little something, Happy birthday." Brodie said as he handed his partner the bottle. Atkins smiled as he stared down at the box. "Good timing, I just finished my other bottle." Brodie smirked and rolled his eyes slightly, he wasn't surprised. Atkins slowly traced his finger around the golden trim of the box, as he stared down at the composite his smile faded. "I could taste it you know." From the tone of his voice, it was obvious to Brodie that Atkins wasn't talking about the scotch. Before Brodie could say anything a young officer walked over to the detectives' desks. "We just gotta' call, two homicides by the abandoned warehouse off of Mott Street, possibly slasher." Detective Atkins and Detective Brodie glanced at each other somberly. "Tell them we're on our way." Atkins said to the officer as he turned back to Brodie. "I told you I could taste it." "Jesus, I think your starting to become psychic partner." Brodie smirked and the two men left the station.

Fifteen minutes later the two detectives pulled up in Atkins' vintage black '65 Dodge Challenger, other than a few scuffs and scratches the car was in great condition. They got out and walked up to the warehouse where the burnt shell of a Cadillac was sitting. There were a few police cars parked with their sirens flaring and an ambulance idling quietly next to them. The detectives showed their badges to the officers on patrol and crossed over the police tape. The two cooked human bodies along with the two dog bodies had already been pulled out and laid down on the snow covered ground. "Wakey, wakey, burnt your eggs and bakey." Detective Atkins said in a very insensitive tone. He hadn't always been this way, but no one could blame him for taking on a much colder approach to death. A forensics officer was on his knees looking closely at one of the human bodies. "What have we got here?" Brodie asked curiously as he and Atkins took a squat next to the blackened corpses. The forensic officer turned to both men. "Judging from the lethal bite around the neck, this one was definitely killed by the dogs. As for the other, the animals don't appear to be the cause of death." "Then what appears to be the cause?" Atkins asked. "His throat was slit." The forensics officer said sternly and Detective Atkins stared at him for a moment, the memory of his wife and daughter was beginning to consume his mind again.

"So what do your guys think happened?" Atkins asked and the forensics officer shook his head diffidently. "Well before my guys could come to a real conclusion. I think you and your guys need to find out exactly who these guys were and what kind of shit they were into." Atkins nodded in agreement as the officer continued. "Now there was a duffel bag found inside the warehouse, it was filled with towels, there was also an empty plastic bag that has what appears to be coke residue inside of it. Best guesses say this was a drug deal gone wrong, or perhaps a faux drug deal gone wrong" "So, what makes them think it was the slasher?" Brodie asked confused. "Well nothing exactly, just that this is kind of his territory. And nowadays what homicide around here doesn't get blamed on the friggen' slasher." Atkins gave Brodie a look of disbelief before turning back to the forensics officer. "That's all they're going on huh?" Atkins asked stubbornly. "Pretty much but either way unless there's some DNA left behind, it makes no difference who it was. It could have been Freddy Kruger for all we know." The forensics officer let out a small chuckle. Atkins and Brodie stared emotionless at the man until he felt the tension and stopped abruptly.

Detective Atkins stood up and walked away from the bodies, Brodie gave the forensics officer a nod and followed his partner. "What do you think?" Brodie asked with slight concern. "What I think is that the Bloomingdale slasher is getting more creative with the ways he kills people." Brodie stared at his partner perplexed before Atkins continued. "I've been watching this guy long enough to know his work is unpredictable, he doesn't have a pattern and he doesn't leave a calling card. Even all the murders he's presumed to be responsible for have no real ties. Just the fact that they're in close range to each other and that before the slasher started his streak, there were barely any murders in this town. Hell that forensics guy is right, anybody could murder someone these days and if there isn't sufficient evidence, it'll get thrown on the slasher's tally..." Detective Brodie stared at Atkins expecting something more to be said "But..." Atkins smirked lightly. "But, I do think he killed these two guys and then for some reason, made it look like a drug deal." "But why?" Brodie asked. Detective Atkins shook his head. "That I don't know. Maybe he's got the same hunch I got, that we're getting closer." "What if the deceased end up being criminals, this could actually be something entirely unrelated to the slasher. Maybe a drug kingpin sending a message?" Detective Atkins shook his head. "I wouldn't doubt they have records but even if they do, a drug kingpin, in this town? I'm sure there's somebody out here making a killing off all the kids that smoke grass, but that isn't exactly the kind of shit that will get you chewed up by a dog. Brodie nodded in agreement.

Detective Atkins looked back towards the bodies and thought for a moment before continuing. "I think the slasher lead them here, might even have set up a faux drug deal just to kill them. As for the dogs, I don't know where the fuck they'd come in." The two detectives shared a moment of silence, they were engaged in thought. "Protection, that's really the only reason I could see two rottweilers being here." Brodie said. "So the guy brought the dogs as protection?" Atkins said and Brodie nodded." "Is this gonna' end up going with the rest of the slashers case files or somewhere new." Brodie asked and Atkins shook his head. "Who knows. It's like the forensics guy said, if there's no DNA, it doesn't really matter who it was." "You really think this was the slasher?" Brodie asked. "I do but I'll tell you what, once we get these composites posted around and we catch the fuck, you could ask him if he did it yourself." Atkins said with a grin and Brodie nodded approvingly. "Will do."

6

Dear Old Uncle Paulie

At about five pm in the Lawson household, Daniel and Michelle were watching TV in the living room. They embraced warmly on a white leather love seat where they had spent most of their evenings. A long time ago when they had first had Nicole, Daniel and Michelle were less loving to one another. At the time Daniel was working a lot more and would take the stress from his day out on his wife. The rough patch had lasted through most of Nicole's childhood years but nowadays she could barely remember it and would often wonder if it had really ever been that bad. It had, it had even gotten so bad that the two weren't even sleeping in the same bed for weeks at a time. Daniel who was too consumed with his work would come home late and sleep alone in the guest room. Michelle was an emotional wreck, she would constantly feel angry and insignificant. All the chaos had eventually lead Michelle to find her emotional outlet in another. Unbeknownst to Daniel, the secret lover that had seduced his wife many years before was now on his way to their house.

Michelle had never told Daniel about her and Paulie for many reasons,

78

the obvious one being that it would destroy him. Though she had committed the unfaithful act, it was never Michelle's intention to hurt Daniel. Things had simply fell into place and it had happened. Sometimes things worked that way, whether you were planning on something or not, things would just fall into place. As time went on and other things fell into place, (Paulie going to jail being one of them) Daniel and Michelle worked through their problems. Nowadays some might say that Daniel and Michelle were a great couple but that would be an understatement. The truth was Daniel and Michelle had become a perfect couple and it wasn't just on the surface as so many couples appear to be. Their sex life was good, they had good communication and they hadn't even had so much as an argument in years. For Daniel it was easy, once he got a promotion, work became less stressful and so did home life. For Michelle it was a little bit more difficult. At first she had trouble with giving up the idea of Paulie, even though it was all so wrong, it felt right. Time eventually healed that though and Paulie became an ever fading memory.

Yes life had been alright, stress free and enjoyed to the fullest, but late last night something had come crawling back through an innocent phone call, something that Michelle had buried deep in her subconscious. Over the years as Paulie had sat in a jail cell, Michelle's fears had vanished gradually. She realized that what she had done was behind her and with Paulie far away, it wouldn't happen again. With Paulie gone, it was like it had never happened and that was just the way Michelle wanted it to be. Michelle had never thought in a million years that Paulie would be back in her life. As time went on the thought of him got pushed further back in her mind, almost like he had been erased from existence. It had never crossed her mind that in all the years passing, Paulie was getting closer to freedom. Even if Michelle would have did the math, she would have shut the thought down knowing that Daniel and Paulie would never talk again, but that wasn't the case. The reality of it was that Daniel and Paulie had talked, they had let bygones be bygones and all her fears would awake in the instant he arrived. What if Daniel some how found out about what had happened, what if Paulie just came out and told him? No he wouldn't, Michelle reassured herself as she sat cuddled next to her husband. But that didn't calm her as something far more fearful slipped into her mind. What if they were alone, what if she was feeling vulnerable, what if she did it again?

Suddenly the door bell rang through out the living room and echoed into the upper level of the house. Michelle felt the dryness that had overwhelmed her throat and swallowed. Daniel glanced over at his wife with a look of silent anticipation. "Is that him?" Michelle asked with disbelief, her voice was hoarse. Daniel looked down at his watch. "It could be." Daniel got up and walked towards the front door, Michelle followed behind him hesitantly. When they got to the door Daniel reached for the knob and opened it. There Paulie stood holding his duffel bag, he smiled and took his freezing hands out of his jacket pockets. Paulie tugged on the rim of his baseball cap as if he was giving some kind of modern day cowboy salute. "Hello Daniel." Paulie said innocently. "Paulie." Daniel said as he smiled affectionately. The two men hugged as Michelle watched in uncomfortable awe. "Come in." Daniel said kindly. Paulie stepped into the house and Michelle closed the door behind him. "How did you get down here so fast?" "Magic little brother, magic." Paulie quipped strangely. "Yea magic alright, you must have drove all night. You're probably exhausted." Paulie smirked. "I'm fine." Paulie turned to Michelle who was staring at him in silence. "And my beautiful sister in law, How are you?" Paulie kissed her on the cheek and Michelle felt goose bumps occupy her skin. She looked back at him with a disoriented gaze. "I'm good Paulie,everything's just great." Paulie nodded. "Good, good."

Paulie pulled off his hat and ran fingers through his messy hair, Michelle watched as he did and felt something inside of herself twitch. He unzipped his jacket and slid it down his shoulders revealing the red

81

Christmas sweater, Michelle's eyes widened and she spoke without thinking. "Is that the sweater I made for you?" Paulie nodded pleasingly. "You bet it is." Michelle could not have imagined the sweater was still in existence. "I can't believe you still have it, I would have figured you got rid of that old thing a long time ago." Michelle was now blushing. Paulie shook his head. "I would never get rid of it, not for the world." The two glanced at each other and Michelle began rubbing the back of her neck trying to soothe the growing goose bumps. "Oh it's ripped." Daniel said as he pointed a finger to the tear on the sweater. "Would you look at that, I hadn't noticed." Paulie lied. "Well I'm sure Michelle could fix that for you, can't you honey?" Daniel said and Michelle glanced at the hole. "I just have to get red fabric but it would be no problem." Paulie smiled. "That would be great, thanks." Paulie pulled off the sweater, revealing his snug white undershirt. Daniel grabbed the sweater from his brother and handed it to Michelle, she took it reluctantly. "Take care of that hun'." Daniel said. For a quick moment Michelle had a feeling of contempt for her husband. She didn't know why and shut it out as fast as it had come.

Nicole who had been studying for a final was now coming down the steps to fetch a drink and proceed on with her work. When she spotted her parents with the familiar stranger she regretted leaving her room instantly.

Daniel turned toward the staircase with a grin. "Look who's here Nicki." He called. Vague memories filled Nicole's mind as she finished down the staircase. She knew who was here, she knew that face, it was her dear old uncle. Paulie stared at the teenager with an awkward but seemingly joyful expression and Nicole countered with her best fake smile. "Hi." Nicole said. Paulie smiled and looked the girl up and down. "Well look at you, you've really grown, haven't you?" Paulie sounded genuinely surprised. Nicole could feel the blood rush to her face with sudden embarrassment. "Yes she has." Daniel added as Paulie continued to stare. "You look just like your mother." Paulie said. "Thank you." Nicole was flattered but couldn't help but feel slightly uncomfortable. Michelle stared at Paulie deeply as if she was trying to read his mind. "Mom..." Nicole interrupted. "Jake's gonna' come over for dinner." Michelle snapped out of her stare and turned to her daughter. She had the thought to have a dispute but didn't care enough to. "Ok, that's fine."

About an hour later, Paulie, the Lawson family and Nicole's boyfriend Jake sat at the dining room table eating a chicken dinner. Paulie finished chewing his meat and wiped his mouth before speaking. "I can't say it enough, this meal is delicious." Michelle smiled graciously. "Thank you Paulie." Paulie turned to Daniel who was now pouring his brother a glass of wine. "Seems like you have everything here Danny boy. A beautiful home, a great wife and a lovely daughter." As the words rolled off Paulie's tongue, envy filled his mind. Daniel nodded as he poured himself a glass of wine. "Well with my brother back, now I really do have everything." Daniel said with a smile, Paulie followed with one and Michelle gave a quick one of her own. Nicole and Jake glanced at each other with goofy smirks. Paulie noticed the mocking grins and turned toward his niece. "So Nicole, you're going to college soon?" Nicole wiped the grin off her face with her napkin. "Yea I've been looking at some schools." Paulie took a sip of his wine and nodded. "Good, stay in school. I never had the time for college, I should have made time though." Paulie said passively before sticking the fork back into his chicken. "What were you busy doing?" Nicole asked though she knew the answer. Paulie glanced at Daniel before turning back to Nicole. "Stuff I shouldn't have been doing I guess." He said somberly. "What kind of stuff?" Nicole continued innocently.

Daniel turned to his daughter with a look of anger. "Nicole." He grunted. Paulie should have been blushing with embarrassment but instead had a simple stern look on his face. "Bad stuff, real bad stuff." Paulie replied before taking another sip of his wine. An awkward silence took over the dining room and Nicole felt herself begin to sweat. Jake swallowed his throat and took a sip of his soda, Michelle stared at her daughter in disbelief. Daniel glanced at his daughter angrily and then back at Paulie with compassion. "Paulie, I'm sorr..." "It's ok Danny..." Paulie interrupted his brother. "I'm no saint. I've done things, I just can't pretend they didn't happen." Paulie's voice was soft and child like. Nicole stared emotionless, she was beginning to regret what she had asked. "But I did the time and paid the price. Believe me when I say, I am a changed man." Paulie was now staring directly at Nicole, his voice was shaking and filled with emotion. Nicole nodded silently in agreement, she was speechless but it was obvious to Paulie that she was sorry. After another awkward minute, Paulie turned to Jake. "So Jake, you're going to college too?" Jake was struck by the question being that he was still shocked by what had just happened. "Ah... Sure, I applied to some this week." Jake had no plans to go to college, in fact he had no plans for the future at all. He was just taking things as they came to him. Paulie nodded. "Good, good and I hope your taking care of my niece." Nicole felt embarrassed but was glad that the conversation had taken a turn for the better. Jake smirked nervously. "You bet I am." Paulie smiled sinisterly. "Good, you seem like a good kid, I wouldn't want to have to kill you." Jake giggled nervously and Paulie burst into laughter. "I'm only kidding kid, lighten up." Jake smiled and the rest of the table laughed as relief filled the once tense room.

Later on, Paulie and the family sat in the dimly lit living room watching old home movies. Daniel smiled as he watched, Michelle sat next to him looking rather tired. Paulie sat on a lone recliner, staring at the screen closely, as if he didn't want to miss a frame. Nicole and Jake were sitting on the other couch closely but not enough for Mr. Lawson to mind. A young Daniel and Michelle were having a barbecue in their backyard on the screen, they were about thirteen years younger. "Look at how young we were." Daniel said with a hint of nostalgia. A little girl with a disproportionate sized head wobbled onto the screen and the camera followed. Michelle giggled. "There's Nicole." Nicole smirked and watched as her younger self ran around the backyard passing several other relatives. Jake began to laugh. "Look how little you were, you had a big head." Nicole gasped before slapping Jake on the arm playfully. "Shut up jerk!" Jake smiled and kissed Nicole on the cheek. Paulie was beginning to get bored, he didn't care for the past and didn't like the way he used to be. Back then he was lost, out doing stupid things for cheap thrills, He had barely known himself.

Daniel abruptly pointed to the screen. "And there's you Paul." Paulie stared a cold stare at his younger counterpart who was sitting in a secluded area with his then girlfriend. The unknown voice holding the camera spoke "Wave to the camera Paulie." The younger Paulie waved to the camera and

86

grabbed the girls arm to do the same. The girl quickly pulled her arm away and said something that sounded like "I'm still mad at you." The two then began to argue and the cameraman slipped away quietly. Daniel smiled. "You and your girlfriend Laurie, you were always fighting. Whatever happened to her?" Paulie shook his head. "Who knows." Paulie fantasized for a moment about tracking her down and killing her for being the bitch she always was, he grinned to himself with the thought. Daniel noticed his brothers smile and thought it was obviously related to the video. "You're not seeing anyone now Paulie?" "Well I see some girls here and there..." Paulie said innocently as he turned toward his brother and Michelle. "But I can't seem to find the right one." Paulie shot a quick unnoticed glance to Michelle and she looked away just as fast. "Your uncles a ladies man?" Jake whispered into Nicole's ear. She began to giggle and just as Paulie, Daniel and Michelle looked over at them, Jake stood up. "Well it was very nice to meet you sir." Jake walked over to Paulie and shook his hand, he then turned to the Lawsons. "I better get going, thanks for dinner." Paulie smiled at Jake. "Take it easy kid." The Lawsons said goodbyes and Nicole proceeded to walk Jake to the front door.

Nicole and Jake stood in the doorway. "I can't believe what you were doing at dinner." Jake said in a whisper. "I know, I feel bad, he really is nice.

At first I thought he was a little creepy, but he's not that bad." Jake nodded. "He seems harmless, I was expecting a lot worse." "He probably hates me now, I feel like an ass." Nicole said. "No, I'm sure he forgave you, he seems like a nice enough guy." Jake said confidently. The two engaged in a quick kiss and then another and another. "Well let me go, I'll call you tomorrow." Jake said apologetically. They kissed once again, this one slightly longer and seconds later Nicole waved as Jake drove away in his parents minivan.

7

Old Flames Burn Again

In the middle of the night, as the rest of the house was fast asleep, Michelle who was in a dream like state, crept down the stairs as quiet as she could. She tip toed down the wooden steps and their tiny creaks echoed through the dark house. Once she was downstairs, she entered the laundry room and flicked on the light behind her. Michelle looked toward the hamper and spotted Paulie's red sweater. The same sweater she had made him all those years ago, the sweater that after all that had happened, he'd kept. She picked it up and smelled it like a curious puppy smelling a flower. Michelle thought back on the day when Paulie had gone away, the day she couldn't stop crying. She had to hide her tears from Daniel, she was so afraid that he would find out, but he never did. As Michelle stood there squeezing the sweater tightly to her night gown covered breasts, a single tear dropped down her eye. Suddenly there was another creak, this time coming from the hall and Michelle spun around startled to face the doorway.

Paulie stood there in the semi lit doorway, he was wearing sweatpants and a white T-shirt. Michelle let out a sigh of relief at the fact that it wasn't

Daniel. As she stood there staring at Paulie standing in the doorway, she remembered the day their relationship changed, the day it had crossed into the wrong. It was probably about a decade earlier Michelle assumed, maybe a month before Paulie was sentenced. Michelle had been cleaning the house, freshening up a bit and trying to keep her mind off a fight she had with Daniel that morning, when there was a sudden knock at the door. Michelle walked over and opened the door and to her surprise it was Paulie. After all those years she could still remember the hairs on the back of her neck standing up when their eyes met. For the last few months before that day, Daniel and Michelle had been fighting all the time and Michelle was starting to take a little too kindly to Paulie's casual friendliness. Though at that point it was hardly casual friendliness, it was blatant flirting. It started as simple compliments and gestures but before too long it had become much more. Long stares, implying comments and most recently a soft comforting rub up and down her thigh after Daniel had fought with her. At first Michelle was a bit startled by these things, but she was never the type to jump to conclusions, let alone tell her husband. After a while she looked forward to seeing Paulie, when he was around she knew he would do something that would make her feel better, make her feel respected.

The sexual tension was building between the two and perhaps in another situation it would have never gone anywhere. On this faithful day however, after being so hurt by Daniel's comments and feeling so vulnerable, the sparks flew. "Come in Paulie, come in." Michelle had said almost nervously. Paulie walked in, he looked calm but a bit shaken. Later Michelle would find out that Paulie had known the law was about to come down on him hard. Perhaps that was another reason for what had happened, they were both in a weird place, stress was high and they needed a release. "Is Danny here?" Paulie asked. He had known deep down that Danny was most likely at work but for some reason he had come looking anyway. "No he's working until seven." Paulie looked frustrated. "Oh damn." Michelle shouldn't of asked but did. "Could I get you a drink Paul?" Paulie let out a sigh as if a weight had been lifted off his shoulders. "You know, I could really use one of those right about now."

After about twenty minutes of the two drinking some Merlot, Michelle abruptly began to wail. Paulie turned to her concerned. "What's the matter, what is it?" She struggled to get the words out as she continued to cry. "We've been fighting so much, he's always so angry at me. I think he despises me!" Paulie grabbed hold of her by the shoulders. "No, how could he, your the perfect wife." Paulie consoled. "He does, I swear we always fight, he puts me down." She wiped some of the tears from her face. "Hey you're great, he'd have to be crazy to put you down." Paulie said as Michelle put her tear covered face on his shoulder. "You're always so sweet Paul, never a bad thing out of your mouth." Michelle said softly. Paulie didn't reply but began rubbing her back up and down, they were now face to face. Paulie's hand slid down her back slowly. "It's okay now, I'm here, it's all fine. I'm here for you." As he continued down to her hips, Michelle looked up at him and kissed him quickly on the lips before pulling away. His hands continued down to her thighs and they stared at each other for another moment before kissing again, this time sensually and longer. Her arms wrapped around him and before they knew it, they had done what was once a fantasy.

Now Paulie stood in the doorway of the laundry room, the last time they were alone together in this house was that surreal day. "You never did tell him, you said you would in that last letter you wrote me." Paulie said softly. Michelle stared for a moment, thinking, she threw the sweater aside. "I was going to tell him but things changed, he changed, I felt there was no reason he should know, it would only hurt things." Paulie stared at her silently. "He's my husband Paul, I couldn't just.." "It's ok, I'm happy for you." Paulie interrupted. He obviously wasn't, there was no way he could be Michelle thought. "We've come a long way, I'm older now. I know what's right now and we rarely fight anymore." Michelle said these things trying to

92

convince Paulie and some part of herself. Paulie smirked "Good, good for you." The look on his face could kill her alone. Everything started going well with Daniel and you forget about me, Paulie thought to himself. That wasn't what was supposed to happen.

Daniel's father had left a nice sum of money to Daniel and not surprisingly, none to Paulie. When Paulie was about to take the heat for the bank robbery (that had actually included two other guys) and the shit hit the fan, Paulie had the idea of pulling an OJ and bailing. He had originally come there that faithful day to talk to Daniel about borrowing the money. His plan was to take the money and leave town but Daniel didn't like this idea at all. For one, he felt that Paulie would get caught and they'd seize the money and mark it as the cash that Paulie's two accomplices had made off with (not only did he go to jail but they got the money, Paulie got them back for that eventually). Also, at the time Daniel had just purchased the house and was looking to put the money into fixing it up for his daughter and loving wife. Paulie quickly turned on Daniel and tried to make a run for it without his help.

When Paulie was finally nailed, Daniel went to visit him and Paulie went off on his brother. He blamed him for not lending the money and told

Daniel he never wanted to see him again. That was when their relationship officially ended. Michelle and Paulie however kept in contact for a few more months. Paulie would tell her that he loved her and that when he got out they would be together. Everything was going good until Daniel began to change his ways (this was probably related to what had happened with Paulie). He was nicer to Michelle and they began to get a long like a real couple. Michelle stopped writing the letters and moved on with her marriage and Paulie was all but forgotten. Left alone in a cell for the remainder of his eight year sentence. If it hadn't been for his new found hobby, he would have probably   lost his mind or maybe that's just what happened. Instead of saying anything more to Michelle, Paulie walked away from the laundry room and disappeared into the blackness of the hallway. Michelle began to cry silently to herself.

8

The Girl Who Knew Too Little

The next morning Nicole sat in her English class trying to pay attention to her boring teacher's boring words. Like her fellow classmates, Nicole was a little preoccupied with fantasizing about the upcoming Christmas break. What Nicole didn't know was that she would be spending her break with the psychopath that was her uncle. Her uncle, she thought about him now. How could she put the guy in the position she'd put him in, it wasn't right and it wasn't like her. He was obviously a changed man and she had hurt him when she had instigated the bringing up of his past, she could see it in his eyes. Nicole reached the conclusion that she would apologize to him, it was the only way to get it off her chest. At that moment Jake snuck up to her classroom door and got her attention. Jake was an avid cutter in school, he never did go to too many classes, especially the week before a break. Jake was a good kid though, just not the school type. He was behind on credits and knew he would never be able to graduate on time let alone go to college. Well, when all else fails, there's the GED, he sometimes thought. Jake signaled Nicole to leave the class room but she couldn't. She looked at the clock and realized there was ten minutes left of class. She signaled to

Jake, he sighed and let it be known that he'd be waiting for her down the hall.

When the bell finally rang, Nicole packed up her books and hurried out of the classroom before anyone else was out the door. She ran to Jake and hugged him and then they kissed. They had a better relationship than others their age and they usually got along well. When they did fight it was about the stupid meager things in life and nothing all that important. Eric and Cindy walked over in the middle of Nicole and Jake's passionate kiss. "Is this all they ever do." Cindy said jokingly. Nicole and Jake smiled and pulled away from each other. "You guys coming tonight?" Eric asked. Jake and Nicole both looked equally confused. "Coming to what?" Jake asked curiously. Eric rolled his eyes. "I told you last week, there's a party at the house tonight, gonna' be the last party there until after Christmas break, the biggest too, everyone's gonna' be there."

Cindy looked a bit down. "Yea everyone except for me." Eric sighed. "It's not anybody's fault but your own. She's going away with her parents for Christmas." Jake and Nicole smirked. "That sucks, well I'm definitely in tonight." Jake said. Nicole was about to say she was in as well and then it hit her. "Damn it, I can't go." Jake's smile faded as he turned to Nicole. "Why?" Nicole had a sad look on her face. "I have to study for my Math final." Eric rolled his eyes unbelievingly. "Well that sucks the big one." Jake smiled at

Eric's comment for a moment before wiping it away for Nicole. "Can't you just study before class tomorrow?" Jake asked and Nicole shook her head. "I can't, if I fail this test I'm definitely failing the semester." Jake turned to Cindy. "How did you get out of your tests Cin?" "Well I told my teachers about vacation a month ago and made arrangements already, I took all my finals today." Cindy said confidently. Jake nodded his head. "Well I guess I'm going alone too." Bewilderment took over Nicole's face. "You're gonna' go without me?" Jake took a second to come up with something to say. "Eric's gonna' be there alone, so I'll go with him." It was obvious that Nicole was now angry. "Well I'm gonna' be alone too, I figured you would come by and help me study." Jake looked at Eric and then back at Nicole. "Babe, it's the biggest party before break..." before he could finish Nicole cut him off. "You know what, do what you want." Nicole stormed off down the hall as the late bell rang and Jake stared speechless as she did. Cindy noticed the bell and kissed Eric on the cheek. "I gotta' go, I'll see you guys later."

Eric and Jake began to walk down the now secluded   hall, Jake looked a bit distressed so Eric put his arm around him. "Don't worry about her man, she'll get over it, but listen while were alone. I got this girl that I've been talking to for like a month online, she's coming to the party tonight. She goes to New Dorp high, I could tell her to bring a friend for you." Eric could immediately tell from the look on Jake's face, that his friend was a little unsure. "I don't know, maybe I should go help her study" "Are you fucking kidding me? Fuck that man, you gotta' live a little. Why do you have to stay cooped up in the house so she could study, she'll be fine without you." "I guess your right." Jake agreed. "Trust me man, this girl is hot and hot girls have hot friends, it's a proven fact." Eric smiled before continuing. "I gotta' get to gym, you gonna' come or what?" Jake took a moment before answering. "Yea I'll be there." Eric smiled. "Great, I'll give you a call later and let you know the deal." Jake and Eric went their separate ways and headed to class.

Later that afternoon in Mesapeena, Detective Atkins sat in a bar alone drinking his sorrows away. The only other person in the bar was Rachel, the thirty year old bartender. Rachel noticed that his glass of scotch was empty and walked over to him. "Another one Detective?" Detective Atkins smiled. "You're not gonna' cut me off?.." Atkins said as he glanced at the face of his watch that read one thirty. "It's not even two and I'm starting to feel a little buzzed." Rachel smiled. "I can't turn down a cop, can I? "Rachel proceeded to pour Atkins more scotch and he grinned. "You're a sweet gal, if you were a little older, I think we'd be perfect for each other." Rachel smirked and held up her left hand. "And if I wasn't married.." Detective Atkins puts his hand on his forehead in shame. "Right, you're married too." Rachel smiled and walked away. The loud ring of the detective's phone sounded and filled the vacant bar. He pulled out the phone from his pocket and looked at the screen which read Brodie. The Detective took a sip of his drink as he picked it up. "What do we got Brodie?" Atkins asked nonchalantly. "Sports bar right outside of town, past Lowell." Brodie said. "I think I know the place, what about it?" Atkins said with another swig of his scotch. "There's been a murder there, it's about forty minutes away but it just made the cut off for our jurisdiction. I'm driving over there now if you wanna' come meet me." "I'm on my way." Detective Atkins said in an instant and hung up the phone. He pulled a fifty out of his pocket and placed it on the bar. "Rachel, I gotta' go, I'll see you soon." Rachel turned to Atkins. "Where are you going in such a hurry?" Atkins turned to her. "Believe it or not, another bar." He smiled and ran out the door.

An hour later Detective Atkins's black 65' Challenger pulled up to the sports bar that Paulie had visited the night before. There were a few of the bar's employees standing in front of the building being questioned by officers. Detective Atkins parked and quickly made his way towards the crowd, his trench coat was blowing in the crisp winter wind like some superhero's cape. The detective turned to a fellow officer who was smoking a cigarette. "Where's the murder scene?" The officer exhaled his smoke and pointed toward the back of the building. "In the back alley, just walk around there." Atkins nodded. When the detective got to the back he immediately spotted Brodie and a few other officer's surrounding a dumpster in the distance, he continued toward them. "So who's the stiff this time?" Atkins asked casually. Brodie turned toward his partner and gave him a sort of hello nod. "ID says Charles Tooze, everyone that knew him here called him Chuck. The employees said he was a frequent visitor, kept to himself, but was well known." Detective Brodie let out a sigh before continuing. "Middle aged, biker type, heavy set. Don't want to judge a book by the cover but probably a low life." Atkins smirked and looked around curiously. "So where is our friend Chuck?" Brodie nodded his head towards the dumpster. "Right in there with the rest of the trash." Brodie said unapologetically. "Show some respect for the dead will ya?" Atkins said with a smile. Detective Atkins walked towards the dumpster and looked in, there he saw the lifeless body of the heavyset bearded man. The large man appeared to have gotten heavier due to the bloating that had occurred in the wee hours. The mark from the piano wire around his neck was now a dark purple color which complemented the yellowing flesh nicely.

Atkins turned back towards Brodie. "Strangled him huh?" Atkins asked. "Yea, not sure exactly where it happened though, could've been out here or inside." Brodie said and Atkins nodded. The two detectives began to walk back to the front of the bar. The officer who was smoking by the front earlier was now walking towards the back, Atkins stopped him. "Hey you got a smoke?" Atkins asked and the officer nodded. "Sure." The officer reached into his pocket and handed the detective a cigarette, "Light?" The officer asked and Atkins nodded. The officer lit Atkins cigarette and Brodie stared on slightly confused. "Thanks." Atkins said as he took his first puff and the officer continued toward the back of the building. "I haven't seen you run out of smokes in months, you always have two packs on you." Brodie said curiously. "Yea well I haven't bought any, I'm trying to quit. I'm just gonna' focus on my drinking from now on." Atkins quipped slickly and Brodie laughed. "That's good, I guess." "So did the forensics guys have anything interesting to say?" Atkins asked. Brodie waved some of his partners smoke out of his face. "They didn't even get here yet." Brodie said and Atkins nodded.

"Forget the forensics guys, I was talking to some of the employees earlier, a bartender I think his name is Larry or Llyod or something. He said that this guy Chuck, was known for selling stuff around the bar." Brodie said. "What kind of stuff?" Atkins took another puff of his cigarette as he asked.

"Mostly coke and heroin, the bartender never stopped him because the guy never caused any problems." "So another coke related death? Maybe there is some kind of drug thing going on." Atkins said regretfully. "Well here's the thing, I asked the guy if there was any new faces that stuck out last night and he remembered this guy in a goofy sweater. He started describing him and I pulled out the slasher sketch." Atkins stared at his partner anxiously. "And." "And he said without the beard, it was him." Detective Atkins threw his cigarette to the snow covered ground. "So the slasher enjoys a little coke from time to time. He scores some off this Chuck guy and then he kills him." Atkins said as Brodie nodded. "Probably the same reason he killed those other two by the abandoned warehouse." Brodie added. "But wait, where almost in fucking Boston here, the slasher never kills this far out, why would he change all of a sudden?" Atkins asked and Brodie smiled. "The same reason he shaved his beard." Detective Atkins eyes lit up. "He knows we're on to him, he's making a break out of town." Brodie nodded in agreement. "Somebody saw that news report after all." Brodie added and Atkins looked at him sternly.

9

It's Beginning To Look A Lot Like Christmas

After Paulie survived the ambush in the library of the   prison, he
began to take on a certain reputation around the place. To take three guys
down at once, now that was something that would earn you respect (amongst
killers, thieves and rapists but respect nonetheless).The on duty guard, who
coincidentally disappeared from the library when the three men managed to
get in was still gone when Paulie slipped away into the prison court yard.
This left the three murders a mystery and ultimately got the missing guard
fired, but the inmates had heard the stories and they knew who had done it.
For the first few nights following the murders Paulie was shaky and nervous,
he thought at first that he couldn't handle the fact that he had killed but deep
inside himself there was something out of place, a yearning. Sure Paulie
wanted to get out of prison, that was a given, but the feeling wasn't related to
freedom. As the days passed by Paulie began to have even stranger urges.
Once during lunch while he sat across from an unknown Spanish prisoner
who was chewing rather annoyingly, Paulie abruptly had the thought of
suffocating the man. He would grab his thick, stale piece of bread, jam it into
the man's throat and hold his nose. Then and only then would the unbearable

103

chomping be subdued. Paulie jumped back into his normal mind set with an unsettling wonder at what he had just thought and what had brought it on.

As the months continued on and the morbid urges showed no signs of ceasing, Paulie began to realize what he needed to do, he needed to feed his impulses. One day while in the courtyard he overheard two Puerto Rican men talking about another man who had gotten on their nerves. The first man had said something to the other about wanting to kill the guy and before the two men had even began to devise a plan, Paulie interrupted casually. "Who's the guy, I'll kill him for you." It was something that the two men had taken as a joke but when Paulie didn't laugh about it, they second guessed their initial reaction. Like the rest of the prisoners they had heard what Paulie had done those months ago and they knew just what he was capable of. Two days later Paulie snuck up on the man in the shower and slit his throat effortlessly, he was in and out of the bathroom quickly, without a trace. When it was said and done, Paulie felt centered and fulfilled. This was when he began to realize the true joy that killing could bring him.

Paulie decided that he needed a routinely planned outlet for his newly found craving. As time went on and he became acquainted with other prisoners, Paulie took on a sort of go to guy persona. However he was far from your average go to guy who got you that pack of smokes or those nude books you really needed. Paulie was into much bigger things, a sort of murderer for hire. Prisoners who knew about his handy work would come to him and offer their best (but mostly petty) trades for the jobs. Most inmates in need of his services would offer him booze or smokes and most every time he would take the stuff for the hell of it. The truth was Paulie considered the job as the pay and other than the guy getting killed, it was a win win for everyone else involved. The inmate would have his man dead and Paulie would get to scratch the burning itch inside of himself. After a while Paulie even did the deeds as favors and all he would ask for in return was protection and a favor of his own, if one day needed.

Paulie would kill whoever his fellow inmates wanted, hell he'd tell a guy that he was gonna' kill someone for him and then that same week somebody would tell him to kill the guy who sent him and he would do it. He didn't have morals and at this point in his life, he couldn't care less about them. Paulie was right in the middle of an eight year sentence and getting out was the last thing on his mind. What was the sense of freedom when there was nothing for you on the outside. Michelle had stopped writing him months after he had gotten here and all the problems in his once mundane life seemed so worthless now. Paulie would sometimes hope he'd get caught by the guards while doing a job and receive a life sentence, that he thought would be easier than trying to resume a normal life after his eventual release. The guards never did get wise, mostly because Paulie was an ideal inmate or at least seemed that way. He was a loner, always keeping to himself and never seeming to cause a problem. These murders would occur randomly and the guards would have their idea of what guy or guys did it but would never have any solid evidence. Paulie was about the furthest thing on their mind, as the guy was in there for robbing a bank without so much as wounding someone. To the guards, the inmates who were dumb to his moonlighting and the entire penal system, Paulie was just a guy trying to do his stint and be on his way.

Over the course of the eight years Paulie had killed roughly thirty people through out the prison, which was hardly a dent in it's population of thirteen thousand. As his prison sentence came to an end Paulie began to have a taste for freedom again. He imagined himself walking through the barbed wired courtyard for the last time and heading for the main gate that he hadn't passed in almost a decade. This abrupt and overwhelming feeling to finally get out made Paulie decide two weeks before his release that he wouldn't take a chance with anymore murders (on the inside at least). He had done his time and what was the point of getting stuck in there forever.

Besides he was curious to see how being a free man felt again and how different the naked breeze on his skin would be compared to that of the barricaded courtyards. Sometimes when you least expect it, life has some irony waiting in the shadows and Paulie never believed that more than the day he saw his two former bank robbing partners being walked to their new cells.

    Paulie couldn't help but laugh at the fact that these two guys had entered the shit house a day before he was set to be released. During lunch time Bobby and Travis spotted Paulie and walked up to his table. They were two well built men, Travis had a shaved head and a scar above his forehead and Bobby looked like a scarier Sal Mineo. They approached Paulie like old classmates who hadn't seen each other in years, goofy smiles across each of their faces. They asked ridiculous questions like how are you doing in here and how much time do we get outdoors daily. Paulie couldn't believe the casualness of their conversation and had to fight off the urge of killing them right there and then. They gave a stale apology for leaving Paulie behind to get busted, said the walls were closing in and they had to get out of dodge. The worst part was they gave some bull about not being able to get in touch with him, but nevertheless Paulie listened closely and humored them. He said he understood and it was water under the bridge. Travis and Bobby had heard

that Paulie was getting out and wished him the best. Paulie added that maybe
when they got out, the three of them could go out for a drink or something,
maybe start doing some stuff together again. Paulie kept his promise to
himself and didn't kill another person, the next day he was released and a
week later he moved to New Hampshire. Sadly, Travis and Bobby never did
get to have that drink, as two days after their reunion with Paulie the two
men were found dead in the showers. They were sodomized by several
unknown prisoners and both of their throats were slit. It turned out that the
owed favors Paulie had saved up had come in handy after all.

Paulie spent the next year taking his murderous impulses through
Mesapeena without a single care. Now Paulie grinned in ironic amusement at
the fact that he was back in his home town, walking through a packed
shopping mall with his estranged half brother. Looking back on the path that
had gotten him here made him feel like he was looking back on some fading
dream. As he walked passed the familiar parts of the mall Paulie thought that
maybe his serial killing lifestyle had been just that, a figment of his
imagination. Perhaps he had never even been inside a jail cell, because being
back here in Darnite was making him feel like he had never left the town.
The air conditioning that filled the mall was barely noticeable as the swarms
of holiday shoppers continued to pump in. Each of them brought their stress,

money troubles, and hot air as they entered. Most of the shoppers looked like brainless zombies going off instinct, they went store to store buying up what ever was put in front of their eyes. Skull caps and scarfs were stuffed into jackets and jackets were stuffed under sweating,hot armpits as the holiday jingles echoed throughout the stores. As the two men continued around the mall, Paulie tried to ignore the uncomfortable heat and perspiration that had started around his neck. This slight annoyance began to brew other feelings, somewhat more barbaric ones and Paulie knew in that instant that his murderous life had not been a dream after all.

Daniel was holding a couple of shopping bags and grinning dumbly at the people going about their holiday shopping. "Thanks for coming with me Paulie, I can't stand going shopping alone." Paulie snapped out of his bored but thoughtful daze. "Hey it's the least I could do and maybe you could help me pick out something for Nicole and Michelle." Daniel smiled. "You know that's not necessary Paul." Paulie turned to Daniel and smiled. "Please, it'll be my pleasure." Daniel nodded in acceptance before continuing. "Speaking of that, I guess I'm gonna' have to get your gift when your not around, anything you need?" Paulie had the urge to answer with the words "Your wife" but instead he reluctantly shook his head. "You've done enough for me Danny boy, let me worry about getting the gifts." Daniel sighed with a smirk. "So

you're going to make it hard for me huh, alright, I'm up for the challenge."
Paulie gave a meaningless smirk of his own and focused his attention back to
the surrounding environment. "I have to piss." Daniel said abruptly after
spotting the mens room. The two men walked toward the bathroom, Daniel
walked in and Paulie put his back against the wall near the doorway and
waited for his brothers return. As Paulie stared carelessly at the holiday
shoppers that passed him his mind came to a sudden halt at the sight of one
shopper in particular. A black haired man who was about his age was
walking with his wife and small son, Paulie knew the man's face well but
could not quite grasp from where.

In another moment Paulie remembered all too vividly who the man
was. He quickly wondered how his memory could have had such a lapse in
the first place. Although he had stored them in the back room of his brain,
Paulie could never come to forget the days he had spent sitting in that hot
courtroom. The nervousness that had filled his mind and left his lawyer
seemingly calm was beginning to boil his skin. Sweat cascaded down
Paulie's face as he sat awaiting his judgment He had spent three days in this
court room listening to his pathetic lawyer try to finagle the jury with his
woeful words and to date, it had been the worst three days of his life. Time
seemed to go in slow motion as Paulie sat awaiting his probable doom. At the

110

time the thought of jail terrified Paulie. He may have done the crime but he didn't look at himself as somebody who belonged in the prison system nor did he look at himself as someone who would do good in the place (well as good as one can do). Without any further warning the judges solemn voice echoed through the stiff courtroom. "Defendant, please rise." He may have said please but there was hardly a trace of pleasantness in his voice.

Paulie stood up and felt sweat trickle down his thighs as he did. He stared straight ahead seemingly emotionless but filled with absolute terror. The judge then turned to the jury and Paulie could have sworn he winked to them but his lawyer later proved that moot. "Jury, what is your verdict?" The black haired man stood up from his seat amongst the group of people and turned to the judge. "We the jury find Paul J Aldo...Guilty of all charges." Paulie's face had gone as pale as a man dying of blood loss and the inside of his mouth was now a desert. Paulie's lawyer slammed his fist on the table in front of them and the judge called for order. At that moment Paulie's brain was barely functioning, not a single thought was passing through and the shock had froze him in place. "Damn it, this is bull shit!" His lawyer yelled as he shuffled his papers back into his bag, Paulie could feel life returning back into his body. "Bull shit for who? You still get paid, I go to jail." Paulie said softly in a strange tone, he sounded like an actor practicing his lines, the lawyer did not retort. Paulie stared as the men and women of the jury headed out of the courtroom, none of them had so much as a sign of regret on their faces.

It all seemed like just yesterday as Paulie stood staring at the black haired man. He could now feel the terror from that day jolting into his head like some kind of delayed aftershock. Daniel stepped out of the bathroom and stared curiously at his brother. "Paul?" Paulie heard him but didn't bother to answer. "Paulie, hello, are you alright?" Paulie pulled his eyes away from the black haired man and looked at Daniel. "I'm fine..I'm fine...I thought I saw somebody I knew." Michelle began walking towards Paulie and Daniel from the opposite direction, Daniel noticed and smiled. "Well here's somebody you know." Michelle smirked and gave Daniel a kiss, Paulie was unaffected by this as he was still shook from seeing the former jury member. "I didn't know you still had shopping to do, you could have came with us." Daniel said apologetically. "I wasn't planning on coming but I figured since I was home I might as well finish up my list." Michelle said. Paulie watched the black haired man and his family enter a nearby store and then refocused his attention to his present company. "Hey Danny since Michelle's here now why don't you finish up your shopping with her, that way I could pick up some stuff for you guys." "I told you that's not necessary Paul." Daniel said with a grin. "Believe me it is." The sincerity in Paulie's voice was overpowering due to the fact that he really did want them to go, though it was for an entirely different reason. "Hey if that's not good enough, while I'm not around you can start talking about what to get me." Paulie added with a giggle. Daniel nodded and smirked. "Alright, I guess I'll hitch a ride home with you honey." Michelle nodded and glanced at Paulie curiously. A great big fake smile came over Paulie's face as he waved the couple goodbye.

When Daniel and Michelle had vanished into the crowded mall, Paulie made his way toward the store the man had entered. He peeked inside and noticed that the man and his family were no longer in there. The old terror that had snuck up on him moments ago had now turned to full blown frustration. Paulie looked around the congested shopping center frantically, hoping to spot the man's now familiar black hair. Paulie's anger wasn't directed so much towards the man as it was to Daniel. If his brother would have just shut up and went off with Michelle, he wouldn't have lost track of the guy. Swiftly another thought that had been dormant for years crept back inside of Paulie's distraught mind. If it wasn't for Daniel, Paulie might have been able to avoid jail. Just as Paulie felt himself beginning to see red he spotted the black haired man and his family leaving a shoe store. The man grabbed hold of his sons hand and continued walking, Paulie sighed heavily and followed the family. Paulie stayed about ten feet away from the family as he followed, it wasn't too far but he figured to them he was just another innocent holiday shopper. As Paulie continued to trail behind the family, a Santa Clause from the salvation army cut in front of him. The Santa was dragging his change bucket stand lazily and Paulie had to stop short to avoid walking into him. Paulie watched as the black haired man and his family proceeded out the exit doors of the mall. "Son of a bitch." Paulie said with a grunt. The Santa came to a halt and turned to Paulie with a look of dismay. "Take it easy, it's Christmas time." The Santa said in a belittling tone. Paulie did not respond, instead he stared at the Santa with a passionate look of rage, his face was now as scarlet as the man's suit. The Santa simply swallowed his throat and continued his desired path.

Paulie hurried to the door where the family had exited, carelessly pushing through people in the process. When he got outside the mall he looked around for the man and his family, he finally spotted them getting into a white minivan. "Shit." Paulie mumbled. He noticed the license plate on the minivan that read "902 1178" and a large dent above the cars back tire caught his eye in the process. He began silently reciting the number back to himself as the family got into their car. As he continued to recite he spotted a teenage girl sitting on a bench, writing something in a notebook. He jogged over to her and grabbed the pen without asking. "Hey!" The teenage girl said mortified. As if that wasn't enough to startle the girl, he then ripped out a piece of paper from her book. The girl let out a gasp and looked around to see if anyone had noticed or cared to say something, no one did. Paulie quickly jotted down the number and gave the scared girl back her pen. "Thanks a million." Paulie said with a wink which left the girl feeling even more unsettled. The girl felt the urge to say something or let out some kind of scream but all she could do was stare in silence. Paulie stood watching the white minivan pull away. "See you around pal." Paulie said to himself. The young girl continued to watch as Paulie stared and thought there was something in the man's demeanor that made her feel threatened, something not quite right. If she only knew the kind of monster she had just come into contact with, she would have surely counted her blessings that night.

10

Investigative Reports

After his shift ended, Detective Atkins headed to the same local diner
where he spent most of his evenings. He sat quietly by himself in an
oversized lavender booth, drinking coffee and eating his watery eggs.
Though he looked calm, his mind was racing, the thought of the slasher
getting away was beginning to eat at him. The waitress quickly walked over
with her coffee pot. "Another cup?" she asked. Atkins looked up at her and
smiled. "Please." She poured him his coffee and was on her way. As he
continued to eat he heard the jingle of the bells as someone stepped into the
diner, Atkins looked up to see Detective Brodie walking towards him. Brodie
was holding a manila envelope, he placed it on the table next to Atkins' food
and sat down across from him, the cheap pleather of the booth made a loud
moan as he did. Detective Atkins glanced at the envelope but didn't seem to
care about it. "What's this?" he asked. Detective Brodie grabbed a piece of
bacon off of Atkins' plate, Atkins stared at his partner with displeasure as he
ate it. "That's the info on the two quote on quote drug dealers that we found
cooked with the dogs." Detective Atkins took a sip of his coffee. "And.."
Atkins proceeded still not seeming to care. "And you were right, nobodies,

116

one of them was a loser junkie of sorts but that's it." Detective Atkins smiled.
"Hate to say I told you so."

Brodie giggled and then got serious. "So you were right about that,
you think we're right about this other thing?" Detective Atkins bit into a
piece of toast and pretended to be confused "What other thing?" Detective
Brodie rolled his eyes. "That the slashers taking a little vacation for the
holiday season." Atkins took another sip of his coffee. "Oh that thing, yea I
think so." Atkins responded casually, the last thing he wanted   was to make
Brodie find out how crazy their last find was driving him. "Okay, so what are
we gonna' do about it?" Brodie asked. "There's nothing we can do, until
another dead body turns up somewhere." Atkins mumbled with some
annoyance. "Great, I can't wait." Brodie added jokingly. Brodie reached for
another piece of the detective's bacon and Atkins stuck his fork out ready to
stab his partner, Brodie threw his hands up in defense. "Woa' take it easy
partner." Brodie said apologetically with some shock in his voice. "Don't
ever touch another man's bacon, you got that!" Atkins added sternly. Brodie
smirked and at that moment his phone started ringing, he shook his head with
a grin and walked away to take his call. Atkins watched as Brodie picked up
his call, the nervous smirk still running across his face. Atkins was now
smiling at the thought of what he had just done. As Brodie continued to talk

117

on the phone Atkins noticed the smirk on his face had faded into a grimace, Atkin's followed with one of his own. Detective Brodie finished his phone call and walked back over to Atkins with confidence in his face. "That body your waiting to turn up, does it have to be dead?" Detective Atkins stared baffled by his partners words.

When Atkins and Brodie got back to the station there was a young attractive woman with a large burn mark on her face sitting in hand cuffs. There were another two detectives sitting in front of her asking questions. Atkins picked up the girl by the arm and he and Brodie began walking her to the interrogation room. "We'll take over from here boys." Brodie said apologetically as the other two detectives stared dumbfounded. The three entered a dimly lit interrogation room and Detective Atkins pulled a chair and sat the hooker down. Brodie grabbed two more chairs and both men sat across from her. Atkins slammed the sketch composite of the Bloomingdale slasher on to the table. "Tell me what you know about this guy." He said sternly. The woman was almost in tears as she replied. "I don't know anything, I swear..."Brodie cut in without warning. "The other two detectives said you noticed his picture on the wall and started asking questions about why he was wanted. Then when they mentioned he was a killer you played dumb." The woman's eyes were now drenched in tears, she said nothing and simply stared. "What's her name?" Atkins asked and Brodie looked down at the sheet of paper he had in front of him. "Lila." Brodie replied. "Lila, you were picked up for prostitution and you will be charged with it if you do not comply with us, do you understand that?" Atkins spoke very calmly. "I don't know anything!" Lila wailed. "Listen to me and listen to me good, this son of a bitch has killed a lot of people and as long as he's a free man, he isn't going to stop. Do you want him to hurt anybody else? Do you want to be responsible for him staying on the streets?" Lila continued to cry and touched the burn on her face. "No..." "Did he do that to you?" Detective Atkins asked pointing to the burn. Lila nodded wildly. "Don't let him hurt anyone else, tell us what you know." Detective Atkins pleaded. "We'll protect you." Brodie added.

Lila did just what the detectives asked, she told them all she knew about Paulie (though his name was one of the things she didn't know). She told them he had picked her up a handful of times and that he drove a car she remembered as being black or dark colored. Lila said she wasn't an expert on cars and didn't know the exact model but thought it might be a Mercedes or a Cadillac. She also told them about how the last few times he had picked her up it had been very violent. Atkins and Brodie were shocked and downright disgusted to hear how aggressive the man had been with her. "Why did you keep on seeing him?" Brodie asked curiously. Lila took a deep breath and then replied. "The money... the money was always good, I'd put up with his bullshit and I'd have the money." "When was the last time you saw him?" Atkins asked. "It couldn't have been more than a day or two ago, I loose track of the days sometimes." Lila added. Detective Atkins stared at the burn on the young woman's face. "Was that when this happen?" He asked. "Yes it was." She replied in a somber tone. "I wanted to tell someone but what was I supposed to do, come to you guys?" She continued, the detectives glanced at each other thinking of the irony of her words." So I went to my pimp, but he didn't care, all he cared about was the money. He told me I must have done something to deserve it." Lila began to cry again. Detective Brodie put his arm around her as she did. "It's ok." he said sincerely. Detective Atkins lit up a cigarette. "So where does this creep live?"

Fifteen minutes later the three were well on their way. Detective Atkins sped down a dark and winding road with a look of vengeful anxiousness in his eyes. His loud siren blasted through the night sky urgently, it was accompanied by the flashing red bulb that was now stuck to the Challenger's hood. Detective Brodie who sat shotgun, glanced over at his partner and felt his stomach sink. He pulled his seat belt down until it clicked into place, Atkins noticed and a smirk crept onto his face. "You better do the same honey." Atkins called to Lila who was sitting in the back seat. Lila looked at Atkins with some disbelief before sighing and pulling the seat belt over her chest. As Atkins sped up, he glanced at his rearview to see if his back up was still with him. He spotted the red and blue lights in the far distance and grinned to himself again, the patrol car was keeplng up better than he had expected. "It's a right up here." Lila yelled abruptly over the roar of the engine. Atkins jerked the wheel right and the back tires screeched loudly. "The place on the left." Lila said and Atkins threw the car into park without hesitation. A moment later the patrol car came speeding around the turn frantically and nearly smashed into the back of Atkins' Challenger before swerving toward safety. Atkins was too distracted to notice or care.

Detective Atkins turned back to Lila who now looked a bit nervous. "Stay in the car." He ordered and Lila nodded her head without the thought of objecting. Though she felt safe with the two detectives ,she couldn't help but feel frightened by the thought of that horrible man. If he found out it was her who lead them here, he would kill her for sure. Atkins and Brodie stepped out of the car and looked up at the building. It was a beat up old apartment building that sat in the middle of a broken down and secluded neighborhood. The building wasn't huge, only three stories but it towered over the few houses that it shared it's street with. The other two apartments

had constantly changed tenants and as of two weeks ago the inhabitants of
the middle floor had been kicked out leaving it vacant. The gray stone cobble
that covered the exterior of the building was now mossy green and
reminiscent of a rotting old family mausoleum. Lila had told them that
Paulie's apartment was on the first floor and Atkins noticed the lights were
off on all three levels. He turned to Brodie and the other two officers who
were just joining them as he pulled his revolver from his chest holster. "I'm
going in first, follow my lead." Brodie and the others nodded their heads,
pulled their guns and awaited the detective's first movement.

Detective Atkins began to creep towards the concrete steps that lead
up to the slasher's apartment. As Atkins came to the sidewalk he realized that
these steps were undoubtedly the ones Lila said she had fallen down after the
coffee incident. He glanced down at them solemnly and began to fantasize
about the comforting feeling that would come with finding this maniac off
guard. Perhaps he'd be asleep, no it was only eight, he couldn't be asleep,
Atkins dismissed the thought. Maybe he was eating dinner or watching his
favorite television show, wouldn't that be perfect. Right when he's enjoying
his devilish life, burst in the door and throw him against the wall, he wouldn't
even know what was happening. As Atkins footed up the first few of the icy
steps he realized that it wouldn't stop at throwing him against the wall. Once

he saw the man he'd begin to beat him to a pulp, he'd be helpless to his inner rage. Brodie and the other guys would have to pull him off of the bastard and at that moment who knew if anything would be left.

The pleasure of killing him, Christ it would be divine, Atkins thought as he came up to the door with Brodie and the others right behind him. This was it, this was his moment. Detective Atkins held his gun up tightly as he looked back at the other officers and signaled them to go on his count. One, sweat began to fill his palms and he could almost feel his hands around the scumbag's throat. Two, he had the thought of bursting in and immediately firing a bullet into the slasher's head. His blood would spray onto his walls and Atkins would feel a weight lifted, even if just for the moment. Three, it was time to make all of his fantasies a reality. Detective Atkins kicked in the door and pointed his gun forward, Brodie and the other two officers followed suite. Atkins stared in disbelief at the sight, no one, not a soul in the dark apartment. Other than the initial sound of the men busting through the apartment, there was a dead silence. The four men stared cautiously into the dimness, listening for foot steps but hearing only the creaking of the wood that held the old place together.

Detective Atkins let out a disappointed sigh and flicked a light switch to his right. Paulie's messy living room illuminated in a yellowish hue that came from a lone bulb on the ceiling. Brodie and the other two officers followed Atkins lead into the midst of the apartment, their guns still held up in precaution. Detective Atkins glanced around the empty room before turning to the two tense looking officers. "You, go check out the bedroom. And you, go get the girl." Atkins ordered sternly, the two officers reluctantly nodded and were on their way. Atkins continued to snoop around the living room for anything out of the ordinary and Brodie slipped into the nearby kitchen. He gazed awkwardly at the shabby folding table that sat in the center of the room, it was accompanied by one plastic white lawn chair. Brodie then turned his attention to a banged up green fridge that sat in the corner. He opened it and all that resided was something that looked like a hamburger, some potato salad and one half eaten slice of pizza. The measly amount of food still managed to cause a stale stench that filled the small kitchen quickly and Brodie slammed the door in disgust.

Brodie continued around the counter and glanced into the sink which was nearly filled with empty beer and soda bottles. Atkins, who had found nothing out of the ordinary in the living room joined his partner in the kitchen. Brodie noticed an overturned sugar bowl and stared at it curiously. "What's with this?" Brodie asked as Atkins stared confused. Brodie moved closer and noticed the residue of the white substance was far too thick to be sugar. He pressed his finger around the dome shaped interior and swiped it along, picking up the last of the powder. Brodie cautiously licked his index finger and felt the tip of his tongue go numb. "This is sweet, but it ain't sugar. I guess that proves your theory." Brodie said confidently, he was expecting his partner to rejoice and show approval of the find. Atkins' eyes however were fixated on the other insignificant objects that made up the filthy kitchen. "Still doesn't point us in his direction." Atkins said without a trace of interest. Before Brodie could say something else, one of the officer's stepped into the kitchen. "There's some evidence that he might of bailed in the bedroom, if you guys want to take a look." The two detectives followed the officer without a word.

The three men stepped into the lamp lit bedroom and Atkins immediately felt the thick hot air from the unventilated room stick to his skin. The bedroom was just as messy as the rest of the apartment and there was a stale smell of sweat lingering. The smell Atkins thought was probably the remnants of what Lila and the slasher had done nights before. There were clothes thrown around on the floor and another larger pile sitting on the sunken mattress. The closet door hung open and the inside seemed scarce. "Looks like he did some closet cleaning." Brodie said. "Yea, maybe he

125

decided to donate his clothes to the salvation army." Atkins said sarcastically.

Atkins and Brodie continued around the bedroom as the second officer came walking in with Lila. "Sorry Detective, she was afraid to come in. I told her the house was empty, it is empty right?" Atkins nodded. "It's empty Lila, he's long gone." Lila stared at Atkins diffidently for a moment before reluctantly nodding. "The night you were here, did he say anything about taking a vacation? Or anything regarding going away somewhere?" Atkins asked. "No, nothing, we didn't really talk much, I know he wanted me to stay. Some nights he would want me to stay and watch TV with him, but after the sex I just wanted my money, I didn't want to be around him anymore. I went to go and that's when he..." "So he liked to watch his TV." Atkins interrupted Lila knowing she was about to bring up the painful memory that had left the savage scar on her face. "As much as the average person I guess." Lila said and Atkins grinned wanting to add he was hardly the average person, instead he nodded his head. "So he sees the sketch of himself on the news, packs up, shaves and gets the hell out." Atkins said to himself in an aloud thought. "Checks off everything on our list, but still, where did he go?" Brodie added. Detective Atkins turned to the two officers. "You two, rip this place apart for anything with a name on it, a phone book, a

126

receipt, whatever." The two officers nodded and headed back into the living room to start their thorough search. "What do you need me to do?" Brodie asked generously. "Take my car and take the girl home, then call headquarters and tell them to get the call logs on this phone. I want both outgoing and incoming." Atkins said. Brodie nodded. "Anything else?" "Yea...Don't scratch my car." Brodie smirked and was on his way.

11

Old Ways

It was almost eight forty when Paulie pulled up to   the neighborhood liquor store. There were several cars parked outside, most with their engines left running. Paulie had spent the rest of his time at the mall enjoying a cookie   from the cookie stand and browsing the department stores aimlessly. At one point Paulie had found himself looking through woman's lingerie, gazing deeply at the bras and panties that hung on display. The sophistication of the garments represented made Paulie realize how long it had been since he was with a real woman. Sure since getting out of prison he had been sexually active but paying for it was different, and when it was free it wasn't consensual. Paulie stared at a mannequin and immediately thought of Michelle's breasts in place of the white plastic ones that inhabited the bra. Sure enough the two thoughts connected in his mind as they should have before, Michelle was the last real woman he had been with. The recognition of that fact made the longing for her body that much worse.

When the sales clerk came over and asked if he needed any help, Paulie had told her he was just browsing for something for his wife. The woman gave him a devilish smirk and walked away. It had actually crossed Paulie's mind to perhaps get Michelle something from the store for Christmas, but he decided that buying your brother's wife lingerie wasn't the kind of thing that would come off as normal or even subtle for that matter. When he grew bored of window shopping Paulie left the mall. He spent the next hour driving around and rediscovering the old town that he had almost completely forgotten. He knew he would be late for dinner and when he saw the liquor store in the distance he felt it was at least half of an alibi to where he had been. He could just tell them the truth, that he was taking in the old sights around town, there was nothing wrong with that. But some part of himself was cautious, it was the same part of him that didn't tell anyone in Mesapeena his real name or that he had been in prison. It was the part of himself that held in the horrendous secrets of his everyday life and sometimes the meager things in life got pushed into the darkness as well. It was just a force of habit, if you're constantly lying, you were apt to lie pointlessly every once in a while.

Paulie parked in front of the liquor store and stepped out of his blue Cadillac. He looked around for a moment at all the other cars in the lot and shook his head. People drink too much, he thought. He entered the crowded liquor store, pushed passed the line and headed for the back. The angry and impatient faces that filled the store stared forward at an overweight young female cashier, she was counting a customer's change as slow as a tortoise. Paulie made his way to the wine aisle and began looking through the large selection on display. His eyes searched around nervously for something familiar and just as he was growing weary and a bit annoyed he spotted a bottle of Secret Garden Vineyards Merlot. Paulie immediately remembered it had been Michelle's favorite, he picked up the bottle and stared at the pale green label. When she had still been writing to him and when her mind was still set on leaving Daniel, she would ask Paulie what they would do when he got out. Paulie would write back and tell Michelle that when he got out they could start a new life together. He would fill her mind with romantic fantasies, they could sit by a fireplace drinking her favorite wine and making love all night. The words in Paulie's letters would give her goose-bumps and fill her with excitement, longing and fear. Paulie grinned selfishly to himself before walking over to the large line.

The overweight cashier was still ringing as slow as she could and the men and women on line continued to mumble things and look at her like they wanted to strangle her. Paulie on the other hand seemed surprisingly distracted, he was busy thinking of Michelle. He wanted her and couldn't help but feel that he deserved to have her. After all the years away from her, his desires had come crashing back. He glanced down at the bottle of wine and grinned. Bringing the wine back to the house would surely evoke some kind of feeling in her like the old sweater had. The entrance door swung open and a thirty something business man in a gray suit walked into the crowded store, he had slicked back brown hair and a tie to match it. His hair glistened under the store's fluorescents and so did the face of his obviously expensive watch. He was wearing one of those blue tooth pieces around his ear and he might as well have been screaming into it. Paulie distracted by the man's blather turned to him with a look of annoyance. "Yea, I just stopped by the liquor store, it's fucking packed." The man moaned into his ear piece. Without an ounce of regret the businessman pushed through the people in line and headed down the first aisle, still talking in the process.

The man gave a quick look around the selection before impulsively grabbing a bottle of Bourbon. He walked back up to the line and grabbed a twenty four pack of Coors from a massive stack as he did. When the man got to the back of the line there was a woman being rung up by the cashier and Paulie was now next. "Next time plan ahead and get the stuff in advance Jay." The man whined into his ear piece. As the business man stood impatiently in line, he took a tally of how many people were in front of him. Including the man that was next, there were six people ahead, the business

131

man let out a long sigh and stared at the overweight cashier with utter hatred. "I can't fucking believe this. This fat pig on the register is slow as shit." The man's voice was louder and more obnoxious with each spoken word, everyone including the cashier had surely heard his comments. Suddenly the business man stepped off the line. "Fuck this." He shouted loudly. He charged up to the counter bumping into people in the process. When he came to the front of the line he pushed through Paulie with his shoulders and he stumbled back lightly. Anger and dismay rushed over Paulie's face. The business man slammed forty dollars on the counter and the overweight cashier stared at him in awe. "Keep the change!" He shouted as he stormed out of the store unapologetically, the crowd of people stared in amazement.

The woman in front of Paulie finished paying for her liquor and shook her head at the thought of the business man's uncalled for behavior. Paulie stared into oblivion, no longer thinking of Michelle but instead reflecting on what had just happened, he noticed he was next in line and walked up to the cashier. Paulie placed his bottle on the counter and the overweight girl let out a sorrowful sigh before ringing him up in the register. "That'll be sixty five." The sad cashier said. Paulie pulled out his money and handed the girl a hundred, as she took it Paulie noticed a cheaper ten dollar wine on display behind the counter. His mind wandered back to the annoying man who had bumped him. "Let me get one of these too." Paulie said as he pointed to the cheap wine on display. The cashier sighed again, this time with some annoyance and grabbed a bottle off of the shelf. She bagged both bottles, gave him his change and in a robotic monotone wished Paulie a happy holiday. Paulie smiled accordingly and was on his way.

Paulie stepped outside the store and looked around the parking lot casually, to his liking the business man was still there. The man was standing next to his fancy red Porsche in the far distance of the lot. He had parked his car about twenty feet away from the store in order to get a spot that was secluded from the rest of the average cars. He was still talking into his earpiece excessively and was now puffing away at a cigarette. Paulie smiled and began to walk over. "Yea I'm coming right now...No man I got whiskey and beer... Yea, it's all good...No,I ain't smoking in my car, trust me two minutes isn't going to make a difference." The business man conversed. Paulie stopped about five feet from the man and stared at him solemnly. After a moment the man noticed Paulie and stared back at him curiously. "Hey could I help you buddy?" The man said arrogantly. Paulie did not reply, he simply continued to stare, this made the man agitated. "Hey asshole, do you have a problem?" The man spoke strongly but there was a hint of fear in his voice. Paulie continued to stare silently, he was holding the paper bag with the Merlot in it with his left hand. His right hand was tucked behind his back, tightly squeezing the neck of the cheap wine. In that instant the man realized his friend was still on the phone and was asking him what was wrong. "Nothing I can't handle, I'll see you in a little." The man said to his friend before clicking the ear piece off.

Paulie began to smile in a very unsettling manner. "Get the fuck out of here before I wipe that smile off your face!" The man yelled uncomfortably. Paulie placed his bag of Merlot down on the concrete, almost invitingly. "Come over here and do it big shot." Paulie's words were confident and calm and the man's face went rose red. "That's it, I've had about enough of you!" The business man charged at Paulie with his right fist clinched, he swung wildly at his head but Paulie was quick to duck. As the man turned back towards him, recovering from the missed whale, Paulie smashed the bottle of cheap wine over his head. Glass, blood and wine sprayed through the air and the man moaned at the pain of his forehead spliting open like a cantaloupe. The battered business man fell down to his knees and Paulie grabbed him by his now blood soaked hair. He looked the man in his eyes which were now rattling around aimlessly. "Bottom's up scumbag!" Paulie yelled as he jammed the broken bottle into the man's throat. Blood shot out into the cold air and the man hit the concrete pavement with one final squirm before stiffening. Paulie looked back towards the liquor store and saw some cars leaving the parking lot. He knew they were too far away to spot the dead man in the darkness but he dragged the body behind the far side of the Porsche anyway. Paulie crouched down beside the man and pulled out his wallet, he opened it and found a bunch of credit cards with about one hundred in cash. All these rich bastards carry is plastic, he thought to himself as he took the bills and put the wallet back. Paulie noticed the man's car keys on the ground next to his legs, he picked them up and popped the trunk. Paulie looked around cautiously as he quickly lifted the body into the trunk. When he was finished he swung the keys around his index finger, whistled casually and drove off in the dead man's Porsche.

Paulie pulled up to the Lawson household in his Cadillac at nine fifteen. He had driven the body of the business man two miles away from the liquor store and dropped him into a wooded ditch. It wasn't the best place but Paulie knew everybody eventually gets found anyway. He drove back to the liquor store, parked the dead man's car in the same distant spot it had been in and stepped out. Paulie pulled an old shirt from his trunk and wiped down the mans steering wheel, door handles and trunk. The Lawsons were sitting patiently around the dinner table when Paulie strolled in holding the paper bag with the Merlot tightly to his chest. "Paulie, we thought you got lost or

135

something." Daniel quipped with some curiosity. Paulie grinned and made his way to the table. "In this town? Come on. Don't forget I lived here for years." Paulie said as he sat down with the family."What's in the bag?" Daniel asked. "Oh I picked up a little something." Paulie said innocently as he pulled the Merlot out of the paper bag. Michelle's eyes lit up like a flame when she spotted the label, she immediately knew it was no accident Paulie had picked that brand. "Well look at that, Secret Garden, that's Michelle's favorite." Daniel said with a smile,he was genuinely excited by this supposed coincidence. Daniel turned to Michelle to see her reaction, she noticed and put on a fake grin to hide her disbelief "You love that Merlot, don't you honey?" He asked even though he knew the answer. Michelle turned to him still smiling. "It's my favorite." she said. Paulie smiled, he was trying to look surprised. "Well I didn't know that." He said in a fabricated tone and shot a glance to Michelle.

There was an awkward silence that came after, as the three held their idiotic grins. The silence was broken when Nicole spoke up playfully. "So are we going to eat or what?" "Yes, lets eat." Daniel said and the four began to dig into their steak and potato dinners. "Is everything alright Nic? You seem like something's bothering you." Michelle asked. "Everything is fine." Nicole replied quickly." Is Jake coming over tonight?" Michelle continued.

"We got into a fight." Nicole said as she looked down at her steak. Michelle wiped her mouth. "Couples fight, it's only natural honey." Michelle glanced at her husband then at Paulie and then back at her daughter. Paulie wiped his mouth. "If I may say something, as much as fighting is normal, it isn't healthy for a couple to fight all the time." Paulie added and shot a quick look to Michelle before continuing to cut his juicy steak. Daniel nodded and Michelle looked like she wanted to add something but didn't. "Do you guys fight a lot?" Paulie asked. Nicole stared at her uncle, perplexed by his strange and sudden interest in her personal life. Her first instinct was to tell him to mind his own business but when she thought about how mean she had been the night before she realized he was just being nice and let her defense down. "No not really, this is the first one in a while." Nicole added. Paulie shoved a piece of steak into his mouth and chewed it up quickly. "Well I wouldn't worry about it then, sometimes us men need our space, it's kind of childish but it's true." Paulie said with a grin. Nicole followed with a reassured grin of her own. "Yea, you're probably right."

Daniel nodded his head in agreement. "That is true, we sometimes need our space. Now what say we open that wine." Daniel went to grab the bottle from the table but Paulie beat him to it. "I got it." Paulie said as he stuck the cork screw into the top of the bottle. He pulled vigorously and the

vein in his forehead began to bulge, after a moment the cork popped with
relief. "Impressive." Nicole said with a friendly smile. Paulie grinned.
"Practice makes perfect kiddo." Paulie proceeded to pour wine for Michelle,
she stared as the wine dripped slowly from the top of the bottle. A million
thoughts were filling her mind as the red wine was filling her glass. When he
was finished she looked up at him with a forced smile. "Thank you." Paulie
turned to his half brother and began pouring some in his glass, this time
faster than he had poured Michelle's "Thank you Paulie." Daniel said. Paulie
turned to Nicole who was in the middle of cutting a piece of steak. "She
could have some can't she Danny boy?" "Sure, she could have a little."
Daniel said almost reluctantly. Paulie poured some wine for Nicole and she
looked at him like a child looking up at someone who had just given them
candy. Maybe he wasn't so bad, she thought to herself. Maybe he was just a
little weird and at that moment Nicole noticed what looked like blood on
Paulie's sleeve. "There's something on your sleeve uncle Paulie." Nicole said
as she pointed to the stain.

Paulie looked down at his sleeve and noticed the splash of blood on it.
How did he overlook it, he thought to himself. "Oh that, that's a..." He spoke
hesitantly trying to come up with something to say and then let out a nervous
giggle. "I'm a little embarrassed, you see that bottle of Merlot is actually a

138

replacement. Me being the clumsy guy I am, I dropped the first bottle in the parking lot. It must of splashed on my sleeve as I tried to catch it." Nicole couldn't help but laugh, Paulie smirked. "I had to wait on the line again but the cashier was nice enough to give me the second bottle free. I guess she could relate, either that or she just pitied me. I thought my secret was safe, thanks Nicole." Paulie quipped but his face was now blushing with timidness and at that moment he seemed innocent and almost vulnerable. Nicole felt a belated sympathy for Paulie rush over her. "I'm going to say that happen to me next time I buy a bottle, maybe I'll get a two for one." Daniel said with a giggle. Paulie and Nicole joined in with some laughter of their own and Michelle watched somberly as her family enjoyed themselves. Everyone was ecstatic it seemed and she was the only one living in agony, she wanted Paulie gone.

Daniel took a sip of his wine and Paulie and Nicole followed suit. Michelle reluctantly lifted her glass and quaffed more wine than any of them had, she then placed the glass down and stared at it indifferently. Daniel turned to Paulie with a pleasant grin. "Paulie I just want to say, I see how much you're enjoying yourself being back home and all. And Michelle and I have decided, if you'd like that is, that you're welcome to stay here as long as you want." Paulie looked shocked and a little thrilled, Michelle shared the same look of shock but her core feeling was dismay. She stared at her husband in awe. Paulie took another sip of his wine and wiped his mouth with a cloth napkin that sat properly on his lap. "You really mean that Danny boy?" "Sure Paulie. You live so far and I can't imagine what it's like to have no one around." Paulie nodded at his brother's words, it was for the best being alone, but he couldn't go back to Mesapeena now with all the heat on him. "There's plenty of room Paul, it's not a problem." Daniel continued to encourage his brother. "I guess I could stay for a little, I have been thinking about moving, perhaps closer. But what about money? I could take you up on staying here for a while but I'm not gonna' live off of you two." Paulie seemed honest but he was actually hoping he could do just that, he would have it made then. Daniel waved Paulie's words away. "Don't you worry about that. We'll talk to my boss tomorrow, he could use a good laborer, it's real manual stuff but it's something." "That's fine." Paulie said with a satisfied grin, not only did he have a place to hide out for a while, he had a job set up. Pretty soon, he thought,he'd be a regular Ward Cleaver.

Later on after dinner had disengaged, Paulie laid napping on the living room sofa. He had fallen asleep to the old Orson Welles film "Touch of Evil". An artifact of how politically incorrect Hollywood had once been. Paulie always got a kick out of the fact that they gave Charlton Heston a black mustache and a fake tan and tried to pass him off as a Mexican. If it was only that easy to hide the truth in real life he could have gotten a fake mustache and moved back to Mesapeena. The fact was he'd have to stay here and whether he wanted to accept it or not, he had no choice in the matter, he had nowhere else to go. There were two complications in Paulie's subconscious mind and now while his brain was dormant they began to arise. One was the obvious, Paulie needed to kill, it was as simple as that. The impulse had come tonight and he had acted on it in an instant. It had ultimately lead him to disposing a stranger's body into a shallow wooded grave. It was the same impulse that had lead to the large drug peddling biker's death nights before and it was undoubtedly the same impulse that had created the notorious Bloomingdale slasher. The question that lingered in Paulie's suppressed thoughts was when would he feel the urge to do it again?

The second complication was in a way more problematic, the contributing reason for that was that Paulie was ignoring it. Sure on the surface Paulie was having his lustful thoughts of Michelle but what Paulie didn't know yet and what his subconscious mind barely knew was that sex would not be enough. Paulie wanted Michelle for himself and just as he had joked with the idea of him soon being a regular Ward Cleaver he had a fleeting glimpse of Michelle being his June. In a way it was his return to innocence, a return to a time to when he wasn't the slasher. All of those old feelings about Michelle had come back and the fantasies they had once had were now seemingly reachable again. Could they run away together? Would she actually do it? Her words told him no but her demeanor was different all together. There was something about it, something about her, she was nervous and uncomfortable but there was something there. Paulie thought that she was afraid of the lustful feelings of her own and for that he believed she wanted him gone. Out of sight, out of mind.

Michelle was cleaning some dishes absently when Daniel strolled into the kitchen. "Hey honey, did you make coffee?" Daniel asked innocently. Michelle didn't turn around, instead she stared up at the now fogged window above the kitchen sink with a look of utter contempt. "No" she said simply. Daniel was about to ask her if she could do so when he felt a sudden uncomfortable feeling radiating from her. "Is there something wrong Michelle?" Michelle continued to stare at the hazed window for another moment before whipping around hastily, Daniel winced. "Why didn't you at least ask me Daniel?" Michelle said angrily, her hazel eyes were gleaming wildly. "Ask you?" Daniel's face was filled with ignorance. "About Paulie staying." Michelle said sternly. Disbelief came across Daniel's face. "I didn't think I had to ask your permission for my brother to stay for a little longer."

Daniel said with a sharp annoyance. "How long is a little Daniel? He could
be here for months!" There was a light screech in her voice. "What is the big
deal? You and Paulie get along fine..." Michelle tried to ignore the irony of
what her husband had said. "And from the looks of it Nicole seems to be
taking a liking to him as well." Daniel finished. "Forget it, just forget it."
Michelle said unwillingly and stormed out of the kitchen. Daniel stood
shaking his head for several moments, bemused by what had just occurred.
Paulie, who had woken up seconds before Daniel had entered the kitchen
now laid wide awake with a grin that showed no signs of faltering.

12

The Real Break

Detective Atkins strolled into the station around ten the next morning. He had searched the slasher's apartment until around midnight for some kind of ideal clue but had found nothing. There had been several smudged finger prints left sporadically around the house but that was nothing new. A while back some smudged finger prints had been found at one of the murder sights, when the results finally came back five weeks later there was no found match in the state's system. After giving up on the search, Atkins sat in the apartment for another hour hoping that maybe the slasher hadn't taken off and that he'd just walk through the door. The detective couldn't help but grin as he sat there in the darkness. Wouldn't that be something, he thought, he'd have the slasher all to himself. If by some chance the slasher did walk in the apartment Atkins would probably shoot him right there and then. The minute he'd see that fuck come through the threshold he'd squeeze the trigger of his .45 and blow his head off. Then what, he wondered. He'd probably laugh to himself for a while and stare down at the carcass solemnly until finally calling Brodie. He'd tell him it was done and hang up the phone, as simple and vague as that. Then he'd head home, pour himself one last glass of scotch, swig it and put the .45 to his temple. He'd blow his head off just as he had the slasher's, his work would be done, nothing left to live for then. Ultimately Atkins came to his senses and called it a night. He headed back to his house and proceeded to drink himself into oblivion. Atkins accompanied his brand new bottle of Blue Label with a remedy of four Vicodins, he slipped into his self induced coma at dawn.

Brodie had come back to the slasher's apartment around nine only to bail a half hour later. Atkins didn't blame him though, he had a wife and kids to worry about, Atkins was the loner. As a matter of fact the closest thing he had to family anymore was Brodie. Atkins had already set it up in his will that Brodie would get what ever measly things he had when he did eventually die. Among those miserable properties was of course the Challenger, something that Brodie had always admired. After all the kid had done for him. as far as being there and such, it was the least he could do. But Atkins wasn't dead yet,he was a bit hung over and dry mouthed but that never stopped him from coming to work before. He was two hours late, that was new and it would probably cause some fuss with the chief, but he hardly gave a shit at this point in his life about what his superiors had to say.

Detective Brodie watched as Atkins walked over to his desk and oozed into his chair, he smirked. A few moments later Brodie walked over with a fresh cup of coffee in his hand. "From the looks of it, I thought you could use one of these partner." Brodie said with a smile. Detective Atkins looked up at him with a strained grin. The rims of his eyes bore thick black bags and the inebriated detective looked like he had just been punched by the middle weight champion of the world. "Thanks kid." Atkins said genuinely. "So what did you find?" Brodie asked as he took a seat on Atkins' desk. Atkins rubbed his bruised looking eyes as he answered. "Nothing, a few smudged finger prints but I don't have to tell you that'll get us nowhere." Detective Brodie frowned and nodded his head. Atkins took a sip of his coffee and noticed that Brodie's frown was now a cocky smirk. "Having a peachy fucking morning Brodie?" Atkins asked with some aggression "Oh I'm not bad, hanging in there." Brodie spoke calm and cool. Atkins stared at his partner with a look of bewilderment as he took another sip of his coffee.

"So what about you Brodie, what do you got?" Atkins asked. "Well first things first, I managed to get in contact with the building's landlord early this morning." Atkins yawned quietly and nodded his head. "I asked for his infamous tenants name and he says he ain't got one." "No shit." Atkins replied rather unenthusiastically. "Yep, says the guy never gave him a name." "He rents a guy an apartment without even knowing his name?" Atkins said

146

in a baffled tone. "Well the landlord said the slasher made a sort of set of terms with him. Landlord says the guy told him he didn't want to be bothered for anything, whether it be that the water wasn't going to be working for a day or what, also he didn't want any paper work or record kept of his stay. Oh and no money trail, whatsoever." "And this moron gives the guy the place just like that?" Atkins asked, he was dumbfounded. "Well the slasher offered to pay him in advance, he gave him three months in cash and said after that he'd give him an envelope for another month and a half at the end of each month. The landlord said he had no choice, he couldn't rent the place for shit and here he had a guy willing to just hand it to him without complaining or being late or any of that bad tenant crap."

Atkins nodded and a light grin was still showing on Brodie's face. "Judging from that stupid grin I hope you have something else to tell me." Brodie's grin broadened "I also found out about that thing you wanted me to look into, the phone numbers." Atkins' eyes lit up, with all the drinking last night he had forgotten what he told his partner to do. Atkins quickly tried to look calm as it wasn't his style to be easily excited. "Yea, and..." Atkins said stubbornly. Brodie leaned forward eagerly. "Well most of the outgoing calls were pizzeria's and other stuff like that. This guy orders a hell of a lot of take out." Brodie giggled as he said it, Atkins sat stone faced waiting for him to

147

continue. "And the incoming we're mostly telemarketing and other salesman types, the same strange numbers that probably pop up on every person's caller ID a hundred times a day. I was just about loosing hope until they found a number that called two nights ago." Brodie said excitingly.

Atkins still seemed somber enough, but he could barely contain his eagerness and his eyes didn't lie. "The numbers private and we can't really get an exact pin point or an address yet but it came from a town in New Jersey. Darnate, no Darnite, yea that's it." Brodie finished. "So are they going about a direct trace? Did we get a duration on the call?" Atkins said hastily. "We got the duration, it's just about seven minutes." Brodie added. "That's something, seven minutes, is definitely something." "I know." Brodie said and the grin that once sat on his face was now gone. "What is it Martin?" Atkins asked heedfully, he could see there was something wrong. Brodie closed his eyes and rubbed his brow. "Chief doesn't think it's anything." Detective Atkins sat up and stared at his partner with a look of shock. "He doesn't think it's anything?" Atkins repeated dubiously. "He says for all we know, it could have been a prank caller." Brodie said apologetically. Atkins slammed his coffee down in a rage, he hardly even felt the hot liquid splash on his hand as he did. He stood up in an instant and made his way for the chief's office, Brodie sat watching in awe.

Chief Redding sat at his oversized oak desk reading over a large stack of papers to the left of him, he was bespectacled but was hardly a delicate looking man. His shoulders were broad and though he was only five ten he radiated a certain kind of intimidation, mostly through his dark, sober eyes. Detective Atkins burst through the door rapidly without warning. The chief continued looking over his paperwork for another few seconds before slowly turning up to the frantic detective. Redding stared at his inferior with a dead gaze, his dark eyes were noticeably magnified in his large specs. "Atkins, you could knock sometime." Redding said placidly as Atkins closed the door behind him. The chief signaled Atkins with his chubby palm to take a seat, but the Detective didn't acknowledge the offer. "Why aren't you following the lead?" Atkins asked abruptly. The chief's eyes snuck back down to his paperwork before looking back up at Atkins apathetically. "What lead are you referring to Detective?" Detective Atkins raised a pointed finger to his superior. "You know damn well what I'm talking about, the number from New Jersey, the one that called the son of a bitch. Why aren't we going any further with it?" "Let's not forget who you're talking to Atkins so put that God damn finger down." Redding barked back. Atkins moved his hand back to his side, he barely even noticed he was pointing it at the chief.

149

"Now as for your so called lead, that could have been a couple of kids pressing buttons for all we know." Redding said firmly as he waved the thought away with his hand. "Or it could have been someone the slasher knows, maybe an accomplice, maybe someone giving him a place to hide out." Atkins added and the chief shook his head disapprovingly. "That psychopath doesn't have any accomplices, you know it and I know it." Redding said. Detective Atkins stared at his chief in silence for a moment. "Chief, with all do respect, the call lasted seven minutes. That's gotta' be..." "Forget about it." Redding cut in. "Wait for something else to turn up and that's an order." "Nothing else is going to turn up chief! He's gone! We've been to his place, it's abandoned" Atkins said sternly and began to raise his voice a bit. "You don't know that for sure. We'll have some men stake it out tonight and see what happens." The chief added with a bit of a yell himself. Detective Atkins shook his head in disbelief. "Nothing is gonna' happen! I was there most of the night and..." Detective Atkins stopped in his tracks, knowing he had said too much. Chief Redding stared up at the detective with a look of shock.

"Since when do we have unauthorized stakeouts Detective?" Atkins sighed and began. "Chief I..." Redding cut Atkins off. "And what the hell were you going to do if he did show up Robert? Ruin your career! Ruin your life!" The chief was now bellowing at the top of his lungs. The detective closed his eyes in frustration and began to think back on the previous night's fantasy. If the slasher had walked through that door in his apartment, he would have blew him away without hesitation. Atkins was about to agree with his chief, about to come to his senses and give up on the lunacy but then something fell out of his mouth as effortlessly as a dead leaf falls from a withered winter branch. "My life is already ruined." Atkins' words were robotic. Chief Redding stared at the detective with a look of dismay, he didn't know what to say but Atkins spoke first. "He's gone Chief, I don't know where to, maybe Jersey, maybe somewhere else. I have to find him." The detective's words were calm but full of emotion, his eyes were glassy and filled with pain. Redding slid off his glasses and rubbed at his eyes and forehead with two open palms before turning back to the detective. "Well send out the composites to the surrounding states, they'll..." "They'll what? They'll hang the sketch on a board next to a million other faces and then what. He's not stupid, he'll slip through the cracks, he wont make himself seen. How many more people are going to die before he gets caught?"

Chief Redding stared at Atkins solemnly "I'd rather have him somewhere else than have him ruining more lives here." Atkins stared emotionless at the chief. "And if you're thinking about going to chase some

151

murdering psychopath out of our jurisdiction, well then you better forget it because there's no way I'm letting it happen under my watch. I know how you must feel Robert but I can't have you on this case anymore, it's too personal and God knows I don't need this man hunt to end in unnecessary blood shed. He'll be caught, you'll get your relief." Detective Atkins shook his head in disbelief and some disgust. His mouth formed a grimace that slowly turned into a sickly grin. "The only thing that's gonna' give me relief, is knowing that bastard is dead." Atkins words were sincere and cold and Chief Redding couldn't help but swallow his throat at the sound of them. "If you're not going to help me find him, I'll do it myself." There was a thick silence in the room as Atkins waited for some kind of reaction. "You say killing him is the only way, and if that's the case I can't help you. I'm responsible for my department's actions and I can't be a part of that.

The chief extended his hand, Atkins looked down at it and knew immediately this wasn't the gesture for a handshake. Without hesitation Atkins handed his gun and his badge to his superior. They stared at each other for another moment before Atkins nodded and was on his way. The door shut behind him and Chief Redding let out a sigh. "Good luck." He said sincerely before going back to his large stack of papers. When Atkins walked out of the chief's office Brodie was sitting by his desk, he immediately got up and rushed toward his partner. "I could hear some yelling, what the hells going on?" Brodie asked nervously. "Come by my place when you get off, we'll talk before I go," Atkins said sternly. "Go? Where are you going?" Brodie asked with a hint of a giggle. Before Brodie could get an answer Atkins was walking toward the exit of the police department. In another moment he was through the door and on his way home to start packing.

It was about ten thirty in Darnite when Paulie and Daniel pulled up to the wooded construction site in Daniel's work pickup. There were several bulky men with hard hats and flannel shirts who were chopping lumber either by hand or by use of machinery. Paulie was dressed in a flannel work shirt that he had borrowed from Daniel. Daniel was wearing his regular white collared shirt and tie, as he was co-supervisor on the work site. Daniel walked over to another man who was wearing a similar shirt to his and began talking to him. This man was the head supervisor Mike, he was a short, stocky, balding man with a thick mustache, Paulie stood nearby waiting in silence. "He's a great worker Mike, I think you'd really be able to use him out here." Daniel said profoundly as his boss stared at him with an uninterested look. "We're pretty loaded up here Dan, I don't know if we need another guy." Paulie couldn't help overhearing but didn't seem to care, he was too busy thinking about how long it would be until his first local victim popped

153

up in the woods. "You got any experience?" Michael called. Paulie snapped
out of his murder indulging trance and moved closer to Daniel and Mike. "I
did work like this out of state for about six months" Paulie said and Michael
nodded. "It doesn't have to be long term, just for a little." Daniel added with a
shrug of his shoulders. "Alright but I can't guarantee you more than a
month." Michael said and Daniel turned to Paulie smiling. "I think that will
do." Daniel added. "Alright then." Michael said as he shook Paulie's hand.
"When could I start?" Paulie asked. "No better time like the present."
Michael replied matter of factly.

Two hours later Michelle sat comfortably in the living room watching
"Dr. Oz" and drinking the rest of the bottle of Merlot her secret ex lover had
brought. Daniel and Paulie were busy at work and Nicole was still at school.
This left Michelle with the house to herself and she used that opportunity to
drink to the point where she would no longer be thinking. No longer thinking
of Paulie, or Daniel,or the inconvenient fact that Paulie could be there for
another five months seemed almost impossible, but she had to do try.
Suddenly the house phone rang, it might have startled her a little but the
soothing wine had already crept into her bloodstream and began to calm her
(well that and the obviously charming Dr. Oz). She picked up the phone and
saw that it was Daniel's work number, she stared at it curiously. Why was he

calling her? Probably to try and smooth things over, she thought. She didn't care nor did she want to hear his voice right now. Michelle threw the phone to the couch and took another sip of her favorite wine as the answering machine picked up. Daniel's voice was clear and sounded slightly concerned. "Hey it's me." Michelle sighed at his voice. "I guess your at the store or something. Listen I don't want to fight, maybe tonight we could go out to eat and talk about things. Just the two of us. I gotta' get back to work so I'll try back again later, I love you." The message ended and the beep sounded. Michelle stared at the answering machine emotionless, her mind was full of those thoughts she was trying to avoid.

Daniel and Michelle were not the only ones who weren't talking, Nicole and Jake were still in their own immature war. Sure it was a childish one but Nicole was still thinking about it while she tried to study for her upcoming final. The final, that was the problem, if she didn't have the final they would have never fought. Was she wrong for being mad at Jake for wanting to go to the party without her? Maybe, and maybe she overreacted a bit. Nicole sat by herself in the silent but surprisingly crowded library as she contemplated these thoughts. The end of the semester was the time of year when all of the students said they would clean up their acts and do what they needed to do, nevertheless most of them would fail. Some like Nicole did have a fighting chance but with all that Jake crap still in her head, she felt her chances of passing were getting slimmer by the minute. She had seen Jake the period before, walking to his history class. He had looked at her with a loving but empty gaze and when the late bell sounded he simply shook his head and was gone. Nicole thought that he seemed sorry enough but felt she wasn't the one who should break the ice and start talking. She knew she was better than that and wasn't about to run back to him like the average emotionally challenged girlfriend. Thinking about it now, she barely cared if he went to the party, let him have fun, she thought. And the realization that she no longer cared about it made her even more distressed, maybe she had overreacted.

Meanwhile in the lunch room, Eric was telling Jake about the probable "hotties" he had coming to tonight's party. "Man from the looks of her pictures online, this girl is fuckin' right!" Eric said enthusiastically and Jake shook his head in embarrassment at how loud his friend was being. "And she said she's gonna' bring a friend." Eric added with a grin. Jake smiled with discretion. "I don't know man, what about Nicole?" Eric rolled his eyes. "Forget her man, has she even tried to talk to you since she flipped out for no apparent reason." "No, not yet." Jake said with some optimism. "Then fuck her! She doesn't care about what you want. She wants you to stay in the house and study with her, while me and the rest of our friends are getting hammered..." Eric cringed humorously. "Now that's just plain selfish." Jake was about to speak but Eric cut him off. "Has she even let you look at anything downstairs yet?" Eric asked condescendingly. For a moment Jake looked angry that his friend had even brought this up but grinned anyway. "Nicole's a really nice girl, she's also a good girl. Which honestly Eric, is pretty fucking hard to find. Nowadays, everyone's a whore." "How is that a bad thing?" Eric said quickly. Jake laughed and pushed Eric on the shoulder. "Hear me out, she doesn't have to know anything. You come to the party, we meet up with the girls. We have a few drinks, get smashed and see what happens. If you're feeling her, maybe you'll be able to do some smashing of your own and if not what ever, I'm not forcing anything. Just be a wing man." "Alright fine." Jake said reluctantly. "Alright! It's gonna' be a good night." Eric added playfully.

Back at the work site, Daniel sat in a trailer looking over some blueprints for the construction that was going to go on in the next few weeks. Suddenly he began to think of Michelle, she had still not called him back and it had been an hour since his second call. She was probably still mad he thought, but mad at what? Why was she so strange when it came to having Paulie stay over. In the past they always seemed to get along, perhaps it had

157

something to do with him being in prison for the last eight years. Maybe it frightened her, that could be it, but Michelle afraid of Paulie? That didn't sit right with Daniel. The trailer door opened and Michael the head supervisor walked in holding a cup of coffee. "What's up Danny, everything alright in here?" Michael asked routinely. "Everything's good here Mike. Anything you need?" Daniel asked respectively before turning back to the blueprints. Michael did not answer right away, instead he stared out a large window that faced the workers. "No, no I'm fine..." Michael sounded uninterested as he continued to stare through the glass. "Jesus Christ, your brothers a real animal with that thing huh?" Michael said abruptly. "What?" Daniel asked confused before standing up and looking out the window with his boss. There he saw Paulie outside swinging an old rusted axe frantically into a large tree that was now laying across the ground. As he continued to viciously swing the axe into the thick trunk, the other workers began to gather around and stare on in confused delight. Daniel heard his brothers loud moans and grunts through the window. The passion in Paulie's eyes and the sounds he was letting out gave Daniel a chill up his spine. He swallowed his throat nervously and in the next moment he didn't know why.

13

A Productive Night Part One

Daniel and Paulie had gotten home from work around five. Paulie went right to sleep, it had been a month since he had worked a real day of work and it had taken a lot out of him. Daniel immediately talked to Michelle and began to patch things up. He apologized and said he should have gotten her opinion before asking Paulie to stay a while. He reassured her that he didn't want to fight and that they had come too far in their marriage to go back to those days. Michelle agreed passively, as she was no longer interested in the discussion. Daniel smiled happily unaware that his wife was now full blown drunk. She had finished the bottle of Merlot and thrown it in the trash with hopes that Daniel would forget there was some left. Michelle was not in tune with the conversation Daniel had with her and she nodded most of it and basically "yessed" him to death. She filled the rest of the conversation with about twenty five "You're rights" and ended it with a playful kiss on the lips. She wondered warily if he would smell the alcohol on her. She had done a good job of brushing her teeth and sucking on some mint lifesavers but Michelle thought the wine might still be lingering. If it was, Daniel didn't happen to notice, his mind was still too consumed with the thought of why Michelle had gotten so mad in the first place. He didn't care to share his thoughts, thinking it would only cause more of a fight. Shortly after, Daniel called the local fancy (and very expensive) Italian restaurant Pino's and made a reservation for eight o' clock. The couple had dined there several times in the past, mostly to celebrate pointless anniversaries, year after year. It was Michelle's favorite restaurant and he thought going there would surely close the case.

Later at about seven thirty, Daniel and Michelle were both getting ready for their night out. Nicole strolled in the front door with a fresh bag of taco bell, her pre study cuisine, and headed into the kitchen. Moments later Daniel came walking down the steps in a fine olive colored suit that matched his dark complexion, he spotted Nicole eating her dinner across the way in the kitchen. Daniel smiled and walked up to his daughter. "Wow Dad, you look real sharp." Nicole said and accompanied it with a thumbs up. Daniel smirked. "Thanks pumpkin. You gonna' be alright tonight?" "Dad, I'm not ten, I'll be fine." Nicole said slightly annoyed. At that same moment Paulie walked out of the guest room he had been sleeping in for several hours and let out a large stretch and yawn. Daniel noticed him and realized he had totally forgotten about his brother being there. "Oh Paulie, wow, I completely forgot to tell you. Michelle and I are going out to dinner so you're going to

have to grab something tonight." Daniel spoke apologetically. Paulie walked
into the kitchen. "That's ok, I'll just order something for me and Nicole..."
Paulie stopped abruptly when he noticed Nicole was eating already. "Sorry."
She said innocently with a full mouth. "I'll get something, don't worry."
Paulie said with a dumb smirk.

"How do I look?" Daniel asked his brother as he straightened his tie.
"Sharp Danny, real sharp." Paulie answered amusingly as he brushed off his
brother's shoulder. At that moment, Michelle who was wearing a stunning
violet colored dress and a pair of stilettos to match began to walk down the
steps. Nicole, Paulie and Daniel all turned to stare as she approached the
kitchen where they were standing. "Honey you look beautiful." Daniel
proclaimed. "Wow mom you look gorgeous." Nicole added. Michelle smiled
at her compliments and began to blush. "I'll say it again, you're one lucky
man Danny boy." Paulie smiled and stared at Michelle deeply as he said this.
Michelle began to feel uncomfortable and the smile across her face quickly
faded. "Well I gotta' start studying, have fun guys." Nicole said as she got up
from the dinner table, she kissed her mother, then her father before hurrying
up the steps. "See you later Uncle Paulie." Nicole called out as she made her
way to the top of the stairs. Daniel turned to Michelle. "Well, we better get
going. If you need anything Paulie, don't be afraid to call." "Please I wouldn't

want to ruin your evening, go ahead have fun. Don't even think about me."
As Paulie said the last words he shot a look to Michelle, she quickly looked
away. "We'll try not to." Daniel said with a smirk not knowing the severity
Paulie's words meant to his wife.

Paulie walked the two to the front door and opened it for them. Daniel
walked through first. "Thanks Paulie." Paulie didn't reply, instead he simply
winked at his brother. As Michelle walked out the door she stared at Paulie
with an aggravated look. She suddenly knew the reason she didn't want
Paulie here. It wasn't because she hated him and it wasn't because she was
afraid of him. It was because in a given situation, she might do something
she would regret. As Michelle stared at Paulie for another second she
wondered if and when that given situation might occur. "Have a good time."
Paulie interrupted her thoughts and she heard herself reply awkwardly. "We
will." As if to rub it in his face. Paulie closed the door behind them and they
were gone. "Now what the hell am I going to do." Paulie said to himself
aloud.

At the same time in Mesapeena, Detective Atkins was in his house
packing some clothes for the trip he had ahead of him. He suddenly heard a
knock at the door and walked over. He opened it and as expected it was

Detective Brodie. "Come in Martin." Atkins said and his partner entered.
Atkins continued to rummage through his drawers for any last additions.
Brodie watched his partner silently, trying to figure out what to say to him.
"What are you going to do?" Brodie asked cautiously. Detective Atkins
looked up at his partner with a look that said, you already know what I'm
going to do. "I'm going to Darnite and I'm going to find the man who killed
my wife and daughter." Detective Brodie rolled his eyes annoyed. "And then
what?" "Then what, well I don't know. I haven't thought that far, I'll just have
to see how things play out." Detective Atkins smiled eerily. "What about the
chief, what did he have to say?" "Forget the chief, he wants to wash his
hands of this whole slasher thing and that's ok with me. If that's the way it's
gotta' be, I'll do it myself. I don't need anyone."

   Atkins' words were stern and Brodie couldn't help but feel that he
should lend a hand. "I could..." Brodie began and Detective Atkins
immediately shut him down with a word. "No." Brodie stared at Atkins as he
continued to pack, after another moment Atkins sighed and looked back at
him. "Listen, I didn't mean that towards you. You're a good kid and I know
you've got Lorraine and the children to worry about." "Robert, I want to
help." Brodie added. "I can't let you, you're not going to ruin your job and
maybe even your life because of me. I won't let it happen. My life on the

163

other hand, nothing to lose there." Atkins grinned and Brodie shook his head.
"But...if anything should happen to me..." Dismay came over Brodie's face
and he interrupted. "What are you talking about? Don't talk like that." "Shut
up and let me finish." Detective Atkins said with a bit of annoyance and
Brodie stared at him like a child who had just been yelled at by his father. "If
anything happens to me, then you could help me, then you could find the
bastard and bust his ass for me. Understood?" Brodie nodded in agreement
and spoke hoarsely. "Whatever you say partner."

"Good." Atkins added. "You sure there's nothing else you need me to
do?" Brodie asked curiously. Detective Atkins lit up a cigarette. "Oh yea, you
could help me pack the rest of my shit." Brodie nodded and saw that Atkins
already had two large duffel bags of clothes packed. "What else do you need
to bring?" Brodie asked curiously. Atkins grinned and walked over to a large
oak armoire that sat awkwardly in the corner of the detective's bedroom. He
opened it up and revealed an extensive collection of about ten different guns;
two of which were shotguns, four different kind of handguns, two revolvers,
one machine gun, and one rifle. Detective Brodie's face dropped when he
saw his partner's secret collection. "Jesus Christ! Since when did you become
Rambo?" Detective Atkins smirked and let out a small giggle. "I got a lot of
time on my hands partner, doctor said I should get a hobby...So I got one."

Detective Brodie smiled uneasily and Atkins grabbed another duffel bag from his closet. Atkins grabbed one of the long necked western looking revolvers and placed it into the bag while Brodie continued to stare at the collection in awe. "Are you trying to compete with the station's artillery?" Brodie asked and Atkins smiled. Brodie pulled a silver finished nine milometer from the armoire and gave it a closer, intrigued look. Atkins noticed and grabbed the gun from his partner and placed it into the bag, Brodie smirked.

Detective Atkins instinctively grabbed one of the shotguns and placed it into his bag. He glanced at the second shotgun still sitting in the armoire. "Why don't you keep that one for yourself." Atkins said as he turned to his partner. "Really?" Brodie asked. "Yea sure, who needs two shotguns anyway." Both detectives smiled and Atkins zipped up the bag and closed the armoire. Outside, Brodie gave Atkins a hand loading the three bags into his trunk. After that was done Atkins flicked his cigarette into some snow in the street and the two detectives stared at each other in silence. "Do me a favor partner." Brodie said. "Yea?" "Be careful." Atkins nodded and for a moment he thought maybe he should give Brodie a hug, instead he extended his hand and Brodie shook it firmly. Brodie gave Atkins an accepting nod and Atkins got into his Challenger. A moment later the Detectives tail lights were just a flicker in the nights horizon. As Atkins continued toward the main intersection he spotted his bottle of Valume sitting in the cars cup holder. He picked up the bottle and gave it a light shake, he judged from the sound that there were only maybe two or three left in the plastic. Without contemplating any further he rolled down his window and chucked the bottle out. The bottle jumped onto the slush covered street and landed camouflaged in a soft pile of snow.

Paulie was hungry and decided to get in his car and go grab something. After almost a half hour of passing up some local restaurants he ended up settling on McDonald's. Nothing better than a big mac, he figured. Now he drove in his Cadillac listening to Keith Richards sing "Run,Run Rudolph." and picking at the rest of his french fries that sat on the passenger seat. He didn't know what to do, he was bored out of his mind and knew he couldn't sit in the house the whole night especially with Nicole upstairs studying. He'd loose it, hell he might even get so bored he'd kill her and that he couldn't afford to do. So he drove around aimlessly, eating his french fries, hoping to find something to distract him from the boredom. When suddenly and quite divinely he did. It was funny the way life worked itself out, Paulie often thought. Like tonight for instance, with all the boredom and such, to stumble across the white minivan he saw yesterday at the mall. He grinned sinisterly. There it was, sitting in a driveway, the white minivan. He was almost sure it was the same one because of the dent that was over the back wheel but he pulled the piece of paper from his glove compartment to end any doubt. Yep that was it, 902 1178, that was the one. He smiled to himself grimly and pulled his car over to the side of the street about ten feet from the house where the van was. He turned off his head lights, sat in the shadows and began to watch silently. He glanced at the clock and noticed it was barely nine, he sighed and pushed back his seat to get more comfortable.

Across the street and a few feet in back of where Paulie's blue Cadillac sat was an unfinished house. If Paulie's windows were down, he might have heard the muffling of loud music coming through it. This was the same house that Nicole and Jake had partied in with their friends a few nights before. The same house where tonight the biggest party before the holiday break was happening. Teens began loading inside the house through the back garage to avoid any attention they might bring to a cop patrolling through the neighborhood. It would seem slightly out of place for thirty kids to be pouring into the front of an ownerless house. Luckily for the teens (and for Paulie) no cops appeared to be around. The party was set to get underway at around ten but inside there was already a crowd of about fifteen boys and girls who had decided to come and pre-game early. Jake and Eric were two

167

of those early birds. The boys walked in and were greeted by some familiar faces from school. Jake and Eric were praised for bringing extra alcohol. They had managed to get Jake's older cousin Jackie to buy them some of it, the rest had come from Eric's father's liquor cabinet. He was a slight alcoholic and with the elaborate stash he had, Eric didn't think he'd miss a few bottles. Other than some minor things like not having electric, the house was pretty much finished. Some walls were still naked without paint but none of the drunken teens seemed to mind (at least the toilets worked, that was important). Most of them brought candles and flash lights and the house was now reminiscent of some strange dimly lit church or religious vigil.

Jake looked around the semi crowded house nervously. "So where are these girls?" "Relax, they'll be here, I told them to come at ten so we would have time to get a little buzzed, I'm more charming when I've got a little alcohol in me. Like Don Juan Maraco." Eric said jokingly and Jake giggled. "What if they don't show." Jake asked. "They'll show, didn't I tell you to trust me?" Eric asked. Jake didn't look too thrilled by Eric's guarantee. "What's your problem man, you having cold feet?" "I don't know, I feel wrong. Nicole trusts me, what if someone sees us and tells her?" Eric sighed. "Look no offense but Nicole is kind of a nobody in school, no one's gonna' be anxious to tell her." Jake looked like he wanted to defend his girlfriend but knew Eric was right. Eric continued. "Just have some drinks with me and relax. Be my wing man, ok?" Jake let out sigh and spoke reluctantly. "Alright, I'm your wing man." Eric smiled and slapped his friend on the shoulder. He grabbed two beer cans, popped them open and handed one to Jake. Eric smiled and Jake began to drink his worries away.

14

A Productive Night Part Two

At a quarter past ten Nicole was deep into her studies, she laid in her quiet room reading the suggested pages in her text book over and over again. When she had first started, Jake was on her mind and she couldn't seem to shake the thought of him. What was he doing? Was he still mad? Was this the end of their relationship? What if he was seeing someone else, maybe that's why he didn't care for calling her. No it couldn't be, he would never, she reassured herself that was not the case. She fought through the rest of the negative thoughts in her mind and tried to focus on what was important, her math final. She sighed as she flipped to the beginning of her textbook and started over. Algebra, geometry, trigonometry, what did all this bullshit matter, she often wondered to herself. When in life was she going to need to know the square root of something. If she could have it her way, you would learn all the basic math early in life and that would be it. Once you were done learning addition subtraction, multiplication and division, you would be done unless of course you chose to keep learning it, but who in the world would choose that option. She felt her mind beginning to wander into this fantasy and caught herself. Nicole sighed and turned the page refocusing her attention back to her studies.

Pino's restaurant was packed tonight and that was no surprise to Daniel and Michelle as it was always that way. There was a delay on their reservation and they spent the first hour having drinks at the bar. Michelle was almost fully sober when they had got there and was anxious to have another drink. She restored the drunkenness that she had worked on earlier in the day with three vodka martinis and Daniel got his blood flowing with four martinis of his own. When the hostess finally did have a table ready for them at around nine fifteen, Michelle and Daniel were both pretty tanked. They sat down and enjoyed some more drinks as they put in their orders. Now at almost ten thirty they were eating their main courses, laughing and enjoying each other's company. Michelle was surprised by this as she was almost sure the dinner would be a disaster. But the alcohol seemed to keep her mind off certain things, certain things that had to do with her brother in law. She ignored the insignificant thoughts that were trying to creep into her mind, ate her pasta and attempted to be fully engaged to her husband.

The party in the unfinished house was now fully underway. The music was louder now and trying it's best to escape and spread into the rest of the neighborhood. Paulie didn't hear it, as a matter of fact Paulie didn't hear anything as he was now passed out in the drivers seat of his Cadillac. He was drooling away in his slumber and probably dreaming of hacking up someone. One things for sure he wasn't having nightmares, homicidal psychopaths never had nightmares, why would they? It was ten thirty when he awoke suddenly to a child's playful scream. When he opened his eyes he saw the black haired man from the jury holding his small six year old son up in the air. The wife was standing there smiling at her husband's antics. The three were standing in front of the house and it seemed like they were about to leave and go somewhere. Damn, Paulie thought to himself. The father and son playing had not changed his attitude on what he wanted to do, he was going to kill the man regardless. He thought for a moment that maybe if they were going somewhere he could follow them and wait till he got his chance to kill the man alone, but what if he never got the chance? He'd have to kill them all, he sighed with this thought. One body was easier than three but three was better than none.

As these horrific thoughts casually crossed Paulie's mind, the wife and boy kissed the black haired man and walked down the driveway to the white minivan. They gave one last wave, got into the minivan and pulled away, the man walked back into his house. Paulie was in awe as he watched this occur, he laughed to himself, life did have a way of working it self out. The man was home alone, this would be like taking candy from a baby, Paulie thought. He stayed seated in the car and waited another few minutes for the man to settle into his house and get comfortable. Maybe he'd catch him while he was sleeping, Paulie thought, now that would be fun. He'd wake him up and then slash his throat. Then it hit Paulie, he didn't know if he had anything to kill the guy with. He figured he could do it with his hands but wanted it to be a little more gruesome than that. The thought crossed his mind to just go in the house and try to find a knife or something, but what if he ran into the man while he was looking around? Then he'd be forced to kill him with his hands anyway.

Paulie got out of the car, walked towards the trunk and popped it open, he began to look for a weapon. He spotted the gun that he had taken from one of those foolish drug dealers but knew immediately guns were no fun, not when it came to murder. Murder was something that had to be done right, it had to be done slowly and sensually. He pushed the gun aside and continued to look through the trunk. He passed on a worn wooden Louie Ville Slugger and a tire iron amongst other things. Then he picked it up, a slightly rusted flat head screw driver. That was it, that was what he would use. He spotted an old baseball cap and some stained work gloves and grabbed them before closing the trunk. Paulie put the baseball cap on his head and slid the brown gloves on his hands. He stuck the screw driver in his back pocket and began to slowly approach the house. He gave the surrounding houses a quick glance but didn't see anyone, it was almost eleven, he didn't expect to see anyone. It wasn't that late but Darnite at midnight was practically a ghost town.

Paulie snuck pass some bushes and made his was around the side of the house. It had crossed his mind for a moment to break in from the front, but he figured that would be too risky. Paulie didn't know where the man was and for all he knew he could be standing right there in the first room. He spotted a few low windows as he made his way around the side of the house, but when he tried to slide one open he found it was locked. Paulie felt anger rush over him and for a second was about to smash one of the windows in with his elbow. He came to his senses and knew the last thing he needed to do was make any alarming noises that would get the man suspicious. Paulie continued around to the backyard and saw some children toys scattered around, covered in dirty snow flurries. A slide, a big wheel and a swing set, this would make your average person uneasy about proceeding with what Paulie was about to do, but then again Paulie wasn't your average person. As he continued around, he spotted some concrete steps that led down to a door to what he assumed was the basement, Paulie sighed in relief.

Michelle and Daniel were on their way back to the car in Pino's parking lot, both were full with food and alcohol. It was turning into a a chilly night and though the drinks had helped them to try and forget about the crisp wind, Michelle was still walking hastily to get to the car. She was a few inches ahead of Daniel when he grabbed her shoulder. Michelle stopped awkwardly and nearly tripped over her expensive stiletto's, she regained her balance and turned around. Daniel was staring at her timidly, Michelle stared back curiously and just as the word "what?" tried to sneak out of her mouth he kissed her. It was a quick kiss, innocent and awkward, sort of like the way two junior high school kids would have done it. Then Daniel gave her another, this time longer. Before Michelle knew it, they were going at it like high school lovers. The kiss was now full of passion and want and Michelle could feel Daniel's hands moving around her body. She first felt the warmth of his hand around her soft breasts and without even thinking her hands wrapped around him and slithered down his back. Neither of them were thinking about the cold now, they could feel themselves warming and their horniness building. They stopped kissing abruptly and rushed to the car. They got in and drove away with plans to continue their sudden lust for one another elsewhere.

At the unfinished house Jake and Eric were now pretty buzzed. They

175

were gathered around with some friends from school and were both currently laughing hysterically at   something one of their buddies had said. Jake was calm now and had stopped worrying about the whole situation, he realized Eric was right and that he wasn't obligated to do anything he didn't want to. Nicole hadn't called him anyway so why should he worry about her, they could be broken up for all he knew. These thoughts seemed to make perfect sense now, Jake thought as he took a sip of his current beer. Eric nudged Jake and broke his drunken train of thought as he pointed out two pretty girls walking towards them smiling nervously. Jake looked up and swallowed his throat before giving Eric a sort of panicked, here goes nothing look. They walked away from the friends they were talking to and walked up to the girls.

Eric gave the blonde haired girl a hug and friendly kiss on the cheek. "Hey Rachel, it's great to finally meet you. You look even prettier than I imagined." Eric wasn't lying, both girls were beautiful and definitely out of Jake and his leagues. Rachel blushed as Eric continued. "Who's your friend?" The brown haired girl smiled and answered herself. "Hi, I'm Amy." Eric nodded. "Well Amy, this is Jake." Jake had a dumb grin on his face and extended his hand, both girls gave each other an awkward glance and proceeded to shake Jake's hand. There was suddenly an awkward silence but before it could put a dim on the conversation Eric cut in. "You girls wanna' get some drinks?" The girls looked at each other and nodded. "Sure" Rachel said confidently and the four headed off to where the drinks were. Jake who was obviously very amused by Amy, had all but forgotten about Nicole.

It had taken Paulie a few minutes but he had finally managed to pick the basement door open with his handy dandy screw driver, the same tool that in a few minutes would help him do something else. He opened the door slowly and walked into the basement. The basement was dark and cold and had that smell all basements have, one of dust and junk. Paulie moved forward but could barely make out where he was going, he took each step on the concrete floor carefully and felt around with his arms to make sure he wouldn't walk into anything. Just as Paulie started to think his path was pretty much clear, he tripped over something that felt like a chair. Paulie let out a groan and as he did he could feel dust shoot up his nose and tickle the inside of his nostrils. The first two sneezes snuck out very quickly and Paulie had no time to muffle the noise. When he felt the third coming he quickly put his arm to his face to avoid making another sound. After the third sneeze Paulie stopped in his tracks and listened cautiously with hopes that he hadn't been heard.

The silence coming from upstairs reassured Paulie that the man hadn't heard. Paulie continued to move and noticed some light coming from a door cracked at the top of a staircase, he crept towards it. Paulie walked up the staircase as quietly as he could but since it was made of wood, almost every step let out an unpleasant creak. Paulie's tongue hung out of his mouth as if it was helping him to focus and sweat was slowly sliding down his nose. He pulled down the rim of his hat to scratch an itch he had on his forehead. As he came to the top step he crouched down on his knees and peaked an eye through the barely open door. He couldn't see much other than a small piece of the kitchen, he began to hear some footsteps but could tell they were coming from another side of the house. For a moment they began to get closer and Paulie pulled himself back from the cracked door. Abruptly the footsteps seemed to change direction and began to fade to the upper level, thump by thump. The man was now upstairs.

Paulie let out a small sigh of relief and wiped some sweat from his face before slowly pushing the door open. The door creaked madly and Paulie realized he would have probably been better off just opening the door at a moderate speed. He got to his feet and stepped out of the darkness. The kitchen was large and modern looking. There were a few food related paintings on the walls, one of a full fruit bowl and one of a chef cooking up something. There was also fancy lettering above the stove that read "Food &

Family". Paulie didn't like the cleanliness of the place and something about it all made him feel a little uneasy. Paulie spotted a wooden knife holder on the counter and there was a brief moment when he wondered if he should replace the screw driver. He pulled the rusty tool from his back pocket and stared at it for a moment before deciding to keep it. Paulie walked through the kitchen and into the living room, the footsteps continued above but they showed no sign of coming back down, at least not for now. He looked at some photos that were framed around the house, photos of the man smiling with his family, everyone happy. Paulie's uneasy feeling was now an angry one. As he stared at the pictures of the happy family, whether he wanted to admit it or not, he felt a bit envious. Suddenly Paulie heard what at first sounded like a toilet flushing from above. He soon realized this was more close to the sound of water filling up a bath tub.

Nicole had taken a break from her studies when she realized her mind was full of thoughts of Jake. She wondered why he still hadn't called her and her fears managed to get the best of her. She finally gave in and dialed his number into her phone, nothing, a few rings and then the voice mail. Nicole sighed and reluctantly went back to her studies.

Jake had left his phone in Eric's car but that might have not made

179

much of a difference as he was now in an intimate make out session with Amy. They had began talking and after a few drinks Amy thought it was a good idea to kiss him and she did just that. Jake instantly had the thought to try and stop her but before he knew it, he was kissing her back and was defenseless to her beauty. Eric and Rachel were also beginning to get a little hot and heavy. Eric was now dry humping Rachel from behind as they danced to the music being played. Many of the other guys and girls there were doing the same, some even lit up joints which made the dark house even hazier. Eric shot a look to Jake from across the room, a smile that said, see I was right. Jake smiled back. His friend was right but neither that, the beautiful girl in front of him or the fact that he was piss drunk could stop the feeling of guilt that began to overwhelm him. What was he doing, Jake wondered, this wasn't like him. Though he was a good looking kid that never had a problem getting girls, he never thought of himself as a user. He loved Nicole and cheating on her was something he didn't think he'd ever do, but here he was doing it. Amy went in for another kiss and Jake stopped her casually and handed her another beer, he grabbed one for himself and they began drinking silently.

Paulie continued to snoop around the house for a few minutes after the water had turned on. He knew if the man was drawing a bath that it would be best to wait for him to get in before making his way upstairs. After another minute the water stopped and Paulie realized that he hadn't heard another footstep. He began to creep up the main staircase calmly and carefully. The stairs immediately began to creak but Paulie was too focused to worry about that now, he continued up the stairs and could now hear the man singing to "Easy Like A Sunday Morning" to himself. The man sang out of tune and a bit hoarsely. Paulie was now at the top of the steps and couldn't help but smile at the irony in the song the man was singing. It may not have been a Sunday morning but this was going to be easy alright. Paulie started slowly down the hall and noticed the door was left slightly opened, the steam from the hot water had began to sneak out of the gap along with the man's soft lonesome vocals. Paulie approached the doors crevice cautiously and got down to his knees slowly. He peeked through and saw the man laying in the bath lazily, his head was leaned back and rested on a small bath towel. His eyes were closed and he seemed relaxed and invulnerable to the impending doom.

Paulie smirked arrogantly and proceeded to open the door as slowly as he could. For a minute he thought he should open it quickly to avoid having another sound like the door downstairs but before Paulie knew it, the door was moving slickly across the white bathroom tile. Paulie stopped when he felt there was enough room in the doorway for him to enter, the man was still in the same position as he was a minute earlier and showed no signs of incoming movement. The bathtub was about six feet away from the doorway and Paulie made it across the space, snake like and effortlessly. He came to the bathtub and stood over the man as he continued to sing peacefully to himself. Paulie reached into his back pocket and pulled out his weapon of choice, the rusty flat head. He fixed the rim of his hat one last time and stared at the man with a certain hunger, like he was about to eat a four course meal. The man sang the final lyrics and those were his last words. "Peek a boo mother fucker!" Paulie screamed hauntingly. The mans eyes shot open and he let out a bewildered gasp, at the same time Paulie raised the screwdriver up in the air. Before the man could let out another sound Paulie began to stab the screwdriver into the bath water and into the man's torso. Viciously he continued, up and down, up and down. Blood began to mix in with the soapy water as the man wailed in horror, probably shocked and confused by his unexpected demise. The man was completely out of it as the screw driver continued to puncture his vital organs, he could barely comprehend what was happening to him let alone come to the realization of who was doing it. This didn't matter to Paulie much, he didn't care if the guy remembered him or not. All he wanted was for the man to stop breathing.

The now completely red water began to splash out of the tub as Paulie continued in the stabbing motion. The man was now squirming and Paulie thought he was either trying to get away or just convulsing. Finally the man's movement ceased and after a few extra stabs, Paulie stopped and stared down as the man's head slid into the water and the splashing slowly came to a halt. Paulie was out of breath and had not even noticed his hat had fallen onto the floor in the intensity of the situation. When Paulie had finally caught his breath, he looked around the bathroom and noticed the mess he had made. About half of the tub's water had splashed out onto the tile and some was even soaked in a small white rug under the toilet bowl. He had not thought of the mess this was going to make, and even more carelessly he had not thought if he should take the body with him. Well, there was no reason to take it now, he thought. Not with the blood water all over the bathroom, everyone would know there was foul play even without a body. Instead of wasting anymore time thinking useless thoughts, Paulie wiped the blood stained screwdriver on the increasingly red rug and put it back into his pocket. He grabbed his hat off the floor and stormed out of the bathroom.

Eric, Jake and their dates Rachel and Amy had decided to get some fresh air, as the inside of the house was now filled with cigarette and marijuana smoke. Neither of the four liked the smell of cigarettes and Eric

183

was the only one who didn't mind the smell of pot as he was an avid user. They were now standing in front of the house conversing when Eric began kissing Rachel. Amy took a cue from them and began kissing Jake, once again he felt the desire to pull away but didn't. Even though Jake felt dirty all over, he went with it. Directly across the street Paulie was making his way down the steps and back into the living room without delay. He came to the front door, reached for the knob and turned, the door opened without hesitation. Paulie laughed aloud at the fact that the front door was unlocked the whole time. He could have simply walked in instead of prying the basement door. That wasn't important now, Paulie thought as he made his way through the doorway and began his descent down the concrete steps that lead to the front sidewalk.

Paulie was running on pure adrenaline and though the wind had grown colder than it was before, he could barely feel it slapping him in the face. Jake was still making out with Amy when he made eye contact with Paulie and complete fear ran through his body. Fear wasn't the first thing he felt though, that first feeling was that same strange feeling everyone has when they see someone they know out of their normal environment. Sort of like when you see a coworker when you're at the mall, for a moment you almost don't recognize them without their normal surroundings and then it hits you. When it hit Jake was when he felt afraid, he pulled away from Amy and swallowed his throat. Paulie stared at him emotionless, not realizing at first who he was but only thinking there was a witness who spotted him at the scene. When it did hit Paulie, a small piece of him thought "Oh no, I know him." But the other part, the insane part, told him it was all fine.

Jake moved away from Amy, grabbed Eric from Rachel without regard and pulled him away from the girls to discuss the situation. "What the hell!" Eric said loudly. "Shut up and listen..." Jake whispered in a serious tone as he continued. "That guy across the street..." Eric looked around and noticed an unfamiliar man wearing a dirty baseball cap standing on the sidewalk, staring in their direction. "The creep in the shadows? What about him?" "That's Nicole's uncle." Eric gave another glance and then turned back to Jake. "Are you sure?" Eric said disbelievingly. "Yes I'm sure, that's her uncle Paulie!" Jake's voice was louder now but neither of the girls were paying much attention as they were deep into their own conversation. Paulie smirked at Jake and began walking across the street. "Oh fuck, he's coming over here." Eric said without the slightest bit of sympathy in his voice.

Jake stood there in utter shock and felt his mouth run dry. In another second, Paulie was standing next to the four teens. Paulie smiled at Jake, he

185

knew the boy thought he had been caught red handed cheating on Nicole but
the truth was Paulie didn't give a shit about that. All Paulie cared about was
his own situation, with the boy being here with another girl Jake wouldn't be
too anxious to tell anyone he had seen Paulie, and that was something Paulie
could count on. "What the hell are you doing here kid?" Paulie spoke as
casually as ever. Jake swallowed his throat in fear before speaking, he was
sweating and so was Paulie but Jake thought Paulie's sweat seemed out of
place and unrelated to the current situation. "Hey Paulie, how are you?" "I'm
good...Who are your friends?" Paulie asked out of nowhere. Jake hesitated
before speaking "This is Eric...and this is Rachel and Amy." The group of
teens waved at the strange man cautiously. Paulie waved back innocently and
as he did he noticed he still had on his "work" gloves. He removed them
carefully and thought the teens would just assume they were for the weather.

"Huh, Nicole's not gonna' believe I saw you here..." Paulie said and
Jake swallowed his throat once again. "Actually I'll just leave that to you,
you could tell her you saw me." Paulie added and a shot of relief settled over
Jake's body. "Hey by the way I got something for you kids." Paulie walked
away to his car and the rest of the group looked over at Jake curiously. "What
is he doing man?" Eric asked in a nervous whisper. "Who is that?" Rachel
asked. "That's a friend of mine's uncle." Jake said and the two girls nodded

their heads approvingly. The group of teens watched as Paulie went through his trunk, they didn't know what to expect. Finally as if out of thin air, Paulie pulled out a dented box of beer. "Well look at that!" Eric said surprised. Paulie walked back over with the beer in his hand, he handed it to Jake. "They've been sitting in my trunk for about a month, I figured you guys could get more use out of them then I could. With this weather it's like a freezer in that trunk anyway so their cold enough." Of course the beer was the young business man's from the liquor store and it had only actually been sitting there since last night but that didn't seem to matter. Eric smiled and the girls followed with their own. Jake smirked cautiously as if he was unsure if it was ok to do so. They all thanked Paulie excitingly. Jake turned to his girlfriend's uncle. "Thanks." "No problemo kid, just don't tell anyone I gave you those alright. Oh and don't forget to tell Nicole I saw you cause lord knows I'll forget" Paulie chuckled, winked eerily and headed back to his car. Eric grabbed a beer out of the box. "See Jake nothing to worry about, he's a pretty cool guy that uncle Paulie." Eric said as he and Jake watched Paulie get into his Cadillac. An uneasy feeling came over Jake as he watched the car disappear into the night, Paulie saw him kissing Amy and Paulie should have cared.

Daniel and Michelle had tried to find a nearby motel but their desire for one another was at a boiling point. Daniel placed his hand on Michelle's vulnerable thigh and began to rub it softly. His hand then crept to her inner thigh and she closed her eyes and began to moan. "Stop somewhere..." Michelle said softly. "Anywhere." Five minutes later Daniel parked the car in a secluded parking lot and he and his wife were now in the back seat of their car going at it full force. Daniel wrapped his arms around Michelle and began to thrust. Michelle closed her eyes and let out a passionate moan, Daniel kissed her softly on her neck and whispered into her ear. "I love you." The car was steamy and Michelle could feel the leather seats on her bare skin. Without reason and out of nowhere, Paulie came to her mind. Before she could even comprehend why her mind had wandered, she was imagining him making love to her instead of Daniel. She remembered herself back in the living room the day Paulie had come to see Daniel. She remembered how they had kissed and how Paulie had made love to her right there. Daniel whispered in his wife's ear again. "I love you." Michelle opened her eyes. "I love you." she said. Michelle closed her eyes tightly and felt the tears running down her face.

15

The Road Ahead

Detective Atkins had been driving for four hours when the fatigue finally hit him, he thought he could drive to Darnite in one shot. Seven and a half hours didn't seem like a lot before but now as his eyes were getting heavy he thought differently. The last thing Atkins wanted to do was sleep but he had to get some. Better safe than sorry he thought and proceeded to turn onto the next exit. The exit showed a sign for a said to be "Elegant Motel" called the Great Palace. Moments later when the Detective pulled up to the motel, he realized there was nothing elegant about the place. It was big, so that was probably why they called it the great palace but there was nothing nice about it. The buildings color was an unattractive brown and the curtains that hung in each of the windows were a sickening piss yellow. The only thing that looked half decent was a sports bar that was attached to the main level. The place seemed to be packed and a blue neon sign advertised "Good Beer and Good Food". A simple and modest approach, Atkins thought, but also surprisingly drawing. Well it was either the sign or the fact that he hadn't eaten in close to six hours, one of the two.

After he had booked a room for the night, Atkins walked down to the sports bar for his much needed burger and beer. The bar was old looking but clean, much nicer than the actual hotel. There were about fifteen people scattered around, some sitting at booths and the rest sitting at the bar. The place felt more like a smaller Applebees than a real bar but Atkins liked the environment, it was inviting. He took a seat at the bar and the bartender immediately walked over. "What could I get you?" Atkins picked up a small menu that sat in front of him and glanced at it briefly. "I'll take a cheeseburger with the works...and a Coors." The bartender nodded and walked away to put the order in.

Later on, after Atkins devoured his cheeseburger and ordered his fourth beer, a woman about ten years younger than him sat down beside him, she ordered a beer as well. The woman had a worn look to her like she'd been through a lot but her allure was still there, especially in the eyes which were a beautiful blue. Her hair was dirty blonde and put into a ponytail, a style Atkins found very attractive in women, especially his late wife. The woman turned to Atkins. "I don't know who would actually stay at this shit hole but the beers good, don't ya' think?" Atkins smirked and placed his room key on top of the bar. "The burgers ain't bad either." He added. The woman couldn't help but giggle. "Sorry I've just never talked to anyone here who was actually staying in the motel. I always thought it was a good way to start a conversation." Atkins turned to the woman with a sincere smile. "It's ok, I'm just passing through, needed somewhere to rest my head for the night and I thought this place would be better than my back seat." The woman grinned. "I hope it is. I'm Cheryl."

Detective Atkins put his beer bottle down and held out his right hand. "Robert." The bartender brought over Cheryl's beer and she took a sip of it. "So Robert, where are you from?" "Mesapeena." "Mesapeena? Where's that?" Detective Atkins drank the rest of his beer and signaled the bartender for another. "New Hampshire." Cheryl nodded. "So why are you traveling? Business or pleasure?" Detective Atkins thought for a moment before answering. "Business, the unfinished kind." Cheryl smirked. "I see." The bartender walked over and put Atkins' beer onto the bar. Atkins went to reach into his pocket to pay the man but Cheryl slapped a five on the bar before he could. "This ones on me." The bartender took the money and walked away. Cheryl smiled at Atkins as he stared at her with confusion and some annoyance. "You didn't have to do that." Atkins said. "It's ok Robert, there seems to be a lot of pain behind those eyes and it's the least I could do." Atkins smiled. "So tell me a little about yourself Cheryl." Cheryl smiled and took a sip of her beer. "And I got the next one." Atkins added.

16

About Last Night

Paulie had gotten home from his murderous activities at around a quarter to twelve. By the time he got back to the house Nicole had fallen asleep. She had waited for Jake to return her call but when her eyes got heavy and the call never came, she closed her text book and gave in to her weariness. A half hour later Daniel and Michelle had gotten home from their dinner and back seat love making session (though love for Daniel was the furthest thing Michelle was feeling). They walked in the house, headed up the stairs and got undressed. Neither of them said much to each other as they settled into the bed, Daniel faded into his sleep quickly and was snoring within minutes. Michelle laid awake for two hours, her brain going crazy. She knew she wanted Paulie and that made her feel sick, at three o' clock she finally slipped into her night's slumber. But Michelle's lustful thoughts for Paulie didn't stop there, when she fell asleep she became a prisoner to her subconscious. She spent the remainder of the night tossing and turning at the dreams she was having about Paulie. Paulie who was right downstairs in the guest room but who was still so far from her. She wanted him, she needed him. Michelle dreamed that she had snuck downstairs and made love to him

192

right there in the guest room, she enjoyed it thoroughly.

The next morning Nicole woke up around seven. Math was the first class of the day for her so she quickly reviewed her notes and headed off to school. She was still concerned about Jake but tried her best to make algebra the main focus of her mind as she took a seat in the classroom. In the end, she found most of the test to be easy but drew blanks several times throughout. Overall Nicole felt "eh" about her performance and figured worst case scenario she had passed with a sixty five, but that she thought, was good enough. Since today was the last day of school before Christmas break and Nicole had taken the rest of her finals already she decided to cut out early. She didn't do it a lot and had already told her parents she might, so what the hell. She was back in her bed by nine twenty and with a few meager thoughts of Jake rambling through her mind she fell back to sleep.

About an hour later Nicole woke to her phone ringing, she jumped up immediately knowing it had to be Jake. She looked onto the screen of her cell phone and saw his name. Nicole sighed before picking it up. "Hello." She spoke in a weak and strained tone. "Hey baby." Jake said a bit too cheerfully. "Do you still hate me?" He added. Nicole couldn't help but smirk. "No, did you go to the party?" For a minute Jake was about to answer yes but something in him panicked and felt it was best to lie. "We were gonna' but Eric ended up having to watch his little sister. So I went there and we drank some beers and watched a movie." A part of Nicole wanted to challenge what Jake had said but she didn't feel like picking another fight. "I called last night, why didn't you answer?" "Did you? I get shitty service in Eric's, you know that." Nicole knew that to be true, especially in the basement. Whenever Eric, Cindy, Jake and herself were hanging out at Eric's, cell phone service was a constant problem. She had gotten into an argument with her mother not too long ago because Michelle thought she was ignoring her calls.

Then there was a quick knock at Nicole's door and it opened, Daniel peeked his head through. He looked tired and a bit hung over, Nicole thought. "Your mothers making breakfast, be downstairs in ten." Nicole nodded and Daniel closed the door. Nicole wondered why her father was home and quickly remembered that he had off for the holiday as well. "Did you go to school?" Nicole asked already knowing the answer. Jake laughed. "No babe, my break started today. Do you wanna' get something to eat, maybe some pancakes?" "My moms making breakfast, why don't you come over instead?"

Ten minutes later Nicole sat at the table with her father as her mother finished preparing breakfast. "Jake's gonna' come over mom, do you have enough?" Michelle turned around to her daughter."Yea, I'll just make another omelet. At that same moment, Paulie walked into the kitchen, he looked well rested and more relaxed than he did in a long time. He took a seat across from Daniel. "Good morning Paulie, you look like you got a good night's sleep." Daniel said and Michelle who had bags under her eyes glanced to see for herself. "Yea I slept like a baby. Must be that bed." Paulie said confidently even though it was a lie. The truth was killing the man from the jury had felt like lifting a great weight off his shoulders. It wasn't so much the man as it was the murder. The last guy he killed, the snobby business man, was done in a hurry. Paulie didn't even get a chance to enjoy himself, but this one was a vicious kill that left a bathroom covered in soapy, bloody water. It was everything Paulie enjoyed and he savored ever puncture.

Paulie felt relieved and settled (for now at least), he hadn't felt that way since before he got into town. Paulie thought he might actually be getting comfortable here. There was a ring at the door bell and Nicole got up to answer it. "That's Jake, I got it." Paulie had a strange look on his face, he looked almost excited to see how nervous poor Jake was going to be. Michelle filled up five plates and set them on the table, egg omelets, home

fries, and two thick pieces of toast on each. "Michelle this looks delicious."
Paulie said. "Thank you." Michelle felt flattered. Nicole and Jake walked into
the kitchen and Michelle and Daniel greeted the young man. "Good morning
everybody." Jake said as he sat down next to Nicole, he shot an
uncomfortable glance at Paulie. "How you doing there Jake?" Paulie asked.
"I'm pretty good." There was a tense feeling between the two, one that could
not be picked up by the others. Michelle turned to Daniel and pointed to the
small TV that sat on a stand next to him. "Could you put on the news, I heard
a storm is coming and I wanna' see if it's gonna' hit during the party." Daniel
turned around in his chair and pressed the TV power on. A newswoman was
talking about some ordinary, warm hearted story and everyone began to dig
into to their plates.

"You guys got a party to go to?" Paulie asked Daniel and Michelle
suddenly. Daniel wiped his mouth. "Actually we forgot to tell you, every
year we have a little bit of a holiday get together. Nothing huge, just a few
friends and family, we rent out a Knights of Columbus hall. You're invited of
course." Paulie nodded. "Yea count me in, that sounds like some fun." Daniel
smiled. "Yea it will be, it's tomorrow night at eight. Jake you're more than
welcome to come as well." "I might just take you up on that offer Mr.
Lawson." Jake said. Moments later as they finished their breakfast the

weather man finally came on screen, he spoke with perfect fabricated cheer. "We're going to have some light flurries starting late tomorrow night at lets say ten and they're going to continue into Christmas Eve. They'll get a tad heavier through out the day and through the night right on into Christmas morning. So this is going to be a white Christmas indeed." "Great, snow." Nicole said sarcastically." "At least it will miss the party." Michelle added as she began to clear the table of plates.

A serious and distinguished looking anchorman was now on the screen, he spoke sternly. "And now onto our top story, a missing man in Darnite..." Everyone at the table focused on what the Anchorman was saying, Paulie rose from the table. "I'm gonna' go get some fresh air." Paulie walked out through the back sliding door and stood on the backyard porch. The anchorman continued. "Thirty two year old Eathan Mathers of Howell, who was reported missing two nights ago is still without a trace. Ethan was last heard from by a friend when he was leaving a liquor store in town." The liquor store is shown on the screen. "That's Tom Snyder's place." Daniel said in an astonished tone before the reporter continued. "Eathan's car was found in the parking lot with nothing out of the ordinary about it. Friends and family of the man are begging police and the people of New jersey to step forward if they see or have seen the man."

Suddenly someone handed the anchorman a piece of paper, he looked down and read over it for a moment. The color soon left his face and a sickened look took over. The anchorman stuttered as he began. "This just in, horrifying, breaking news. A thirty seven year old father and husband has been found murdered in his home on Stapleton Drive." "Oh my god!" Nicole said appalled, the rest of the table let out a mutual gasp. "We're going to go to our man on the scene Chuck Walsh, Chuck..." A suited reporter with a heavy winter jacket and skull cap stood in front of the house where an ambulance and several cop cars were parked. "I'm here in front of the house where the man's body was found early this morning."

It immediately struck Jake that it was the house directly across the street from where the party was the night before. He wanted to say something but instead swallowed his throat and glanced at the back porch where Paulie was standing with his back facing him. Paulie had been in front of that house last night, but why? Jake wondered uneasily as the reporter continued. "Details are still sketchy but from what we have heard the wife and son had headed over to the wife's mother's house as she was said to not have been feeling well. They spent the night and when the two returned this morning they found the man in the bathroom, he was stabbed viciously. The victim

198

and families name are being held but the people here on Stapleton Drive who knew them are in shock. One man I was talking to has said that the man was as friendly as could be, just a genuine person."

Nicole put her hand over her mouth and gasped. "Wait a minute, that's how I know Stapleton Drive, that's where the house is, where the party was." Nicole said to Jake in a nervous squeal. "Thank God you didn't go, you could have bumped into the killer and god knows what he would have done." Nicole gave Jake a hug to calm herself down. "What the hell is happening to this town." Daniel yelled angrily. Michelle sighed and got up from the table to wash the dishes. Jake was still hugging Nicole when he decided to take another glance at Paulie. When he did, he saw Paulie peaking in through the glass window door, staring at the sight of the familiar house on the TV. Jake stared at him and terror began to rise through his body. In that same instant Paulie turned to Jake and stared at him with an empty and horrific gaze. This sent goosebumps all through Jake's body and he could feel his mouth go completely dry.

17

A Tricky Situation

Jake spent the next hour laying on the living room couch trying to relax with Nicole, but his mind wouldn't let him ease up. Paulie had gone off to do whatever he had to do and Jake was left to reflect on the horrifying and undeniable truth he had realized. Paulie had killed that man, there was no excuse or explanatory thought in his mind which begged to differ. He stared emotionless at the TV screen as he and Nicole watched a romantic comedy on one of the movie channels. His mind was chaotic and he immediately began to think about telling Nicole. Jake suddenly remembered that he had told Nicole he hadn't gone to the party. It would be hard enough to tell her out of nowhere that her uncle was a killer but to go back on a lie in the process, she would loose it. It would start calmly, she'd ask "Why did you lie in the first place?" Then the realization would hit her instantly, "You did something there, you cheated on me. That's why you lied." It crossed Jake's mind that maybe telling her about her uncle would overshadow the minor lie. Nicole might be so shocked that Jake saw Paulie that she'd put the stupid white lie on the back burner.

200

That could happen but it was unlikely, Jake knew Nicole and he knew that when she heard he had lied she'd probably tell him to leave. Jake would stutter and try to elaborate on Paulie but Nicole wouldn't let him. Then what? Jake nervously wondered these thoughts as his breaths grew   increasingly heavier. Better yet, what if she did listen and it wasn't true. What if he told her all of this and then by some outrageous circumstance it ended up being faux. If he was wrong then what? She along with the rest of her family would hate him, no, loathe him. Jake began to wonder, what would be worse, if he was wrong or if he was right? If he cut out the medium Nicole and went directly to the police and they didn't have any hard evidence, what would happen? Paulie would be released, free, If he was in fact a murderer he might even go after Jake afterward.

Jake snapped back into reality as Nicole let out a cough. He was beginning to feel like he was in a bad horror movie, his girlfriend's uncle was a murderer? As ridiculous as it sounded when he spoke the words internally, he knew it had to be true. There was no way that some minor thing was going to pop up and explain everything. This wasn't a movie and maybe if it was there would be that one thing that explains it all. That thing that has everything end on a happy note with everyone smiling, but Jake knew there was no happy ending in sight, this situation could only end badly. Nicole

201

began to laugh at a funny scene on the TV screen. This interrupted Jake's thoughts again and he stood up suddenly. "Listen babe, I'm gonna' go." Nicole looked at Jake with a confused and sad look. "Why, what do you have to do today?" Jake hesitated for a second before speaking. "Nothing, I'm just not feeling well." Nicole's look turned sympathetic. "Are you ok?" "I think I'll be alright, I just a got a bit of a headache that's all." Jake kissed Nicole and as he walked towards the front door she called to him "Jake!" Jake turned around curious at what she would add. "Be careful." Jake looked at her confused and a bit startled by her words. "There was a murder, remember." Nicole added casually and Jake swallowed his throat and continued to the door.

Jake had gotten to Eric's house at about noon, he rang the doorbell twice and after no answer noticed the family car wasn't in the driveway but spotted Eric's car parked across the street. Eric had drank a lot at the party and chances were, he was still in bed sleeping it off. Jake rang the bell one more time before giving the door knob a spontaneous turn. It was unlocked, it was probably always unlocked, Jake thought. He had just never tried before. That was what some people did when they thought they were living in a safe town. Jake made his way upstairs to Eric's room and found him dead asleep in his messy bedroom, he was snoring loudly. Jake began to shake him vigorously."Eric get up!" After a few moments Eric opened his eyes and stared at Jake dumbfounded. "What the hell are you doing in my room man?" "Did you hear about the murder?" Jake asked urgently before quickly assuming Eric had not. "Murder, what are you talking about?"   "Some guy was murdered on Stapleton drive, across the street from where we were last night." Eric let out an idiotic and cruel laugh. "Holy shit. So this is why you come barging in my house?" "Nicole's uncle was there, don't you remember?" Eric sat up in his bed and stretched. "Oh right, so?" Jake was surprised by Eric's calm reaction. "He was in front of the house where the guy was murdered!" Jake exclaimed. Eric rolled his eyes in disbelief. "So what are you saying, he killed him? You realize how ridiculous that sounds right?" Jake sighed. "What do you mean, he was there, I know it's crazy but..." "Listen Jake, I know he was there but for fuck sake you really think the guy would kill someone just like that." Jake's eyes began to drift around the room, he didn't know what to think anymore.

"Murder is a big deal man and you're just going off an assumption. Does the guy give you any reason to think he's a murderer, did he show you his knife collection or something?" Eric quipped with a giggle. "This isn't a joke Eric, there's a guy dead!" Jake was beginning to become exasperated with Eric. "Alright man, calm yourself." Eric begged and Jake closed his

eyes in frustration. "I don't know what to do, I was thinking about telling
Nicole the truth. That we went to the party and that we saw her uncle, I
wanna' see what she thinks." Eric's calm look turned to sheer puzzlement.
"Are you kidding, are you going to tell her what you did with Amy too?"
Jake shook his head. "Of course not, I'll..." "You'll what? She's going to be
very curious to why you lied in the first place and you and I both know she'll
get the truth out of you."

Jake rubbed his brow soothingly. "Than what am I going to do?"
"You're not going to do anything. You think her uncle killed this guy because
he was in the neighborhood? Hell we were in the neighborhood, did we kill
him? God knows how many other people were around that we didn't see."
Jake felt some relief creeping into his bones. "I guess that's true, but the guys
been in jail before you know..." Eric laughed. "What does that have to do
with anything, the guy that grooms my cat at Petco did five years in prison,
does that mean he's killed someone?" Jake burst out with a laugh and Eric
smirked. "I'm sure her uncle is trying his best from ever being back inside a
cell and you want to get the poor bastard in trouble for something you're not
even sure he did." "I guess it is kind of ridiculous when you think about it."
Jake said calmly. "Thank god you're coming to your senses. Listen, don't
even think about this stupid shit anymore. Watch they're gonna' catch the nut

who really killed this guy in a few days and then you're gonna' be kissing my ass for saving yours." Eric said confidently. Jake didn't answer, he simply nodded and tried to push what ever thoughts lingered to the back of his mind. "You good?" Eric asked. "Yea, I'm good." Jake answered quickly with a forced smile. "Great, now get the hell out of my house before I call the cops and tell them you broke in. I need to sleep off the rest of this hangover." Jake laughed. "Alright, I'll see you later."

18

Behind Schedule

Atkins opened his eyes and stared at the ceiling of his mediocre motel room, he was exhausted and his head felt heavy. He noticed some light coming in through the shades and reached for the night stand for an alarm clock. He picked up the clock and saw that it read three pm. "Jesus fucking..." Atkins began but before he could finish swearing he heard the flush of a toilet. Atkins looked up at the bathroom door, heard the faucet run and then saw the knob turn, he was in utter shock as the door began to open. When Cheryl walked out it had all come back to him, well most of it. "You're up." Cheryl said with a smile. It was about time, she thought. "Why didn't you wake me?" Atkin's asked. "You looked so peaceful, I didn't want to intrude." Detective Atkins smirked and sat up in the bed. He began to remember piece by piece what they had done. After he had finished his burger, they ordered beer after beer for each other and talked about their problems. At first Atkins kept with his secrecy but once Cheryl opened completely to him about her ex husband, he felt safe telling her what he had been through. Her husband was a drinker who was a bit too touchy, he left her with a sixteen year old son with leukemia and almost nothing else. The son passed about a year ago and Cheryl tried her best to keep it together. She wasn't doing bad, Atkins thought, but she'd find herself at bars almost every night drinking the pain away. Pretending to be cheerful and crying almost every time she drove home intoxicated.

Though he couldn't remember exactly what he told her, he knew they had bonded. They were two broken down people and what else but fate could have brought them together. What were the chances in all of the world that he would run into this pain filled and fragile woman. After the two got sick of the beer taste in their mouths they moved onto to straight Jack on the rocks. Something Cheryl didn't prefer, but did a good job of taking down three and a half anyway. Since they were both avid drinkers their tolerance was as high as it could be, and by the end of the night they may have been shit face drunk but sloppy they were not. They headed up to Atkins room at around four in the morning with half finished glasses still in hand. There they kissed and made love, love that neither of them had made in what felt like ages. Love that had felt so right and had been so fulfilling. The kind of thing out of a passionate romantic film, the kind of thing that almost never happens.

Atkins stepped out of bed and let out a large yawn accompanied by a

massive stretch. "I want to come with you." Cheryl's voice was soft but firm.
Atkins glanced at her with dazzled confusion. In another moment, as he
stared at her blue eyes he remembered telling her everything. About his wife,
about his daughter and about the slasher. Atkins quickly began getting
dressed. "You can't come. It's not safe." Atkins said and as he did, it crossed
his mind that this was the first time in a long time that he felt he had
something or someone to loose. It may have only been one night they had
spent together but Cheryl was genuine, Atkins could see it in her eyes. He
finished getting dressed and reluctantly made his way to the door, fighting
the feelings that were beginning to arise inside of him.

"I have to go now." Atkins said somberly. Cheryl nodded
understandingly with a smile "Will you come back? On you're way home,
maybe for another drink?" Cheryl asked with some uncertainty and Atkins
smiled. The detective thought the woman was remarkable, she was definitely
someone he would like to get to know better, someone he would love to
spend more time with. The truth was right now he couldn't give her that time.
He had something to do and he intended on doing it. The detective thought of
saying all of this but instead simply said "Maybe." Cheryl rolled her eyes.
"I'll be here, come and find me." Atkins nodded and without a word or so
much as a hug headed out of the room. As he drove away from the Royal

Palace, Atkins thought that seeing Cheryl again was no longer up to him.

19

Storm On The Horizon

Later that afternoon Daniel returned from his last minute Christmas shopping venture at the mall. Nicole and Michelle had gotten home a few minutes earlier, after finally seeing the new Julia Roberts movie everyone was raving about. While the house was empty, Paulie had done his share of snooping around but had cut it short after he started feeling tired. The excitement the recent murder had left him with had began to take a toll on him and he was exhausted. He turned on the TV, put the living room sofa into recline and had fallen asleep within ten minutes of his lounging. As Daniel walked in the house and greeted his wife Paulie still laid sleeping. "Honey come here, I want to show you something." Daniel said in a slight whisper to his wife who was cleaning the kitchen with a look of boredom in her eyes. Michelle put the rag she was wiping the counter with down and walked towards the hall with her husband. They came to four oversized shopping bags that Daniel had placed on the floor. "Take a look at this." Daniel reached into one of the bags and pulled out a brand new shiny axe with a large red bow placed on it's wooden handle. "What do you think? It's for Paulie." Michelle looked a bit confused by the gift. "What is he going to do with that?" "Remember what I told you the other day? How he's been chopping trees at work and how the equipment we got is kind of old. I figured this would work better."

Michelle forced a smile across her face. "Daniel, I thought you said the job wasn't permanent." Daniel placed the axe back into the bag. "I know I did, it's not, but he's real good at chopping, he even prefers it over using a machine. It's probably a hobby of his back home, I think he'll get use out of it if he's working with me or not." Michelle nodded. "Whatever works. I have no idea what I'm going to get him." Michelle looked a little more bothered than she should have by this. "The axe will be from both of us. If you want, make him another sweater, he'd like that." Daniel said absently as he grabbed his bag from the hall. Michelle began to grin. The sweater, she had completely forgotten about the torn sweater. She could fix it up tonight and maybe even give it to him at the party. As Michelle went over the plans in her mind she didn't hear her husband say he was going upstairs.

Meanwhile in her bedroom Nicole was on the phone with Jake who tried his best to sound under the weather."How was the movie?" Jake asked even though he was uninterested. "Good, sad but good, how are you feeling? Any better?" There was a moment of silence after Nicole asked her boyfriend the question. Silence, Jake was obviously too consumed with something to pay attention, probably an X-box game, Nicole thought. "Hello? Are you there?" Nicole asked in an aggravated tone. "Ah yea, sorry, I'm just getting a little tired." Jake said with a fake yawn. Nicole sighed trying to fight her annoyance. "Hey I wanted to ask you, where does your uncle Paulie live anyway?" Nicole was a bit confused by the strange question and made a face though Jake couldn't see it. "I don't know, somewhere in New Hampshire, Mesapine or something. Why do you want to know weirdo?" Jake forced himself to sound casual. "Oh, eh, no reason, just curious. Listen babe I'm gonna' try to take a nap, I'll give you a call when I wake up." "Ok, I love you." Nicole said with feeling. "I love you too." Jake replied distracted.

When the two hung up the phone Jake went back to what was distracting him. He had the words "Murderers who got off." In a Google search bar on his computer screen. He had been thinking a lot since he had left Eric's house and if his crazy suspicion was true there had to be more to Paulie's criminal record than he had heard. A petty criminal who had served his time wasn't just going to decide to kill someone out of nowhere. Especially in the vicious way the news had said it was done. If it was in fact

Paulie that killed the man, he would have had some experience in the field. Even if it was one murder, there had to be something other than the small crimes that landed him in jail. Jake was a big fan of all the Law & Order police shows and if he learned anything about murder from them, it was that they were either done in a premeditated fashion or in the heat of passion. Was this   premeditated? How could it be? Jake wondered. Than again was a murder of passion more plausible? Jake dismissed everything Eric had said for a moment and narrowed it down to the murderer being Paulie. If he did it, it had to be planned. There was no reason why he'd be by the house and there was no explainable circumstance that would have the murder occur impulsively. Jake added the words New Hampshire to the end of his search and clicked the button.

Jake scrolled down the screen clicking links that caught his eye, none of which lead him anywhere. Jake abruptly back spaced on the search bar and thought for a moment what he should write next. After a moment of thinking he typed in Mesapine New Hampshire and clicked search. The search came back with zero results but directly under the search bar was a link that read "Did you mean Mesapeena New Hampshire?" Jake immediately realized this had to be the place and clicked the link. Most of the pages that came up were basic web-sites about the towns in New Hampshire,

212

there was nothing too specific. Jake revised his search once again by adding murderer gets off to the end making it, "Mesapeena, New Hampshire murderer gets off". Jake browsed through the results which were the opposite of what he hoped for. One title read "Machete Murderer gets life sentence", the rest of the links were about murderers who had been caught. Jake sighed and wiped the search bar clear. He rattled his fingers over the keyboard while trying to think of what else to search. Instinctively Jake typed the words "New Hampshire killer" into the bar and slammed on the enter key.

Two million results came back and Jake began skimming through them with a close eye. Four pages into the results Jake came to an article titled "New Hampshire slasher continues his reign of terror without a trace". Jake clicked the link and was directed to a New Hampshire based news site that called itself "The New Hampshire Bulletin". Jake read the page long story that talked about the recent murders of two men. Jake grimaced as he read the details of how their charred bodies were found along with two rottweilers in the shell of an old Cadillac. The reporter then went on to say that most of the local papers were stating the slayings were drug related but that inside sources who wished to be kept anonymous claimed this was most likely another notch in the "Bloomingdale slasher's" belt. When Jake was finished with the article he scrolled down to a discussion board, where he

213

began to read people's thoughts on the story. One of the most recent comments to the page was from a woman who said she saw a special about the slasher a few nights ago and that after the special they showed the first composite of the man. Jake swallowed his throat as he scrolled down the page with anticipation of the image. There wasn't one, just more comments of people asking for someone to post it. Another comment was from a man from South Arden saying that there was probably some in New Hampshire police stations and that some should be popping up around the rest of New Hampshire soon.

Jake scrolled down to a button at the bottom of the page that read "Related Stories". He clicked the link and felt his blood go cold as twenty more stories related to the Bloomingdale slasher popped up. Jake spent the next hour and a half educating himself on the murders of the mysterious New Hampshire serial killer. He read in graphic detail how he had spent the last year terrorizing the otherwise quiet town of Mesapeena. With each article Jake read he became more and more intrigued and equally unsettled. There wasn't anything that pointed specifically to Paulie but Jake couldn't shake the eerie coincidence that the man resided right where all of this was happening. Eric's disputing comments came back to Jake's mind and he felt a certain helplessness overwhelm him. Without physical evidence it was all still just a wacky suspicion. But suspicion or not Jake felt he had to say something about what he'd read, especially to Nicole. Jake would have to go back on his lie of not being at the party but after reading about all the lives that were taken in Mesapeena, he felt his predicament would prove insignificant in the big picture.

Jake didn't know how Nicole would actually react and didn't know what would become of their relationship but it didn't matter, he'd have to tell her and see what she thought. If there was even a chance Paulie was responsible, Nicole had to know. After Jake had decided that he was going to tell Nicole, he felt as if some weight had been lifted   and actually felt like a better person. Then suddenly, just as he was beginning to feel a boost of positive energy, something that had come to his mind before snuck back in and settled cozily. If he was right about Paulie being a murderer, his life could be in danger. If Paulie killed the man, then he was probably thinking that Jake might be curious to why he was in the neighborhood the night of the murder. If Paulie thought Jake was going to say something, whose to say Paulie wouldn't kill Jake. Jake felt his stomach turn and his brow perspire.

For the first time in a long time Jake felt genuinely frightened, goose skin formed on his arms as he felt a chill down his spine. Jake tried to calm his nerves down, he told himself that if he was careful he'd be fine. He thought about going back to Nicole's tonight and telling her but quickly realized that was a huge no,no. Paulie would be there and if he had any secrets to keep, he'd have a close eye on Jake. He had to tell Nicole in a safe place, somewhere where they could be in private. Jake had already told his parents that he was feeling a little sick, so he knew they wouldn't approve of Nicole coming over. Then it hit him, the Lawsons' Christmas party. It was tomorrow and Paulie would be there but he and Nicole could surely find a place where they could be alone so no one would overhear. Besides Paulie would probably be too busy socializing with guests to watch Jake (if he was in fact watching him). Jake could spend the time he had now trying to find out more information on the slasher and figure out just how he was going to tell Nicole. Jake took a deep breath and began searching through Google once again. This time he added "Bloomingdale slasher New Hampshire" into his search before hitting the search button.

20

A Heads Up

Detective Atkins had hit a lot of holiday traffic as he came closer to his destination. He finally passed the "Welcome to Darnite" sign at eight that evening. His body felt drained from the drive and he thought it would be better to get some rest and start his day off early tomorrow. When Atkins sat up in bed the next morning he realized it was the first time in months that he had not drunk himself to sleep. It wasn't a conscious choice, he knew he had no alcohol with him and when he laid back on the bed his slumber was instantaneous. Atkins stood up and stretched, for a moment he felt an unyielding desire to get a drink inside of him. The detective noticed an unfamiliar face as he glanced into a minute mirror that hung on a mantle. The face was lively looking and well rested. The black bags under his eyes that his face had come to necessitate were no longer visible and there was a certain youthful shine to his eyes. The stranger the detective saw in the mirror was probably a combination of a few things (his stress relieving night with Cheryl being one). Atkins felt it was mainly related to the fact that he had gotten a good night's sleep without drowning his liver in certain liquids. With this realization, Atkins shut down his growing urge to get his hands on a drink and made a silent vow to himself that he would stay sober. Atkins had something important to do and giving up on alcohol (if at least for now) was the only thing that could assure he would be his sharpest self. He got dressed into a button down and slacks and threw on his trench coat. He freshened up a bit and complemented his newly enhanced features by shaving the stubble that he had let grow around his face. Moments later he walked out of his room ready to greet the challenging day that lay before him.

The Lawsons' Christmas party was set for seven thirty that night. Michelle and Daniel had headed over to the Knights of Columbus hall at around ten to start their decorating. They had planned to have a DJ playing holiday music, an open bar and a vast buffet made up of various kinds of food ranging from Japanese to Italian. Tonight was an evening that they had both been looking forward to for the last month. The yearly event was something that had grown to be as important to them as Christmas itself. It was a night of drinking, laughing and enjoying the company of the friends and family they rarely saw. Though Michelle seemed to be fully engaged with her decorating duties, her mind was solely consumed by Paulie. She wondered how he would react to the welcome home surprise everyone would give him when he walked in. Michelle further wondered how Paulie would react to receiving the freshly sewn sweater. When she did, the faithful but vulnerable woman that lingered inside of her thanked God there would be plenty of people around.

Meanwhile Nicole sat in her room trying to get some of her school assignments out of the way early. She accepted the fact that not doing them now would only be prolonging the inevitable. She had called Jake an hour before expecting him to be asleep but was surprised when his weary voice answered. They didn't talk about much, Jake sounded a bit strange and Nicole asked him if he was feeling any better. Jake told her he felt good but was still very tired. Abruptly Jake asked if Nicole was home by herself and she quickly told him that she thought Uncle Paulie was downstairs sleeping. Jake was silent for a moment after that and Nicole thought he had fallen asleep. Nicole felt annoyed and just as she was about to say something to Jake he spoke up. He told her he had to go and that if he didn't talk to her he'd just see her at the party. Nicole was about to say something but before she could she heard the other line click off, she sighed.

While Jake was stressing about what would happen when the time came to talk to Nicole, Eric was home enjoying the start of his holiday recess. He sat in his bed going on his third hour of "Call Of Duty" for x-box without a care in the world, this was a good morning he thought and tonight would prove to be even better. Eric's parents were friendly with the Lawsons as they had lived next door to each other several years earlier. Eric and Nicole had even gone to the same elementary school and spent their childhood years playing freeze tag and man hunt along with the rest of the neighborhood children. Back then their parents were both in the same ball park, getting to know the struggles and joys of early parenthood and with that the couples immediately hit it off.

Through barbecues and birthdays the Lawsons and the Bernards had made a bond that had lasted through the years. Even though they didn't get to see each other as much as they used to, they made time to get together any chance they got. Eric and his family had attended each of the Lawsons' Christmas parties since they had started throwing them five years ago, but going to the Lawson party wasn't what was going to make Eric's night good. As a matter of fact, he wasn't going. Like Jake, Eric had been telling his parents that he was feeling under the weather but for reasons entirely different. Eric's motive, to get the house to himself. He had told Rachel that he had the house to himself tonight and invited her over. His plan was to get her nice and drunk and get her to make some bad decisions. Suddenly there was a knock at Eric's door, he shut his TV and threw his x-box remote on the floor before answering hoarsely "Come in."

Detective Atkins had began to feel some regret for leaving Cheryl but quickly brushed it off. Regardless if it was lust or something else, he knew like the urge for a drink, it had to remain dormant. As he drove into town he noticed a small general store with a sign in the window that read fresh coffee, he parked his car without hesitation. To the detectives best knowledge, he didn't think caffeine was something that would disrupt his plans of catching the slasher. Atkins walked into the store and straight up to the coffee station where he poured himself a tall cup of flavorless, original black coffee. He scooped a spoonful of sugar out of the bowl and mixed it rapidly into his coffee with a red plastic stirrer. Atkins flipped the metal lid of the sugar back into place and for a moment he was back in the slasher's apartment feeling the white powder residue on his fingers.

Atkins shook the thought and headed to the counter where he was greeted by an elderly clerk. "How are you today sir?" the thin and brittle looking man asked joyously. Atkins took a generous sip of his coffee, it was still boiling hot but by the way he drank it you would think his mouth was impervious. "Not bad, yourself?" Detectives Atkins said pleasantly trying to counter the mans overly jovial tone. "I've been better myself, but I can't complain. Big storm coming tonight. Gonna' start around nine or ten, they're

sayin' it might go all the way through Christmas day." "Is that so." Atkins
said without much interest. "Yep gonna' be like a Bing Crosby song or so
they say. I haven't seen you in here before ,you just visiting for the holiday or
new in town?" Detective Atkins couldn't help but smile at the innocent mans
intrusiveness. "Just visiting." The old man nodded knowingly. "I thought so,
there's a lot of people coming in and out of town right now. You're lucky you
made it in before the storm started, smart man."

"Is it really suppose to be that bad?" Atkins asked as he took another
sip of his coffee. "Who knows, you know these dense news people. One
minute they say it's gonna' be a blizzard then it ends up being a rain shower.
Stupid bastards, I think they do it to get people crazy, get them out of their
houses and into the supermarkets." Atkins smirked and nodded his head in
agreement. "Anything else besides the coffee?" Detective Atkins looked up
at the cigarettes on display. "Yea let me get a pack of Marlboro reds..."
Coffee and cigarettes, Atkins thought, he could live on just that. As the clerk
grabbed the pack Atkins noticed a local newspaper called the "Darnite
Digest" he picked one up. "One of these too." The elderly man nodded his
head and calculated the sale into the register. "That'll be six fifty, sir." Atkins
handed the man a ten. "By the way, is the local police station far." Atkins
added and the old man took on a tense look. "Everything ok son?" It was the

222

grimmest tone Atkins had heard from the man through the whole conversation. "Oh yea, everything's fine. I actually know someone who works there, that's who I'm visiting." The old man let out a sigh of relief. "I feel bad for your friend that works at the station, they probably have their hands full with that murder. What a shame for the family, right around the holidays. Just like that." The old man shook his head in disbelief. "Murder?" Atkins asked. "Yea guy got murdered night before last, a father, a husband, sad. I don't want to keep you with my petty recount, it's all there in the paper you got anyway." Atkins now had an uneasy expression on his face. "Now as for the station, you come out of the parking lot make a left, take it down to the second light make a right and then you're gonna' come to a stop sign make a left there and take it all the way down. The police station will be on your right." "Thank you." Atkins said and left the store.

Seconds later Detective Atkins sat down in his Challenger and began to browse through the newspaper as he continued to swig on his coffee. As he went down the front page he came across a bold headline that read "Father and Devoted Husband Murdered in Cold Blood." Seeing the thick black letters made it official and Atkins could feel his stomach sink. The slasher was here, there was no doubt now. He proceeded to read the gruesome nature in which the man was killed, that was the slasher's way, Atkins thought. He

223

wasn't surprised when he got to the end of the article and read how there were no leads, possible motives or suspects. For a second he could have sworn he was back in Mesapeena. As he continued to skim down the front page he came across a smaller article that read "Darnite Man Still Missing". The disappearance had happened only a few days ago and this tidbit of information got the detective's wheels turning. The murder was obvious but the disappearance of the man could have been anything. It didn't matter anyway, he thought. He'd have to talk to the officials in town and tell them what he knew, he could throw the missing man out there too and see what they thought. If Atkins could have it his way, there would be a door to door search for the slasher going before the end of the night, but he knew that wouldn't be easy to persuade.

With Paulie unaware of any of the possible threats or impending doom that might be coming his way, he felt close to great. Though he wasn't itching to kill anyone at this particular moment, he was beginning to feel a small desire for it sooner than he thought he would. After Paulie ate his small breakfast of Cheerios he began to feel a bit antsy. He sat on the couch, turned on the TV and tried to relax a little bit. Even with Nicole upstairs it was like he had the house to himself, she was quite as a corpse, Paulie thought. As he continued to flip through the channels Nicole's boyfriend came to mind. Poor

Jake, Paulie thought with a grin. The kid didn't seem stupid so Paulie could easily assume that Jake had made the connection that he was right outside the house where the murdered man was found. The murder, that was all they were talking about on the news today, you'd think that nobody had ever gotten murdered in Darnite before Paulie showed up. He wondered if Jake would talk and reminded himself that he was a bright boy. The smartest thing that Jake could ever do would be to just keep his mouth shut.

Paulie wasn't particularly afraid though, he figured Jake really didn't have any proof besides actually seeing him. Worst case scenario he'd probably just have to kill Jake and that was hardly the worst outcome considering his desire for blood was growing. Paulie abruptly remembered that the party was tonight and figured he should probably go get something to wear to the occasion. He didn't need anything fancy but he knew it was either go out and buy something or get stuck wearing Daniel's clothes again and boy did he hate doing that. Paulie left the house around one and was about to head to the mall but realized the day before Christmas eve would mean complete madness. Instead he chose a local men's clothing store that he remembered going to years earlier.

Detective Atkins pulled up to the Darnite police station at around ten

225

after one. He felt confident with a case but couldn't help but feel a little nervous. He knew that without a badge and without the backing of his department there was a good chance he wouldn't be taken seriously. The best thing he had was an expired photo identification with the words Detective across the top, it wasn't much but he'd have to take his chances. Atkins walked into the station with his head up, he looked like a man on a mission and he was just that. The station was pretty empty compared to the station back home. There was one officer sitting at the front desk and a maybe seven or more sitting at their desks. It was a small and dim building that didn't have enough windows. The heat was blasted a little too high and Detective Atkins could feel sweat begin to form around his inner thighs. He looked around and noticed most of the cops were busy but didn't seem too stressed, they were either on the phone or clicking away at their computers. He cracked a condescending smirk at a thought, this is what a police station should look like in a small town, not the madhouse the station was back home. The detective knew all that craziness at his was due to the slasher and wondered what this place would look like after a few dozen more murders.

Atkins walked over to the elevated front desk, there sat a tall, goofy looking officer with a name tag that read Stevens. The officer was reading a magazine and didn't care to notice Atkins presence. The detective waited a moment before letting out an annoyed cough. Officer Stevens looked up at Atkins with a displeased and baffled look, Atkins felt that was probably the way he always looked. "Could I help you?" The officer asked especially stern, as if to make up for his previous action or lack of. "Is your chief in?" "Yes, is he expecting you?" The officers words were uninviting and a bit condescending, he looked Atkins up and down as if he was sizing him up. Atkins felt contempt brewing for the man but ignored it. "No...but you'll need to tell him it's urgent." Detective Atkins accompanied his demand with the expired ID that read Detective, to look more professional it sat under the clear plastic window of his dark brown wallet. The officer stared at the ID for a moment, if he was a better cop, he would have probably asked for the badge but he wasn't and he didn't. The same idiotic and confused look from earlier spread across the officer's face. "I'll see if he's available." The officer stood up from his chair and walked down to a large office that sat in the corner of the station. He knocked on the door and poked his head in. Detective Atkins watched and listened curiously to the undecipherable words being spoken between the officer and the faceless resider of the corner office.

After a moment longer the officer began to walk back towards Atkins with a look on his face that was unreadable. For a second it crossed Atkins' mind that if this chief was anything like his, he wouldn't give the time of day to some unknown out of town detective. Before Atkins could think of a plan b, the officer sat back down and pointed towards the office."You could go right in Detective." Atkins couldn't help but smile at how nicely that had worked out for him and with a quick thanks to the officer he proceeded to the chief's office. Detective Atkins walked in and found a heavy set man who looked to be in his early forties sitting down at a desk talking on a phone. The man waved Atkins in and pointed to a chair that sat in front of his desk, Atkins nodded and sat down in the chair. The Chief spoke calmly into the phone. "We'll find 'em, I promise, your job now is to keep your friends and family calm Mr. Blake." As Atkins waited he wondered how old the Chief was. He was probably fifty but thought he could easily pass for late thirties, early forties. Nice to have such a stress free job, Atkins thought. There were no big crimes in Darnite let alone serial killers and that made being a police chief here real easy. Being a detective was probably even easier and for a second Atkins quipped with the thought of a job transfer to this quiet town.

The chief finished his phone call and hung up, he immediately turned to Atkins with a light hearted smile. "Good afternoon Detective..." "Atkins, Bloomingdale Mesapeena, New Hampshire." Atkins extended his hand and the chief shook it firmly. "Nice to meet you Atkins, I'm Chief Haim. Bloomingdale, that's a long ways away, what brings you to our town

Detective?" Detective Atkins cleared his throat in preparation of putting an immediate dim on the conversation. "Well unfortunately I wish I could be visiting your fine town under better circumstances." Chief Haim looked slightly confused by the detective's comments but with a gruesome murder in his town and fresh on his mind, he wasn't expecting anything good. "Go on." "You see for the last year there's been a sadistic serial killer running around in Bloomingdale. He kills all sorts of people, completely unbiased, in the sickest ways you could possibly imagine. A while ago the local news papers in my town named him the Bloomingdale slasher." Chief Haim nodded silently not really sure where any of this was going. Talking about the slasher always had a way of shaking up Atkins and he needed something to calm his nerves. He reached into his pocket and pulled out the pack of Marlboro reds he had acquired earlier. "Chief Haim, do you mind if I smoke?" The chief stared at the detective bemused."It's Illegal to smoke in here." Atkins opened his pack of cigarettes and placed one in his mouth anyway."As long as you don't mind."

Detective Atkins lit up his cigarette as the Chief stared in dismay. "Anyway the psycho's been slipping up here and there and just when we finally get some big leads, he vanishes." Chief Haim nodded attentively though he was still distracted by the cigarette. "With all due respect

Detective, what does this have to do with my town?" Detective Atkins took a long, sensual puff of his cigarette. After a moment he exhaled softly making the smoke slowly pass to the ceiling. "We have reason to believe that he may have migrated here." The chief looked almost insulted by Atkins words. "We? Why wasn't I contacted by your department back home about this?" "Well this has become a sort of independent investigation." Chief Haim was about to speak and most likely object to Atkins but was cut off before he could get a word out. "Listen, I've read about what's happened here, there's been a gruesome murder and a disappearance in a town that's normally a stranger to crime. Something's wrong and you know it." "With all due respect Detective, for all we KNOW, that murder and disappearance are completely unrelated." "Maybe they are and maybe they aren't but would you just consider an idea." "What idea would that be?" Chief Haim asked. "Give the town a heads up, tell the local news stations to make some kind of announcement. Mention the possibility of a serial killer, warn folks to be careful. I have a sketch composite, we could make some copies, post them around town. That way everyone will be on the look out for the guy."

"Let me get this straight Atkins, you want me to go before the local news stations and the people of this peaceful town and tell them there's a serial killer on the loose two days before Christmas." "I know it sounds crazy

Chief but there's just no other way. This man is a maniac, I've seen first hand what he could do." "Crazy? No detective it's ludicrous. With all this crap going on here, the last thing I need to do is send the town into an frenzy!" Chief Haim began to raise his voice, he was now as stern as could be. "Chief please, if I'm right and this guy is here. He won't stop with what he has done, he'll kill again the first chance he gets." Chief Haim shook his head in a disapproving manner. "If you won't go out and make some kind of a public statement, at least conduct some kind of search for him quietly. We can't..." "There is no WE Detective, your own guys wouldn't even lend you a hand on finding this guy and you think you can persuade me. This is my town and I'm not going to let some vigilante detective come here and scare the shit out of my people!" The Chief screamed unapologetically and Atkins stared at him in denial of his reaction. The chief took a deep breath and brought down his volume a tad before he continued. "Now hear this and hear it clear, stay in our town as long as you like Detective but know one thing. That title of yours has no meaning here and if you start shaking up my town with an investigation, I'll throw your ass in a cell! Are we clear?" Detective Atkins look unaffected by the chief's threat. "Crystal". "Good, have a merry Christmas."

The Chief got up out his chair and walked towards the office door, he opened it and waited for Atkins to leave. The detective sighed as he stood up and put his cigarette out on the police chiefs desk without a thought. Chief Haim was appalled but did not speak instead he stood staring at Atkins, his face getting more red with each passing second. Atkins began to make his way out of the office before stopping and turning back toward the chief. "You married Chief? Kids? The chief reluctantly replied. "Yes Detective." "You want to know the most disturbing thing I seen the fuck do. He killed a woman and her twenty two year old daughter one night. He tied them up and after raping them one after the other, he cut each of their throats. That woman was my wife and the girl was my daughter." Chief Haim listened to the detective's words, he looked mortified and could feel his mouth run dry. "My god." The chief's words came out weak and hoarse. "No,no. God had nothing to do with that and he'll having nothing to do with what I do when I finally find the son of a bitch. I hope you and your family have a holly jolly one, good night." With that, Atkins was gone.

21

The Eve Of Christmas Eve

At around seven thirty that night Jake had finished getting ready for the Lawsons' Christmas party. He looked quite spiffy in the gray button down shirt he wore with faded blue jeans. He had tried to spend the day relaxing but found himself searching unsuccessfully for more information on the mysterious Bloomingdale slasher. He had practiced how to tell Nicole about her uncle for hours but had found that there was no easy way of doing it. When the time came he just had to spit it out. There was no sugar coating what he suspected and if she wasn't going to take it well then there was no way around that. Jake took a quick glance at himself in the mirror and headed out his door. As he did, something disturbing came to his mind. What if Paulie had a plan? If the slasher and Paulie were one in the same that meant Paulie was a smart man, you can't elude the cops for a year being stupid. Jake began to feel unsettled by the fact that Paulie might not give him the chance to tell Nicole or anyone else for that matter what he had saw. Jake knew he couldn't take the chance without some precautionary measures. Jake thought of Eric and decided he had to make a pit stop.

Ten minutes later Jake pulled up to Eric's house. He left the engine on in his parents minivan, stepped out of the car and rang the door bell. When there was no answer after a minute or so Jake rang again. Another minute later and still no answer, Jake began to look in the blind covered window to try and spot any movements or shadows. He noticed there was a light on in the hall and just as he did, it shut. Jake swallowed his throat and in that same moment the outdoor light that hung over Eric's front door went out as well leaving Jake in the darkness of the cold winter night. Jake began to get very nervous and his first instinct was that Paulie was there. Jake realized that Paulie must have remembered Eric from the other night and somehow found out where he lived. Part of Jake was about to run for the hills and get help but the man, even though young, that lingered deep inside told him no. What if Paulie was about to kill Eric at that moment, he could save his friend, he'd have to try. Jake turned the door knob and was not surprised when it opened. He swallowed his throat in fear once again and began to walk into the dark house. Suddenly out of the complete blackness a flashlight turned on and a shadowy figure grabbed Jake, Jake quickly pushed the figure into the wall and heard a familiar voice say "Fuck!" as the figure dropped to the floor.

Jake flicked the lights on and saw Eric on the floor, he was laughing and holding his head. Jake was perplexed by the sight. "What the fuck are you doing man?" Jake's voice was shaken and still recovering from the scare. Eric got to his feet. "I thought you were Rachel, she said she was on her way, I was going to give her a little scare. So you just walk in my house now, is that your new thing?" Jake couldn't help but smile but immediately remembered the reason he had come and it faded. "Listen I've been thinking about that murder..." "Didn't I tell you to forget that, it's just a coincidence." Eric looked annoyed that Jake was still thinking about it. "Nobody hopes you're right more than me Eric, but I've been doing some research and I found some things that, well it's still up in the air but..." As Jake tried to speak he noticed Eric was rolling his eyes and looking at the clock on his wall. Jake knew Eric's attention span was especially short with Rachel on the way and now probably wasn't the best time to be telling him anything of importance.

"Listen I'm not asking you to do anything crazy, all I need you to do is remember what I said and if something should happen to me..." "Oh come on Jake!" Eric whined. "Will you shut up and listen for once." Eric sighed and glanced at the clock again before turning back to Jake. "Believe me, don't believe me, I don't care either way. I don't know what to believe myself. Just promise me one thing, if by some crazy coincidence something happens to me tonight or any other night, you'll look into it." "This really is ridiculous

235

man." "Don't worry how stupid or ridiculous it sounds man, just say you will." Jake snapped. "Nothings gonna' happen." Eric said calmly. "Just do it." Jake said angrily "Alright man! Jesus fucking Christ!" Eric opened the door to let Jake out. "Now if you'll excuse me I have a guest coming." Jake walked out quietly and then turned back to his friend. "Start keeping your door locked, you never know who's in your neighborhood" Jake said sternly as he proceeded to his car. Eric rolled his eyes and closed the door. Without thinking he did as Jake said and locked it.

Back at the Lawson house Paulie was all ready to go to the party. He was wearing a burgundy colored long sleeved button down with a pair of black slacks that fit like a glove. He had picked the clothes out very fast and was out of the store in under twenty minutes. Now he sat in the kitchen waiting for Nicole who was still finishing up. Daniel and Michelle had already headed to the party to make sure everything was in order for the surprise. Paulie gradually felt himself growing impatient with Nicole's lack of consideration and conception of time. They were already twenty minutes late and it wasn't so much that Paulie wanted to be there on time that was nagging him, but more that if he was too late he'd have to deal with a ton of staring eyes on him. He hated people staring at him and more so he hated a whole room of people staring at him.

Little did Paulie know that tonight every eye in the place would be on him regardless of what time he and Nicole got there. By now the hall was probably filled with anxious people waiting to jump out and scream, most of whom didn't even know or remember Paulie. They were probably saying things like "I didn't even know Daniel had a brother." or "Oh I think I remember him, where has he been?" Surely Daniel and Michelle would never bring up the fact that Paulie was in prison, they wouldn't take the chance of putting a dim on the party or spreading any unflattering stories about themselves and their loved ones. Nicole was ready and had been for at least fifteen minutes but a text from her father that read "Stall him a little longer" kept her upstairs for a while more. Paulie could feel a small splash of sweat begin to trickle around his forehead. It was accompanied by a light sting that came from the combination of sweat and the cheap gel he had slicked his hair with. As if out of nowhere, Paulie felt his urge to kill come on strong, in another moment he'd loose it. Abruptly Paulie heard foot steps coming down the stairs and let out a giant sigh of relief. A moment later Nicole walked into the kitchen, she was wearing a casual looking teal dress with matching shoes. She looked a lot older than she was and Paulie stared at her in silence as he wiped the sweat off his brow. He was struck by how mature and lady like she looked and further more how she suddenly resembled her mother. Paulie

237

didn't say a thing, he simply stared without a blink. Nicole stared back awkwardly "You alright Uncle Paulie?" She asked cautiously. Paulie snapped out of his gaze and smiled stupidly. "Sure Kiddo, ready to go?"

The ride there was pretty much one long awkward silence and luckily for both Nicole and Paulie, the party hall wasn't far. Paulie spent most of the twelve minute ride fantasizing about a way to somehow not attend the party. Sure he had acted like he was roused with the nights festivities to Daniel but that couldn't be further from the truth. Paulie hated social events and getting out of it was something he would kill for, literally. But it was part of the role, he thought, the role of course was that of a normal human being, one who wasn't a ruthless killer. After he and Nicole had gotten into the car Paulie had another brief urge for murder but had forced it away. Paulie knew that if he had another urge at the party he might loose his cool and actually act on his desires. Regardless Paulie thought that maybe after a few drinks he'd be able to maintain himself and prolong the inevitable. As Paulie thought of this, something inside told him that there might be another outcome to drinking. He began to worry that the alcohol might have the opposite effect and would make his urge more powerful. In that moment Paulie had a vision of himself killing each and every one of the party goers one by one, he smiled at the thought and pushed it away. Worrying was pointless, Paulie thought. In all of the things that happen in a person's life, worrying never got anyone anywhere or solved anything. Worrying is simply a series of useless thoughts that consume your mind and eat at you. If something was going to happen, it happened, Paulie accepted that without another thought.

As Paulie pulled up to the Knights of Columbus hall Nicole spoke suddenly. "Uncle Paulie." Her voice was soft and child like and for a moment Paulie had forgotten the very mature looking girl who was sitting next to him. "Yes." "I know when we first met, I mean when you first got here I was kind of hard on you and I just wanted to say I'm sorry." Paulie could tell that Nicole's words were truthful but didn't know what to say himself. He knew what she was apologizing for, the comment she had passed at the dinner table was still fresh in his head but it had hardly hurt him. If he had any emotion he'd probably have some natural affectionate reaction to her kindness. Something like hug or a loving peck on the cheek, instead he cleared his throat nervously and spoke. "That's alright kiddo, don't judge a book." Paulie smiled as his face blushed slightly and Nicole nodded in approval with a smile of her own. Paulie gave her a wink and proceeded to drive his car into the parking lot.

As they pulled in Nicole spotted Jake walking in to the hall and waved to him. Jake noticed Nicole, waved back and then saw that Paulie was driving. Jake swallowed his throat and felt the butterflies settle into his stomach like uninvited guests. He quickly realized that he'd have to wait for Nicole to go in and that meant all three of them would be heading into the party together, the thought of this made Jake cringe. He took a deep breath and waited patiently by the bottom of the staircase that led to the entrance of the hall as Paulie parked the car. A moment later Paulie and Nicole began to walk towards him. Jake turned to face their direction and noticed Paulie staring at him solemnly without so much as a blink. Jake was scared now and he could feel it all over, he reassured himself that no matter how scared he was, at least he was safe. It wasn't like Paulie was going to pull out a machete in front of everyone and chop off his head... or was he? Jake's mind wandered crazily.

Nicole and Paulie reached the staircase where Jake stood like a stone. Nicole hugged him and gave him a quick but loving kiss. "Hey baby, I missed you. Jake cleared his throat before he replied. "I missed you too." Jake turned to Paulie and extended his clammy hand for a casual shake. "Hello Paulie, how are you?" Paulie could hear the nervousness in Jake's tone. "I'm good kid, real good." Paulie extended his hand and the two began to shake. Jake didn't know if it was his imagination or not but thought that

Paulie's grip was a bit tighter than the last time they had shook. The thought made Jake's palm perspire a little more. After another second (one that had felt like another hour to Jake) the handshake ended, Jake swallowed his throat and sighed. "How are you doing kid? Staying out of trouble?" Paulie said enthusiastically as he slapped Jake on the back hard. Jake felt himself flinch as Paulie's hand came down on him. "Trying Paulie." Jake said with a smile. "That a boy." Paulie smiled back. Jake didn't know if there was something different about Paulie or if it was just in his head. Before he could come to a conclusion Nicole spoke. "How are you feeling?" Jake nodded as if he was agreeing to something. "Good, much better." The three then made their way up the concrete steps.

They walked through the door one after another, first Nicole, then Jake and finally good old Uncle Paulie. Nicole smirked and looked back at her uncle as his eyes turned toward the sight ahead. Paulie spotted a crowd of about fifty standing around close together. There was excitement in their eyes and in that brief moment Paulie asked himself what all these people were doing gathered around like a bunch of idiots. Suddenly the voices screamed in unison "Welcome Home Paulie!" Paulie was genuinely shocked and filled with disbelief. He looked around at the faces greeting him and realized that many of them were unrecognizable. Paulie suddenly felt bewildered and mortified. He looked up and spotted a giant banner that read "Welcome Back!" and in that moment Paulie was sure he was dreaming. The rest of the hall was decorated with fake hanging snow flakes, randomly placed bows, mistletoe and icicle lights. An oversized white Christmas tree sat in the corner next to the open bar, it's crystal star kissed against the halls ceiling. Paulie grinned his faux grin and walked toward the crowd where his brother and sister in law stood. Nicole followed her uncle and began saying her hellos to the guests. Jake stood frozen staring at the huge banner that hung from the ceiling. There was a man dead in Darnite and if Paulie was the killer, he was getting a party for it. Jake snapped out of his trance when he heard Nicole calling him to come over and meet some people. He left his feelings behind and proceeded to introduce himself.

Paulie seemed like a regular socialite as his brother began to introduce him to the partygoers. Most were completely new faces to Paulie but there were a few he knew, such as distant relatives whom Paulie had not seen in years. They were all so excited to see him, Paulie couldn't quite understand why but they were. Even the people that didn't know him were excited and acted especially nice, it all made Paulie feel sick. Where were all these wonderful people when he was in prison? Paulie wondered to himself. As he shook hands and kissed cheeks he thought about grabbing the first weapon in sight, maybe something like a butter knife and seeing how many he could kill before someone took him down. As Paulie continued to follow Daniel, he looked across the room toward the bar and locked eyes with Michelle who was talking to another guest. Paulie smiled at her and she followed with a blushing smile of her own. Jake had began to feel his nerves calming, he knew the best thing to do was to take this one step at a time. He walked around with Nicole and tried to somewhat enjoy himself. Paulie was about to take a seat and avoid any other conversing when Daniel grabbed him by the arm. "Let's go have a drink at the bar brother." Paulie smiled painfully and followed his brother to the bar.

Meanwhile Detective Atkins was trying his best to keep quiet as he patrolled around town on his own investigation. He didn't know just where to start but he figured it wouldn't hurt to be on the look out for any suspicious activity. The detective had come across two cars that had New Hampshire plates but quickly remembered it was Christmas time and plenty of people would be visiting their families from out of state. As he continued his patrol he began to feel hopeless. Trying to find the slasher here was like looking for a needle in a haystack. For all he knew the guy could be in someone's house, sitting by the fire and reading a Christmas Carol to their kids. Atkins had briefly thought about forgetting Chief Haim's warning. He was about to go and copy the composites of the slasher and post them himself before coming to the conclusion that it would hurt more then it would help. After finding the composites Atkins had posted, the chief would surely have a composite of Atkins printed up and posted over the slashers. Then as Atkins was conducting his private man hunt, there would be a bigger more public man hunt for him. That was attention he didn't need. The best thing he could do was keep quiet and hope that something turned up.

Back at the party, everyone was beginning to settle in. Some began to dance to the holiday tunes that were being played by the DJ and others sat at their tables conversing with other guests. Jake rose from the table where he and Nicole sat. "I'm gonna' go get a ginger ale from the bar, do you want anything?" "Yea get me a coke. Please." Jake nodded and proceeded to the bar. When he got there he found Daniel, Paulie, and Eric's father Andy drinking some beers. Jake turned to the bartender and ordered the two drinks, Daniel turned to Jake and smirked. "Hey Jakey boy." It was obvious by the use of his name and the tone of his voice that Daniel was a bit buzzed already. "You wanna do a shot kid?" Jake couldn't help but smirk. "I shouldn't Mr Lawson, I drove." Daniel looked surprised by Jake's words. "Now that's a good kid, you hear that? That's my daughter's boyfriend." Jake smirked again as the bartender put the two sodas on the bar. Paulie took a sip of the beer he was drinking and turned to Jake. "You sure you don't want a shot kid, I could always drive you home." Paulie's words had a certain grimness to them and before Jake could process what to say, Paulie spoke again "You only live once."

Jake felt the fear slip back into his stomach as his mouth went dry. He had no idea what to say, he was petrified. Suddenly Daniel spoke. "Would you leave the kid alone, Paulie. He's trying to do the right thing, something we never did." Paulie put his hands up in a surrender like wave and Daniel giggled. Jake stared awkwardly for a moment before letting out a reassuring laugh. "Alright, let's get a shot then, you want one Andy?" Daniel said as he turned to Andy. "Yea I'll take one, Jake have you talked to Eric? Becky can't get in touch with him." "I talked to him before I came Mr. Bernard. I'm sure he's probably sleeping or something, I'm sure he's fine." "That's all he does that friggen kid." Andy nodded in agreement. "Let me get another three shots." Daniel said as he turned to the bartender, Jake walked away with his drinks.

Eric was fine alright, Rachel had just gotten to his house and though he had let her in the house more casually than he had liked to, all of his other plans for the night had followed through. Once Rachel walked through the door they had immediately began to make out and within another few minutes they made their way upstairs to Eric's bedroom. There wasn't much said between the two as they went about it, just an exchange of heavy breathing. When they got to the bedroom the kissing began again and they quickly began to rip each other's clothes off. It was the epitome of teenage lust, no real feeling what so ever, only desire. As they both settled into the bed there was no worry on either one of their minds, just the unexplainable happiness that automatically came with having sex with someone. As they began their lust making, Eric's thoughts were consumed entirely by Rachel. If he had let a fragment of his mind stay on what Jake had said to him earlier and not let his other head take control, Eric might not have forgotten to lock the front door when he let Rachel in.

22

The Finer Things

An hour and a half into the party Daniel, Paulie and Andy were completely under the influence. They had been pounding down shots of Jameson whiskey and Sam Adams beers since the festivities began and they showed no signs of stopping. Paulie had not been this drunk in a long time and surprisingly, he was enjoying himself. Sure there were a thousand other places he'd rather be but he was making do with his current location just fine. Daniel ordered another round of shots for the guys and before they knew it they were clinking their glasses together once again. As Paulie poured the current shot down his throat he realized something, he was no longer thinking about killing. Had it always been this easy? Could he simply drink the urges away? Paulie couldn't remember exactly when he might have last been this drunk but knew it was probably many years ago, before jail and way before his first murder. Paulie began to look around the room curiously, when his eyes stumbled upon Michelle once again. She was now standing by the entrance talking to three women. Each of the four held glasses of red wine in their hands and Paulie wondered if that was something they were doing on purpose. One of the women was Andy's wife Becky who had just about given up on trying to get in touch with Eric. She was a homely looking woman with short brown hair and pale skin.

Paulie stared at Michelle who held her glass firmly and close to her breast. He began to admire the creme colored dress she had worn and was aroused at how well it went with her complexion. Michelle began to laugh at something her friend said and Paulie could feel his excitement growing. He may have been able to fight the thirst for murder off but he was losing control of something else now. He wanted Michelle and the drinks he had been downing with Daniel and Andy had only stimulated his feelings. Daniel and Andy were engaged in a conversation about how the baseball season had ended while Paulie was in his fantasy. Michelle took a sip of her wine and looked towards Paulie's direction before making eye contact with him. Her first instinct was to look away quickly like she had done many times before but something had stopped her. Like Paulie, she had been drinking most of the night away and was just about as drunk as him if not more. Paulie stood his ground and gazed heavily into her eyes. Michelle began to feel goose-skin form down her neck and she swallowed her throat afraid at what she was feeling. Paulie smiled at her and in that same moment, Michelle excused herself from her company and walked out of the hall and toward the lobby, Paulie stared at her passionately as she did.

Though Nicole and Jake were together elsewhere, they were hardly on the same plateau. While Jake was trying to get Nicole alone to break the news to her about her uncle possibly being a sadistic killer, Nicole was busy talking with her cousins and showing off her new boyfriend. She hadn't seen most of them in a while and they were all having fun playing catch up with each other, for Jake it was torture. For almost two hours he had been telling her that there was something he needed to talk about, something serious. Every time he thought they got a moment, she would notice someone else and drag him off to meet them. It had crossed his mind that maybe tonight wasn't the best night to tell her. In fact he was keeping a close eye on Paulie and had began to contradict his hypothesis. Paulie seemed like a normal guy tonight, he was having a few drinks with his brother, maybe Eric was right, maybe it was all one big coincidence.

Paulie could not get Michelle off his mind and when she didn't return after a few minutes he began to get curious. He excused himself from Daniel and Andy who were still fully distracted by their baseball chat and made his way into the lobby. Paulie immediately noticed the lobby was empty but his eyes searched around madly as if Michelle would jump out like a child playing hide and seek. A man walked out of the men's room and headed back into the hall, Paulie then decided that Michelle was probably inside the ladies

249

room. He waited a few minutes for Michelle to come out and while he did his eyes continued to pace around the room. Suddenly he noticed a door about ten feet from the bathroom in the corner of the lobby. The door was cracked and though he assumed it was only a closet, Paulie began to walk toward it anyway. Paulie opened the door and was surprised to see a wooden staircase that lead down. He could see that it was dimly lit down there by what he figured was a single bulb. Paulie looked around one last time to make sure no one saw him before proceeding down the stairs.

Paulie walked down the steps quite carefully as if he was hoping to catch the inhabitant by surprise. When he got closer to the bottom of the staircase he could see Michelle, her back was facing him and she was cupping her forehead and eyes in a distressed demeanor. A single light bulb hung from the ceiling with an old fashioned pull rope dangling next to it. The basement was cold and the gray concrete floor and matching walls made it very tomb like. It had a slightly musty smell to it but it wasn't unbearable. It was actually pleasing and triggering on the nostrils like a smell that you had long forgotten from your childhood. As Paulie stepped down from the last step, it creaked and Michelle spun her head around quickly to spot the intruder. She was startled at first but when she realized it was Paulie she relaxed. Knowing it was him didn't seem to stop the chill from running up her spine. Paulie let his other foot come down from the step and the old wood let out a final settling whine. The two stared at each other blankly for a moment before Paulie broke the silence. "I knew there was something wrong, the way you just stormed out of there."

"I'm fine." Michelle added solemnly and Paulie nodded his head in understanding. Michelle turned away from Paulie and for a moment he caught the vibe that she was mad. She grabbed a bag that sat on a dusty shelf immediately to the right of her, the shelf had been invisible to Paulie before she had reached towards it. Michelle turned around and held the bag out to Paulie, the bag was clean and glimmering red, it didn't fit in with the rest of the worn and dark basement. Paulie grabbed the bag carefully and reached his hand into it. "I was just going to make you a new one, but I figured since you held onto that one so long..." As Michelle spoke Paulie pulled out the newly fixed sweater. The hole he had torn through it throwing the large biker into the dumpster was gone without a trace. The red and green fabric looked brighter now from the fresh wash and almost looked as if it had just been sewn. Paulie stared at it with a strong gaze, and Michelle began to cry. "I just don't know Paulie, I care for you..but so much has changed. I don't know what the right thing is to do...I have these feelings, I don't know if it's lust or something more." Paulie didn't say a thing, instead he moved closer to

251

Michelle as she gazed down at the floor with tears still in her eyes. They were as close as can be when Michelle looked up at him, Paulie stared deep into her eyes. There was silence for a moment and then... a kiss, a quick one which Paulie planted on her lips, it was casual and soft. He continued to stare at her for another moment before kissing her again, this time a little longer.

They stared into each other's eyes before closing them and engaging in a long kiss, a kiss that both knew would turn aggressive and sexual within moments. Without a thought Paulie pushed the sweater back into the bag and dropped it to the floor. He began to pass his hand along Michelle's lower back and slid it slowly to her plump back side and squeezed. Michelle lifted her head towards the ceiling and Paulie began to kiss her neck, she began to breath heavy and moan. She wanted him, she could feel it all over her body and she couldn't help but give in to it. Michelle reached for Paulie's belt and unbuckled it quickly. He lifted her up and placed her on a large sink that sat next to the shelving. He continue to kiss her all over as he slid his pants down his legs. Paulie began to thrust into her aggressively, Michelle wrapped her arms and legs around him tightly and tried to keep her moaning to a minimum.

Michelle could have been screaming off the top of her lungs and no one would have heard her upstairs. Brenda Lee's "Rocking Around The Christmas Tree" was blasting through the hall and was pumping through the walls. Daniel and Andy were now socializing with some other friends from the neighborhood and Daniel was so drunk he had just about forgotten Paulie was even there ten minutes ago. Jake on the other hand had not forgotten about Paulie, he had kept his eyes cautiously on him the whole night and it startled him that he was now gone. He had only been gone for maybe five minutes but Jake wondered if he was up to something. Feeling like this he realized there was no question, he had to tell Nicole. She had left him alone at the table to go talk to her friends but when she got back he wouldn't wait a minute longer, he'd tell her.

The sex had only lasted about ten minutes and when it was done there was a silence in the air that seemed to hang over Michelle's head. Paulie kissed Michelle one last time on the lips before letting out a sigh of relief and pulling his pants up. For Paulie the sex had hit the spot and he was spent, he wiped the sweat off his forehead and began to fix his hair back to the way it looked earlier. Paulie, a man who never let his conscience get a hold of him or even exist for that matter, was feeling fine. He wasn't bothered by the fact that he had just committed adultery with his brother's wife for a second time. Even with his brother being right upstairs, it was no big deal to him, he'd

253

done worse. As Michelle lifted her self off the sink she stared at Paulie with a vulnerable look. Michelle was beginning to feel everything Paulie wasn't feeling, regret included. She stared at this man whom which she had just cheated on her husband with and felt more scared and confused than she had before. What had she done? She wondered to herself. Sure they had done this before, years ago but then it was different, back then her and Daniel were always fighting and it had somehow been justifiable.

Now there was nothing to justify what she had done, her and Daniel were fine until Paulie had shown up again. How could she be so stupid, to give into the lust, to give in to the desires that her younger self once had. How could she be so selfish. Did she think of Daniel? Did she think of how this might hurt him or how it might hurt Nicole if she ever found out. She felt disgusted with herself and felt the urge to cry but fought it forcefully. Michelle had given into her sexual desires and it had been nowhere near fulfilling. The sex was different from what she remembered about it last time, it was rougher and more violent. It felt impersonal and almost hateful. Paulie finished getting himself together and stared curiously at Michelle, he could see something was on her mind. Before he could say a word, he heard the sound of the door upstairs opening. Michelle turned towards the staircase with a look of distress. Her anxiety only grew when she heard Nicole's voice.

"This is the cellar, is it private enough?" Her giggle followed. Paulie and Michelle could hear Jake's reply as they made their way in. "Yea it'll do." Michelle turned to Paulie with a look of horror on her face, as the sound of footsteps came down the stairs she signaled him to a closet in a dark corner of the basement. Paulie was hesitant at first, as he was never much of the hiding type but decided it was probably better off this way. Michelle opened the closet and pushed him inside. She quickly remembered the sweater, grabbed it and threw it in the closet with Paulie before shutting the door. When Michelle got back to the staircase, Jake and Nicole had reached the basement.

"Mom?" Nicole said partly confused, "Mrs. Lawson, why are you hiding from the rest of the party?" Jake said jokingly. "Hey guys, I just came to check if there was a corkscrew down here." Michelle said as she nervously brushed her hair from her eyes. Nicole turned to her mother confused. "Why didn't you ask the bartender, I'm sure he has a corkscrew." Michelle put her hand on her forehead jokingly. "Wow, I didn't even think of that. I feel like an idiot, I'll see you guys upstairs." As Michelle made her way up the wooden staircase, Jake wondered why Mrs. Lawson had not asked them why they were downstairs, he brushed it off and waited for her to leave the basement. Paulie sat quietly in the closet waiting for Nicole and Jake to

255

disappear. Jake watched the door close upstairs and turned to back to his girlfriend. Nicole had been sneaking a few drinks with some of her cousins and being the girl she was, one who almost never drank, she had a nice buzz going on. "So we're alone, what do you wanna' do?" Nicole said in a seductive tone as she walked closer to Jake. Nicole proceeded to put her arms around Jake but he grabbed them and held them away instead. Jake had been wanting to close the deal with Nicole for quite some time but he was man enough to know this was neither the time or the place.

"Listen, what I have to say may come off as crazy but you have to at least consider it..." Nicole stared at Jake bewildered. Jake hesitated unsure of how or where to start. Paulie who sat in the darkness moved closer to the door to get a better listen, his gut told him that Jake was about to mention the murder but he hoped he was wrong. Jake took a long breath and spoke casually and calm. "That murder that happened on Stapleton drive..." Nicole stared at her boyfriend curiously. "What about it?" Jake thought for a moment what to say next and then just came out with it. "I think your uncle Paulie did it." When Paulie heard the words hit the air, he had to fight off the urge of bursting through the closet door and killing the both of them. He put his hand over his mouth and took a deep breath. Nicole stared at Jake emotionless and silent.

Nicole suddenly burst out into a drunken giggle. "What are you talking about?" "I'm serious Nicole, I saw him in front of that house." Nicole regained her composure and stared at her boyfriend straight faced. "When did you see him?" Jake sighed before speaking. "I haven't been completely honest with you..." Nicole continued to stare at Jake but her face was beginning to become more solemn. "I was at that party with Eric, now I don't know for sure, but we saw your uncle in front of the house and that was the night of the murder." "You told me you didn't go." "Look I know I lied but we have to put that aside and look at the bigger picture." "The bigger picture? If you're referring to my uncle being a murderer well than that's just..." "Ridiculous?" Jake shouted. "Exactly." Nicole said wearily. "Listen I was looking up some stuff online last night and there's a serial killer that's still on the loose in New Hampshire." "Are you kidding, you think he's a God damn serial killer? What proof do you even have?" Jake closed his eyes in frustration. "I don't have any proof but I figured I could tell you what I saw and..." "And what Jake?" Jake shook his head. "For God sakes the guy was right there, I mean what is that?" "Uncle Paulie used to live here, he could have been visiting an old friend in the neighborhood, how could you jump to that conclusion?"

Jake stood there silent for a moment reflecting on what he had said so far. He had been sloppy in pleading his case and he wished he could go back and start over. "I was talking to Eric and..." "You were talking to Eric, what is that supposed to help me believe this, is he some reliable source all of a sudden?" Jake rolled his eyes in annoyance. "No I was telling him but he doesn't believe me either, I told him if anything should happen to me that he should..." "He should what?" Nicole said angrily. "I don't know tell someone your uncle was there at the scene of the crime. See what the authorities think." Nicole couldn't help but smile crazily. "I don't know what kind of sick prank, or trick or what you guys are up to, but I don't find it amusing. My father went years without talking to my uncle and now he's the happiest I've ever seen him in a long time, so don't you dare bring me or my family into what ever you two morons are conjuring up." "Nicole were not conjuring up anything, I'm serious about what I'm saying. I wanted to..." "Jake, you sound like a crazy person." Jake stopped dead in his tracks and didn't know what else to say. After hearing it from Nicole's mouth, Jake was suddenly sure he was making a mistake about Paulie. Nicole ran up the stairs without another word and Jake followed her absently, calling at her to stop. Paulie sat in the dark closet and waited for the footsteps to fade away. When they did he stood up,opened the closet door and walked back into the light. Nicole hadn't believed Jake and Paulie knew he at least had that going for him. But Jake, something had to be done about him and his friend.

When Paulie made his way back into the hall he immediately headed over to Daniel and Andy. Daniel turned to his brother and offered him another drink casually. Neither Daniel or Andy acknowledged the fact that Paulie had been gone for almost twenty minutes, to them it had seemed like Paulie had never left. Nicole and Jake were now on completely different sides of the room. Nicole didn't want to hear anymore of Jake's bullshit so she had gone back to her cousins' table and delved into conversation. Jake paced around the party quietly, he thought about trying to talk to Nicole again but knew it was probably moot. He noticed Paulie was back again acting as normal as ever and this only made him fed up. Jake had about enough of playing detective for a night, he was mentally exhausted and didn't see any point of watching Paulie at the party. Even if Paulie was a murderer it wasn't like he was going to get away with killing someone right this minute.

Jake made his way over to where Nicole was engaged in conversation and tapped her on the back. She turned around and stared at him with a stern look. "Yea." She replied in an agitated tone. "Listen, I'm sorry. I'm going to go." Nicole stared at Jake for a moment before replying with almost no interest. "Ok." Jake was about to say something else but instead he nodded

his head and made his way out to the hall. He walked passed Paulie, Daniel
and Andy and thought of saying goodbye to them but felt it wasn't necessary
due to the fact that they were all bombed. Paulie didn't notice him leave as he
was busy taking another shot with his brother and Andy. After they slammed
their glasses down, Paulie took a quick look around and saw that Michelle
was nowhere to be found, he assumed she was in the bathroom freshening up
from their secret sexual encounter.

Michelle was in the bathroom, though freshening up was hardly a top
priority. She had locked the door behind her and was weeping madly at the
sight of her reflection in the mirror. She felt ashamed, used and downright
sick to her stomach, she wished she hadn't done what she did. Doing it had
opened the door for Paulie and she knew it was only a matter of time before
he approached her again. She tried vigorously to wipe away the tears but
found herself crying even more with each passing second. Meanwhile back
inside the hall Paulie's thoughts were the furthest from regret. He was too
busy trying to conceive a plan to find Jake's friend Eric. He knew Andy was
Eric's father but that was all he knew about the kid. He began to feel the urge
coming on and Paulie knew he needed to find the kid. Before Paulie could
think of a way to acquire that information, an opportunity presented itself.

"I'm gonna' go have a smoke and some fresh air, care to join me?" Andy said sluggishly. Daniel shook his head. "I'm gonna' go run to the shitter, I'll meet you back in here." Daniel swiftly proceeded out the door. Paulie's eyes lit up. "I'll come take a breather Andy."

When the two men arrived outside, each took a deep breath of the cool, crisp night's air. The predicted snow flurries had started coming down and were beginning to stick to the ground. Andy pulled out a cigarette and handed one to Paulie, he grabbed it and placed it into his mouth. Andy grabbed another for himself and then proceeded to light both of them starting with Paulie's. The two man headed down the concrete steps and onto the surface of the parking lot where they stood looking out into the night. Paulie inhaled softly and then exhaled the smoke as he stared at Andy whose back was now facing him. Andy stared off into the parking lot as if he was searching for something. "You believe that fucking murder on Stapleton?" Andy glanced at Paulie before turning to face the cars again. "Yea, crazy...sad too." Paulie added with a hint of concern. Paulie was about to move in on Andy but right as he was Andy turned around again. Andy was too drunk to notice Paulie was now a few inches closer to him. "I mean this is supposed to be a safe town. I got a kid, Danny's got a kid, your niece." Paulie nodded his head in agreement and Andy turned around again. Paulie searched around quickly for something to help bring Andy to silence. Paulie looked down and noticed a circle of dirt which must have housed several flowers in the warmer seasons. The circle was outlined with a barrier of small red bricks, one of which had cracked in half and was now laying out of place on the dirt.

Andy turned back towards Paulie and Paulie immediately refocused his attention on the man. "I hope when the cops find the son of a bitch, they give the bastard the chair!" "If they find him." Paulie added casually and Andy nodded. "Your right, the way the cops slack off out here, they might as well get the chair too." Andy turned back around and Paulie carefully reached down for the piece of brick. Paulie flicked his cigarette onto the ground as he slowly came back to his feet, tightly gripping the brick to his chest. He slowly extended his equipped arm and at that moment Andy began to speak again. "You'd think we pay them..." As Andy turned around to look at his company, Paulie swung his arm around and smashed the brick into the side of his head. Paulie's swing was swift and he was sure to catch Andy before he even knew what hit him. Andy stepped forward and wobbled for a second before falling down and smashing his face onto the cold concrete. As he laid unconscious Paulie could already see the lump brewing on the side of his head. In any other circumstance Paulie would have unmercifully beat the

262

remaining life out of his victim but here tonight, that wasn't plausible. There were too many people at the party and Paulie couldn't afford to start murdering folks at a social event like this one. Instead Paulie took a quick look around before reaching into Andy's pocket. He then pulled out a worn looking wallet, opened it up and began to search through.

Within a few seconds Paulie came across what he was looking for, Andy's ID. He stopped and smirked as he stared down at the address that read thirty three Ciccone Court, this was all too easy, he thought sickly to himself. Next he placed the ID and the wallet back into Andy's pocket and rolled the unconscious man over. He was sure to place him into a position accurate to where the lump was. When Paulie felt Andy's body was in a good position, he picked up the hunk of brick and laid it under his head. As he laid the brick in between the wound and the ground he continued to look around cautiously, no one was in sight.

Moments later Paulie burst through the party halls door and headed straight toward Daniel who was patiently waiting at the bar for Paulie and Andy to return. Paulie approached him hastily. "Dan, Andy took a fall, he's unconscious." Daniel couldn't help but smile as he thought his brother was joking, as he stared at Paulie's stern eyes he knew he wasn't. "Oh my god,

263

where is he? What happened?" Daniel spoke in a shaky, nervous tone. Paulie did not say anything, instead he simply began to lead Daniel outside. Other guests began to notice the franticness of the two men, one of which was Andy's wife Becky. She could see the color was no longer in Daniel's face from across the room and when they made eye contact he signaled her to follow them out of the hall. Michelle also noticed but instead of moving she simply sat in her coma like drunken state. Nicole who was mingling with her cousin also realized something was wrong. As she stared at her uncle and father rushing out the door with Mrs. Bernard trailing, she wondered what was happening and furthermore what Paulie had to do with it. Jake and his crazy presumption came to mind and she dismissed it just as fast. If she hadn't she may have been able to save two lives.

23

House Calls If Needed

As Paulie lead Daniel and Becky outside to the still unconscious body of Andy, Sharon Smith, a woman who had been engaged in conversation with Becky, ran to the phone and dialed nine one one. When the three arrived outside Andy was no longer unconscious, instead he was holding the side of his head and moving his neck right to left slowly in some robotic manner. "Wha' the ffukk Happ??" Andy's words were slurred and sloppy, It could have been the alcohol he consumed or it could have been a slight concussion from the blow he took. Daniel and Paulie helped him too his feet as Becky stared with tears in her eyes. "You lost your footing when you were coming back up the steps. Wouldn't of been such a bad fall but you landed face first onto that brick there." Paulie said casually. "I don't even remember it." Andy said passively. Becky noticed the large bloodied lump forming on her husbands head and squealed. "Oh my god, is he going to be alright?" "He should be fine. We should get him to a hospital anyway and get him checked out though." Daniel said. "You took the words right out of my mouth brother." Paulie added. At that moment Sharon ran out of the building. "I called the ambulance, they should be here soon."

About ten minutes later the ambulance pulled up to the Knights of Columbus hall. Two paramedics jumped out and went over to Andy who was now sitting on the same steps he had supposedly fell down. After a few moments of customary questioning, they helped Andy up and lead him into the back of the ambulance. Becky tried to get into the back of the ambulance with her dazed husband but was shut down immediately. "Sorry Ma'm, you can't ride in the back." The paramedic spoke with almost no compassion as they closed the doors in her face. The ambulance then pulled away without hesitation. Becky ran to her car which was parked to the far right of the lot. Sharon began to chase after her. "I'll go with you!" She called out to her friend. Daniel and Paulie stared as Becky and Sharon drove away and faded off in the distance. "Do you think we should go with them?" Daniel asked Paulie. "Nah, they'll be fine, he'll be fine." There was a moment of silence as the two men stared ahead at the black winter sky. "I'm gonna' go get a pack of smokes, I'll be right back." Paulie said abruptly. "You want me to take a ride?" Daniel asked. "No, no, enjoy your party, I won't be long."

As Paulie got behind the wheel of his blue Cadillac cigarettes were the furthest thing from his mind. The main focus of it was Ciccone Court, specifically house number thirty three. When he read the address off of

Andy's ID, he knew immediately where to go. It was a small development located directly in back of where the old intermediate school seventy five had once been. They had started building the development right about the time Paulie had been sent away and he remembered signs advertising "A New Life in Ciccone Court". The school that sat in front of the development was eventually relocated, leveled and made into a public park. Paulie had gone there as a child and though the building was old as hell, he couldn't understand why they would want to level it and build a new one elsewhere. It was always about money. Paulie felt that towns did stuff like that to make people feel like their tax money was doing something important, meanwhile it was just being spent on bullshit. Ciccone Court was about seven minutes from the hall so if Paulie was quick, it would be like he had never even left the party. This was something that enticed Paulie and almost challenged him to the task. Slightly drunk or not, murder was something that came natural to him and he was up for the challenge.

Paulie slowed down as he came to a dimly lit house, he rolled down his window to get a closer look at the address. There it was, in out dated but classy gold numbering, thirty three. He drove away slowly and after passing three other houses (a reasonable distance) he parked. Paulie stepped out of the car, grabbed the gloves from his trunk and slowly walked towards the house. This time he didn't bother worrying about a weapon. If he didn't come across something when he got in the house, he would just use his bare hands. When he came to the front of the house, he looked up and noticed a lone light on upstairs. He took a quick look around the house to see where the best place would be to break in. As he thought back on his last home invasion, he remembered that when all was said and done the front door ended up being unlocked. He looked up at the front door of his current location and decided to take a chance.

Paulie turned the door knob and he could feel relief and some disbelief when it didn't put up a fight. He pushed the door open slowly and stared into the dark abyss like living room. All he could see was a few shadows and shapes created by couches, a lamp and some other mysterious furniture. As he continued to look around he spotted the light upstairs, it's yellow glow illuminated the upper hallway weakly. Paulie closed the door slowly and proceeded to walk toward the shadowy staircase. The steps were old and the first one Paulie placed his foot on creaked loudly, he stopped for a moment and looked at the dimly lit hallway anticipating someone. No one came and Paulie continued up the steps. Each step screamed louder than the last, he stopped another two times and after there was no objection to his visit after the second halt, he sped up his pace and finished to the top. When he got there he could see the light was coming from a door at the end of the hall that had been left open. Paulie began to walk toward the room slowly, there was no creaking on the floors this time and this made him smirk with surprise.

When Paulie got to the end of the hall he peeked his head through the threshold and saw Eric laying on his back with his eyes closed. For a minute the morbid mind of Paulie thought he might be dead, but Paulie quickly realized he wasn't when he saw his chest rising. Eric had dozed off, he now lay comfortably on his bed snoring lightly. Paulie walked over to the bed and stared at the young man for a minute as if he was observing him for a science experiment. Paulie slowly reached for an unoccupied pillow that sat to the right of the teen and lifted it over his head. Paulie began to make soft sounds in hopes to wake Eric from his slumber."Psss! Hey, wake up. Eric!" Eric didn't move but Paulie didn't find murdering as fun, when the person didn't see it coming. Paulie began to shake Eric on his shoulder, Eric began to come to and he opened his eyes slowly. When he first saw the shadowy figure standing over him, Eric thought he was having a nightmare. When the waking blur did clear away from his vision, Eric could only wish it was a dream. "Rise and shine shit head!" Paulie quipped. Eric's eyes shot open and before a horrific gasp could leave his throat, Paulie forced the thick pillow

269

over his face. He pressed down tightly, jamming Eric's head into the mattress. Paulie couldn't help but think, what a comfortable way to go.

Eric struggled to free himself from the cushioned doom but Paulie continued to smother him proficiently. After about a minute the struggle had ceased. Paulie continued to hold the pillow over the lifeless body of the teen, he pressed the pillow down with three more thrusts as if to get every last ounce of breath out of him. Paulie finally stopped and took a deep breath of the air that was now solely his. He stared down at the cold figure that lay in the bed. The pillow that sat on Eric's head gave the body an odd look and Paulie couldn't help but giggle aloud. When he did, he was shocked to hear the toilet flush from the hallway. For someone else, who may have been an amateur at this, the sound of the toilet flushing would have lead to a thousand nervous thoughts entering the mind. For Paulie only one thought came to mind and it was a happy one, he had to kill someone else. He could hear a door open and light foot steps began approaching the bedroom. He looked down at Eric's quirky looking corpse and knew there wasn't much of a way to handle his surprise guest.

Rachel who was wearing nothing but a long t-shirt walked into the room slowly. For a split second, as she stared at Eric, she somehow did not see Paulie standing in the shadows. "Ready for round two..." Rachel said sensually. As the words left her lips she noticed Paulie and before her body could give her the strength to run, she screamed and jolted back into the wall. Rachel stood there pale and in horrific shock, staring at the unwelcome guest. She looked down at Eric and part of her wanted to believe that the pillow on his head and this man standing there was all part of some sick joke. Rachel let out a piercing shriek, Paulie stood as still as Eric and stared. Rachel suddenly began to speak or at least try to. "Whaaa, What didd youuu dooo...." Paulie had scared the shit out of a lot of folks but never had he seen fear like he was seeing now, Rachel was paralyzed with it and Paulie couldn't help himself. "Are you afraid!" He yelled from across the room. Rachel began to tremble and Paulie could feel a natural high coming from it. "Yesss..." Rachel answered fearfully unsure of what else to do. Paulie had a thought and then grinned. "Well you shouldn't be...You're on fear tactics." Rachel felt the goose bumps on her skin begin to fade away softly, relief settled over her tightened stomach. She had watched a few episodes of Fear Tactics with her younger brother Mark and was familiar with what they did. She swallowed her throat and proceeded to let a couple of calm words out. "You are?" Paulie began to grin again, the same high he got off fear, he got off giving the naive hope. He let the silence linger in the air for a few seconds as he felt the suspense building. And just as Rachel was expecting

271

that big "yes", the one that would relax her tense body and send a terrible laugh of relief up to her throat, Paulie replied. "Nope." Paulie charged at the girl and she screamed a hideous panic stricken scream.

Rachel's body was heavy as the shock filled it once again, but the will to live that is dormant somewhere in all of us awoke and she felt her feet begin to move rapidly. Before she knew it she was in the hall moving as quickly as she could. Paulie was behind her and she could feel his breath catching up. Tears ran down her eyes as she passed the bathroom, if she had stayed in there a bit longer, it could have been her sanctuary. She saw the stairs in the immediate distance and just as she was about to hurry down the steps, she felt the strangers hands grab her hair. She wailed as she realized the end was definitely near. Paulie pulled her back by the hair and slammed her head into the wall directly behind the staircase as hard as he could. A loud thump rang out and a stamp of blood the size of an apple was left behind on the pale beige paint, her head had split immediately. Paulie grabbed the long shirt the poor girl wore with his other hand and tossed her down the staircase. Rachel tumbled down like a rag doll, hitting every step violently. When she finally landed at the bottom, the crunch of her neck breaking echoed up the staircase to reassure Paulie his work here was done. He looked down at the lock of hair that he unknowingly held in his gloved

272

hand. Blood was also on his hand and on a few of the steps that Rachel had come into contact with. Paulie dropped the hair to the ground and sped down the stairs, he stepped over Rachel's semi naked carcass like he was stepping over something as insignificant as a piece of gum, and in another minute he was gone.

Paulie pulled up to the Knights of Columbus less than ten minutes later. He walked into the building and headed straight for the bathroom. There he washed his hands thoroughly before splashing some water on his face as well. He finished off by brushing his hair back with his hands, he stared at himself in the mirror and knew he looked just as he did earlier, picture perfect. When Paulie walked into the hall he spotted Daniel at the bar with a few other people. He walked over and just as he thought, it had been like he never left. "Drink Paul?" Daniel said as he tried to show interest in a friend's story. "Sure." Paulie said casually. Daniel signaled the bartender for another and Paulie began to pretend to have interest in the man's story as well. Nicole had been in the ladies room with her mother since about the time Paulie managed to slip away. The drinks or the unfaithfulness had caught up with her and she was puking in the toilet for the last fifteen minutes. Nicole stood by her in the stall, rubbing her back in a soothing manner.

Michelle reached over and flushed the toilet as she began to get to her feet. "I think I'm ok now honey, why don't you go back to the party." Nicole stared at her mother with a concerned look on her face. "Are you sure?" Michelle nodded casually. "Yea I'll be fine." Nicole wasn't about to put up a fight, she had been there for what felt like forever. She left the bathroom and headed back into the hall. When Nicole walked in, the first thing she couldn't help but notice was her uncle and father still conversing and drinking at the bar. They had been there all night, between that and her mother's antics she began to think she might have a whole family of alcoholics on her hands. She stared at Paulie carefully as he laughed at something her father said to him. She wondered if there could be any truth to what Jake had said. She began to search her mind for a logical reason for Paulie to be at that house besides murder but couldn't. Just as that thought didn't come up, a motive for murder seemed even more unexplainable. Just as her mind tried to conceive another thought, Nicole spotted her cousin Maria waving her over, she went.

At about a quarter past eleven Becky, Sharon and Andy who now had a white bandage wrapped around his head, stepped out of rotating doors of the Darnite University Hospital. Doctor Barlow had diagnosed Andy with a slight concussion and had given him some medication for the next couple of weeks. He had also advised him to lay off drinking for awhile, until the head aches stopped at least, the doc had said with a laugh. Andy listened but did not comprehend all of what the doctor was saying. When they got into the car he put the passenger seat back and stared up at the ceiling of the car, before letting out a huge sigh. Becky and Sharon each had a look of slight amusement on their faces. "I feel awful." Andy said with a grunt. "Thank God it wasn't worse." Becky added as she began to drive away from the hospital. She turned to the rearview to look at Sharon, who looked like she could fall asleep at any minute. "Do you want me to drop you back off at the party?" "No I'm exhausted, besides it's probably winding down now." Becky nodded in agreement. Sharon lived a block away from them so driving her home was no inconvenience.

Becky pulled up beside Sharon's house several minutes later, Andy was now asleep in the passenger seat. "Thanks for coming Sharon." Becky said sincerely. Sharon waved it away without concern. "Don't worry about it." Sharon turned to Andy and tapped him, he opened his tired eyes slowly and looked silently around the car like a curious infant. "I'll see ya Andy, watch your steps." Sharon smiled as she got out of the car. "Bye.." Andy spoke with strain. "Oh Sharon, if I don't see you, have a Merry Christmas." Becky added cheerfully. "You too." Sharon waved as Becky drove off. Minutes later Becky and Andy had arrived at there home. Andy yawned and set his seat back up, he wanted nothing more than to go straight up to his bedroom and get some sleep. Becky parked the car and the two walked toward the house. Becky couldn't help but notice an unfamiliar green car parked in front of the house, she wondered if Eric maybe had a friend over. As she approached the door she noticed that it was cracked slightly, even in his dizzy state Andy noticed as well. "Did this kid leave the door open again." Andy said in an annoyed tone. The two walked into the dark house, Becky called for her son immediately. "Eric we're home!" Andy hit the lights on and the two instantly noticed the sight that lay at the bottom of the steps. Becky screamed and jumped back in horror knocking down a picture of the family that hung on the wall behind her. Andy swallowed his throat in fear as he stared at the bruised and bloody body of the unknown young girl.

Rachel's bare lower half, which would once turn on any man that saw it, had lost it's appeal. Andy turned away as he couldn't bare to look any longer. He could feel something rising in his stomach and before he could even begin to think of what might have happened to the poor young girl, he saw the thick yellow vomit leaving his mouth. Becky burst out in an uncontrollable cry. "Where is Eric?" Andy wiped his mouth and turned toward the staircase. He could see there was a light coming from where Eric's room was, without hesitation, he stepped over the young girl's body with impulsive disregard and hurried up the steps. "Wait..." Becky called out to him for no particular reason, before glancing at the girls body again and closing her eyes. Andy ran down the hall and through the open threshold of his son's room. He looked down at the peculiar and lifeless position of his son's body and knew he was dead. The pillow that killed him still sat on his face. Andy felt the desire to scream and even cry but his body didn't supply him the strength to do either. Instead he simply stepped out of the room and walked back toward the staircase. When Andy got to where he was visible to Becky, she looked up at him and noticed his face was now completely pallid. He stared down at his wife solemnly trying to keep his eyes from looking at the girls carcass again. "Is he up there?" Becky asked, though deep down inside she knew he was and what was. Andy couldn't help but begin to bawl uncontrollably, his wife's hope quickly faded as he did. Becky began to cry as well and they both knew that their lives as they knew it would never be the same again.

24

An Otherwise Safe Town

By ten to midnight all of the partygoers had gone about their separate ways. Daniel and Michelle had wished each guest a Merry Christmas and said their thanks. Some friends had stayed a little longer to help the Lawson's give the hall a quick cleanup and Michelle and Nicole appreciated that greatly. Daniel and Paulie weren't much of a help, they were busy being men and men didn't clean much. When the rest of the garbage was put into bags, Michelle thanked the couple of folks who stayed and reassured them that they should go, the final guest left and a strange kind of quietness took over the hall. Daniel and Paulie sat at a table looking as tired as ever, while Michelle and Nicole finished a quick sweep around the floor. Michelle turned to her daughter "I'll finish this Nicole, why don't you go put those last garbage bags in the dumpster." Nicole sighed with a bit of annoyance at the fact that her father and uncle had done almost nothing to help them. She smiled at her mother anyway, grabbed the last two garbage bags and headed out the door.

The air outside was freezing and Nicole immediately regretted not grabbing her coat. The snow which the news had said was going to be heavy was seemingly dying down and Nicole thought that wasn't much of a surprise. She headed right for the dumpster and threw each of the bags in before quickly pacing back toward the building. As she did she saw the head lights of a car coming around the dark bend in the road that sat behind the halls parking lot. She stopped in her tracks curious to see who it might be. Nicole thought that perhaps Jake had come to apologize to her, and as she saw the lights coming closer she was almost positive it would be him. When the car started to become visible her hopes were immediately diminished. Instead of spotting Jake's minivan, she began to see an old black sports car with out of state plates. She stared curiously as the car continued slowly down the road. As it got closer, she could feel an uneasiness brewing inside of her. In the darkness of the night she could not make out the face completely, but she could tell it was an older man, maybe in his fifties. As the car continued to creep down the road, a hint of glow from a streetlight illuminated the man's face and made his grim look completely visible. Detective Atkins stared at the young girl cautiously. With the slasher in town it wasn't safe for anyone to be out at this hour, especially a girl this young and vulnerable.

As Atkin's Challenger came up to the building, Nicole could feel an unexpected fearfulness run through her body. The detective was about to pull over and worn the girl about being alone but just before he did, the girl turned around and began to walk toward the building's door quickly. She took one last look back at the car and hurried through the door. Atkins felt that the point of pulling over was probably moot and stayed down the road to continue his patrol. When Nicole got back into the hall where her mother, father and uncle were, she could feel a sweet warm relief pass through her joints. The mysterious man had startled her in a way which she hadn't felt since she was a small child. Days when she would lay in her dark bedroom staring at the closet door, anticipating a certain boogeyman or vampire to appear. Michelle turned to her daughter "Are you ready to go?" Nicole nodded in agreement. Michelle then turned to Daniel and Paulie, she could feel the sickening nervousness brewing again as she stared at Paulie. "What about you guys?" Daniel stood up and Paulie followed him. "Yep, I'll ride with Paulie." The four then left the hall, Nicole followed her mother to their white Sedan and Daniel followed Paulie to his Cadillac. Daniel and Michelle called their casual goodbyes to each other before driving off.

Michelle and Nicole had pulled up to the Lawson house first at a quarter after twelve. Michelle pulled into the driveway and parked and Paulie's Cadillac came up before she could even shut off her engine. Michelle and Nicole got out of the car and started walking towards the front door, Daniel and Paulie trailed a few paces behind. When they got in the house Michelle took off her shoes and turned to the three. "I'm going to bed." She said before marching up the steps rather speedily. Michelle didn't know what she was going to do about her situation but knew something had to be done, the one thing she couldn't do was let it happen again. Sleep was the only thing that seemed logical right now and within minutes of laying down she slipped into a deep one.

Daniel walked into the kitchen with his stomach growling. With the amount of alcohol he had consumed tonight, he had barley even eaten. He turned to his brother with a smile. "You thinking what I'm thinking." Paulie smiled back at him casually. "Let's get cooking." Though Paulie's excitement was a bit artificial, he was in fact very hungry. The night had been a busy one and somewhere between shooting the shit with his brother, screwing his wife in the cellar and killing two random teenagers (all in record breaking time) Paulie had gotten very hungry. He hadn't had a single crumb of food, not even those delicious cock tail weenies he loved so much. Back in Mesapeena Paulie would buy the microwaveable packs at the grocery store and eat them while he watched the tube. Thinking back on that made Paulie feel desolate and slightly homesick.

Daniel opened the fridge and began browsing through it, there was nothing that really caught his eye. Eggs, some old chopped meat and some even older pasta that had been pushed to the back of the fridge. After another quick glance at the leftovers, Daniel shut the door and sighed. He opened the freezer next and immediately spotted something that caught his eye, he pulled it out and showed it to his brother. Paulie stared at the box that read Big Vito's Instant Bake Pizza and smiled. "What do you think?" Daniel asked excitedly. "It'll do." Paulie added passively. Daniel smiled in relief and began to open the box as he set the oven to preheat, Nicole walked into the kitchen and poured herself a cup of water. Daniel held the box up again this time towards his daughter. "You want to get in on this honey? There's plenty." Nicole smiled at the childish antics her father had been displaying. "Thanks but no thanks, I'm gonna' try and get some sleep. You guy's have fun, don't stay up too late." Daniel grinned at his daughter and she headed up the stairs to her room.

After another few minutes Daniel placed the frozen pizza into the oven and whistled a happy tune as he closed the door. Daniel then began looking through the cabinet. "Do you need garlic powder for that Paulie?" "No it'll be fine just like that." At that same moment the Lawson's home telephone began to ring. At this hour, Paulie immediately knew what the phone call was most likely pertaining to. Daniel lifted his head from the cabinet and walked to the other side of the counter, where the cordless phone sat. "Now who the hell could that be." he said in an annoyed tone before picking up the phone. Before clicking the talk button Daniel shot a quick look at the small screen that displayed the number. It read Bernard, Andy. Daniel smirked at the sight and held the phone to his brother. "It's Andy, let's hope he didn't fall again." Daniel quipped before letting out a small giggle and finally answering the phone."Andy, how the hell's your head?" Daniel smiled while waiting for the man's reaction. Paulie watched with no surprise as the smile ran far from Daniel's face. However it wasn't Andy who told him the bad news, it was their neighbor Sharon. She had heard the sirens coming down the street and when she saw them stop in front of the Bernard's, she had thought for a moment that Andy took another spill. When she saw the commotion of other neighbors and heard the horrific screams of Becky she could only wish Andy had fallen again.

Sharon didn't stay on the phone long with Daniel and it wasn't much of a conversation anyway. Sharon had been talking most of it while Daniel would just listen on and gasp. Occasionally Daniel managed to slip in a "Jesus" or an "oh God" if deemed necessary. After taking it all in he could feel sobriety slipping back into his veins. Sharon told him all about how Eric was smothered with a pillow. She told him about the mystery girl that had been thrown down the stairs, who's body, lay bloody, beaten and half naked. She told him how Andy and Becky couldn't stop crying and how they followed the ambulance to the hospital with a false hope that maybe if God was listening, their son would somehow be alive. Sharon knew he wasn't and that made her cry more for them. Andy had dropped his cell phone somewhere in all the mayhem and Sharon said she picked it up. She knew Andy and Daniel were very close and didn't think twice about letting him know about the sudden horror that had occurred. Daniel swallowed his throat at the surreal and shocking news. "Do you think I should go by the hospital?" he asked feeling it was the least he could do. "They have family on their way, you'll probably be better off holding off for now. I'm gonna' head back home myself, though I don't know how I'm going to sleep." "Ok Sharon, I'll talk to you." Daniel was pale and couldn't think of another thing to say after that, so he simply hung up.

Daniel hung up the phone and stared emotionless at nothing, Paulie broke it with pretend concern. "What was that all about?" Daniel's mouth was dry and he felt as if he had to force the words out. "Andy's son Eric was murdered tonight... and a girl, a friend of his." "My god, do you think it was

284

related to that other murder?" Paulie asked innocently. Daniel continued to gaze absently, he was stunned by the question. It didn't occur to him that they may be connected, was there a serial killer in Darnite? Before Daniel could ponder anymore, he realized the frozen pizza was still in the oven. "Shit." He put on oven gloves opened the door and pulled out the pizza. It was slightly over baked and   one half of the pie was a little dark but it still seemed edible. Daniel shut the oven off and placed the pie on top of the counter. Paulie inhaled the delicious scent of the pizza and could hear his stomach growl. Daniel stared at the pizza as he took off his oven gloves and he could feel a growl as well, but his was more of the sickening kind. "I'm gonna' hit the sack Paul, help yourself." Daniel ran out of the room before Paulie could say anything. Paulie shrugged his shoulders, got up from the chair and walked toward the pizza. He pulled a pair of scissors from the draw and began cutting himself a slice.

When Daniel got up the staircase he immediately headed for the bathroom. He swung the door open as fast as he could and gave it another whip closed when he was inside. He had forgotten that the door was old and needed a good push to be fully closed, so instead it stopped inches before touching the doorway, leaving a small crack. Daniel lifted the toilet seat, stuck his head there and began to go to work. All those drinks he had enjoyed

earlier were coming back up rapidly. The vomit was light colored as it was
mostly made up of stomach acids and whiskey. Daniel couldn't help but grunt
every time the spew began to rise in his stomach. It was a slow and unnatural
feeling that left his throat and stomach in pain. As he continued the grunts
got louder. When he finished a minute or so later he began to spit up any of
the remaining phlegm left in his throat. Nicole knocked at the door gently
and pushed it open. She was expecting to see her mother sitting there on the
floor, but to her surprise it was her father. "Dad, are you ok?" For a moment
she was going to mention her mothers earlier regurgitation but instead
decided not to. "I think so, I just drank too much." Daniel wiped his mouth
with his hand and began to get up. Nicole went over and helped him to his
feet, she pushed the toilet seat down. "Sit down, I'm gonna' go get you a glass
of water." Nicole said with concern in her voice. Daniel surrendered and sat
down on the toilet seat. "Ok."

When Nicole got downstairs she smelt the aroma of the home baked
pizza and heard laughter coming from the living room. She went into the
fridge and poured her father a tall glass of ice water. Before heading back,
she took a peek into the living room and saw Paulie watching an old episode
of The Honeymooners, he had the pizza pie on his lap and had eaten half of it
already. Nicole smirked and shook her head before slipping back to her

father's aid. When she got back to the bathroom her father was sitting just where she had left him, he was holding his head with both hands and rubbing it clockwise as if to soothe some pain. She handed him the glass and he smiled as best as he could before taking a sip. "Thanks Nic." He added before taking a longer gulp, Nicole watched him closely as he did. When Daniel was finished he placed the glass on top of the sink and continued to sit on the toilet. Nicole watched as her father stared emotionless at the bathroom tile. She could see that there was something else bothering him. "What's wrong dad?" Daniel let out a huge sigh before answering. "Eric Bernard is dead..." The color immediately left Nicole's face and a look of shock took over. Tears filled up in her eyes and she choked up as she tried to speak. "What?" That was all that could come out at that moment. Daniel shook his head not sure of how to continue. "Someone killed him at his house tonight. There was a girl there with him, she's dead too." Nicole gasped before cupping her mouth and tears began to leak down her face.

She knew Cindy was still away and immediately assumed the mystery girl was someone Eric was cheating on her with. Even Cindy had sometimes believed Eric was seeing other girls, he just never seemed like the loyal boyfriend type. "This happened tonight?" Nicole knew the pointlessness of the question as it rolled off her nervous tongue. Daniel answered anyway.

287

"Yes, while we were at the party." Nicole began to cry. "I'm sorry I had to tell you like this but there is no easy way." Nicole nodded and wiped away her continuing tears. "I'm going to go lay down." Daniel turned to his daughter. "Are you going to be ok?" Nicole looked at her father with a gaze of fear. "I hope so." Just a moment ago she was asking her father if he would be ok, now the tables had turned suddenly. When she got in her room she went straight to her bed and closed her eyes, just as she did, Jake came to mind. Of course Jake, how could she forget about him. She had to call him and tell him Eric was dead before someone else did. She picked up her phone and dialed his number, the phone rang twice before he picked up. "Hi." Jake said cautiously, he was unsure if she was still mad at him.

"Jake." Nicole spoke in a shaky voice, Jake could immediately tell something was wrong. "Nicole what's the matter?" Nicole closed her eyes and took a deep breath. "I don't know how to say this but...Eric's dead." Jake was speechless for a moment, he couldn't even begin to process what Nicole had just said to him. He felt his mouth run dry, he didn't want to believe it but knew there was no way in hell Nicole would lie about something like that. Jake swallowed his throat before speaking again. "What happened?" Light tears began to run down Nicole's face. "He was murdered, him and someone else, a girl he had over." "God, when did it happen?" "My father said sometime during the party?" Jake felt his stomach turn as she said those words. "Nicole I don't want you to get mad and at this point I don't care if you do, but I have to bring it up. Did your uncle leave the party at any point tonight?" Nicole was not surprised at the question, she thought it was something that was probably floating around her subconscious as well. "No, no he didn't. He was there the whole time Jake" Jake couldn't say anything at that moment, he instead let out an annoyed grunt.

There was silence then and Nicole was frightened by it. "Jake..." She said nervously. "What is it?" Jake sighed. "Then I'm wrong, Eric was right, it was one big coincidence. If it wasn't your uncle tonight, who am I to say it was him the other night." There was a child like fear in Jake's voice. Jake began to silently play some things over in his head. "Maybe I was on to something with the slasher thing, but if that's the case that means there's someone else in town." Nicole didn't know what to say and suddenly a thought struck her. "Oh my God." Jake was shaky himself and stopped dead in his tracks and swallowed his throat at the sound of Nicole's voice. "What is it?" He asked quickly. "When we were finishing up at the hall, I went outside to throw away some of the garbage, I saw a car coming around the bend. I waited to see it because I thought maybe it was you coming back. It was an old black sports car and there was something so eerie about it. I didn't

make out the driver's face too good but he was an older guy. Fifties maybe. I
don't know if it was intuition or what but I just got a bad feeling about the
guy, the hairs stood up on the back of my neck." Jake looked into the phone
with a somber glare. "Did you get a license plate number?" Nicole nodded
her head as if Jake was sitting in front of her. "No, I didn't think to....but   the
license plate was weird, out of state, maybe Pennsylvania or New Hampshire
or something."

New Hampshire, it all hit Jake then, how about that for a coincidence.
Jake had been on the right trail when his own stupidity and assumptions had
gotten him into researching the slasher. What he didn't know was that he was
following the wrong guy. Somewhere in town there was another man from
New Hampshire, that man was the Bloomingdale slasher. "That could be the
guy Nicole." Jake said cautiously, so not to scare her. "What are we going to
do?" "We'll have to go down to the police station tomorrow and let them
know." Nicole nodded in understanding and then as she stared at her clock
that read one thirty am, she realized something that was very unsettling. She
spoke it as the words came to her mind. "It's Christmas Eve." Jake felt
disgusted with the realization that it was. "Get some sleep." Jake said sternly.
He didn't say a thing more and simply hung up the phone.

25

Christmas Eve

Detective Atkins had given up on his secret patrol at around one. There was nothing he saw that was out of the ordinary and with it being the night before Christmas Eve, he expected that. Atkins headed back to his room and spent the remainder of the night sitting up in bed, finishing what cigarettes he had left. During his patrol he had stopped at a convenience store and picked up another pack. With all the stress of his current agenda and the lack of alcohol, he had resorted to being a massive chain smoker overnight. He woke up at around ten on Christmas Eve and began to get dressed. As he did, he wondered if maybe the slasher was smartening up. Perhaps he would take it easy with the killing and try to take refuge in Darnite for as long as he could. But Atkins knew deep down if this was the maniac he'd come to know, he'd have to kill again, sooner or later. Atkins stepped outside his motel room and was surprised to see that the snow had stopped. Judging from the meager amount on the ground Atkins thought it must of came to a halt sometime in the middle of the night. It hadn't even been heavy last night and there was maybe three inches on the floor. So much for the storm, Atkins thought, another weather fluke for the books.

Dominick Tartamella

Detective Atkins hated cop cliches but did love donuts, so when he spotted a donut shop while driving down East Willow road he couldn't resist. He parked his car and made his way to the store and couldn't help but smile when he spotted a sign in the window that read "One HOLE of a Donut!". Clever advertising he thought to himself as he realized it was the first time he'd smiled since before meeting the stubborn Chief Haim. He went in and ordered his favored chocolate glazed donut and a large coffee to wash it down. As he waited for his order, he took a look around the small shop. Other than a man reading a newspaper in the corner and another man typing away on a laptop, the shop was empty. Atkins took his coffee and donut, paid, and sat down at a table in between the two men. He ate the donut slowly savoring it as best as he could. When he finished, he took another sip of his coffee and began to get up. As he did he noticed something that stopped him instantly. The man reading the paper was now holding it to his face, the cover page was revealed and the headline read 'TWO TEENS SLAUGHTERED ON EVE OF CHRISTMAS EVE!'. A smaller headline underneath read "Police officials say there is no official connection to previous murder yet." Detective Atkins grabbed his coffee and ran out of the donut shop before jumping into his car. His Challenger's tires slid momentarily in the snow as he pealed off.

Nicole and Jake had not gotten up as early as they planned. It was ten after ten when Jake's phone calls finally woke Nicole. For a moment, when Nicole picked up the phone and looked at the time she had thought she was late for school. She quickly remembered that Eric was dead and only wished for a moment that she did have school and that none of this had happened. Jake picked up Nicole at her house around ten thirty, before anyone else in the house was even conscious. Daniel had trouble falling asleep most of the night and even though he wanted to wake his wife and tell her the horrible news, he didn't. Daniel figured that at least one of them should sleep well. Paulie was still sleeping like a baby and had fallen asleep while watching old Honeymooner reruns. He finished the home baked pizza pie all by himself and shortly after filling up his stomach, he slipped into his temporary oblivion. Nicole slipped out of the house quietly, not to wake or alarm anyone and got into Jake's car. The two shared an affectionate hug and a kiss before Jake proceeded to drive down the street. "What are we going to do?" Nicole asked with some concern. "We'll have to tell the authorities about who you saw, he should be considered a suspect, he was in the neighborhood the time of the murder." Nicole nodded fearfully. "We should also tell them about the slasher and see what they think."

Detective Atkins arrived at the Police station within minutes of leaving the donut shop. Funny how close some stations were to donut shops, it was almost like they zoned them within a certain distance to keep the officers happy. Atkins burst through the door frantically and instantly began to scope the area for Chief Haim. As he searched around the room he noticed there were more officers on duty now, the station was starting to resemble the mad house he knew from back home. He looked forward and spotted the familiar dull-witted face of Officer Stevens. He was standing next to the elevated desk where he sat, his arm was extended with his hand open to halt. He looked more like an oversized mime trying to pretend to be stuck in a glass box than an officer trying to stop someone from going any further. "Hold it right there Detective!" Officer Steven's voice was loud but hardly threatening to Atkins. As Atkins continued with no signs of stopping, Officer Stevens reached for his nightstick, Atkins suddenly felt a loss of control over his actions. He grabbed Officer Steven's by the back of the head and pulled his blonde hair back revealing his giant adams apple. The officer screamed in pain and dropped his nightstick instantly. Atkins then twisted Steven's right arm behind his back and slammed his head off the side of the oak desk he had sat at for the last three years. The slam created an echoing thump through out the station and it was followed by an even louder thud as the large man fell to the ground.

294

After multiple glances of shock and disbelief, every officer in the station pulled their guns from their holster's and pointed them at Atkins in rapid succession. For most of the officers, it was the first time they had drawn their guns in a serious situation. The feeling was in massive contrast to their usual recreational use. "Freeze" many voices hollered the words and Atkins threw his hands over his head quickly to avoid any unnecessary bullet wounds. Atkins stared at his fellow law enforcement members with a cold gaze, nothing in it showed he was afraid. Suddenly Chief Haim appeared from out of the threshold of his office. He had a grimace on his face, to Atkins the look could've meant a million things. "Detective Atkins." The Chief said softly. The room was so tense and quiet at that moment that it could've been mistaken for a shout. "Chief." Atkins spoke calmly and couldn't stop the grin that formed on his face. The rest of the officers weren't sure if they should shoot the man or shake his hand, they all had the same looks of bewilderment as they looked back at their chief. "Put your guns down." The chief said in an enforcing tone. The officers looked back at their chief again with even more confusion, but slowly did as they were told. Officer Steven's was laying on the floor holding his nose, which was now leaking blood extravagantly. "And someone call a doctor here for Stevens." The chief spoke sympathetically and then pointed to Atkins. "Me and you are going for a ride."

By the time Jake and Nicole pulled up to the police station, the chief and their "suspect" for the murders were long gone. Jake and Nicole walked into the police station confidently but still nervous. The officers in the station were back to work and there was almost no sign that there had been any sort of disturbance within the last twenty minutes. "A lot of cops here for Christmas Eve, huh?" Michelle said curiously. "Let's not forget, there were three murders within a week." Jake said in a somber tone and Michelle nodded in agreement. As they came up to the elevated desk, Nicole and Jake were both a bit taken back when the officer seated moved the magazine from his face and revealed his abnormal looking face. Sure this officer named Stevens was probably no movie star on an average day, but today he seemed a little worse than average. His nose was inflamed and both nostrils were stuffed with two pieces of crumpled up toilet paper. There was blood around the rim of his nostrils and on his upper lip. His eyes were teary and there were thick black half moon's forming underneath each one. "Can I help you?" Officer Steven's said while trying to forget about his broken nose.

Neither Nicole or Jake answered right away as they were still both consumed with the way the officer looked. Jake snapped out of it and spoke after about ten seconds. "Hi, we'd like to see the police chief" Officer Stevens

rolled his eyes and sighed. "Is he expecting you?" Jake shook his head before
he spoke. "No but it is important that we speak with h..." Officer Stevens cut
Jake off before he continued. "I'm sure it is. He just stepped out, you could
try coming back later." Officer Stevens spoke in an insensitive tone. "Could
we wait for him here?" Jake tried to sound less annoyed than he was. "I
suppose you can." Officer Stevens said before going back to his magazine
and ignoring the teens. Jake shook his head in disbelief and he and Nicole
walked over to some chairs that were by the entrance. As they did Jake spoke
under his breath. "What an asshole." "That's probably why he looks like
that." Michelle added and Officer Stevens stared at the two while trying to
make out their words.

At around the same time, Chief Haim and Detective Atkins had just
pulled up to the Bernard household in the chief's patrol car. The front lawn of
the house was wrapped in police tape and there was an eeriness to the estate
that made it look haunted. Chief Haim parked the car and he and Atkins
headed in. The chief spoke as they climbed under the police tape. "The
family is staying with relatives in New York, so we got the house to
ourselves for the investigation. These people have a little girl too, she would
have been at the house last night when the horror occurred. Luckily for her
she had a sleep over at a friend's house." Atkins shook his head as he

listened, Chief Haim opened the front door and the two men were immediately greeted with the smell of dry blood in the air. Atkins looked forward and saw the white chalk out at the bottom of the staircase, it was in a twisted, abnormal position. There was still some blood around the floor and walls, though most of it had been taken in for any possible link to the killer. "We didn't go through everything yet, shit if the scene was any fresher, the bodies would have still been here." Detective Atkins searched around with a disgusted look on his face, this was a haunted house indeed, Halloween on Christmas, he thought to himself. "So what happened?" "Well let's head up the stairs to the boy's bedroom and we'll start there." Chief Haim tried to avoid stepping in any blood he could, as he made his way up the steps with Atkins following closely behind him.

The two men came to the bedroom and walked in, the bed sheets were stripped along with the pillows and the blankets. "We brought the sheets and such in for testing, see if maybe we can find a print or something." Detective Atkins grimaced at the chief's words. "You don't know the Slasher, do you?" "No I don't...But you do, that's why we're here." Detective Atkins nodded as Haim continued "So the guy came in, there's no signs of much of a struggle other than the actual suffocation. He must have snuck up on the kid or something, caught him by surprise." "What's the kid's name?" "Eric, Eric

298

Bernard. So he came in and from the looks of it, he smothered the kid with the pillow first." Chief Haim began walking to the hallway, Atkins followed him. "He chased the girl to the hall, smashed her head here and threw her down here." Chief Haim pointed down to the dark stains of blood at the bottom of the staircase. Detective Atkins lit up a cigarette. "This fit the agenda of your guy?" Chief Haim asked hoping it somehow didn't. "It does I suppose, he doesn't have much of a set style though." Chief Haim stared at the Detective for a moment before speaking. "Well I'm sure that it's no coincidence. I'm sorry I didn't take your word for it earlier. After our meeting, before you came back, I gave your department back home a call to find out what was what. The guy I spoke to there was very helpful, Brodie I think his name was. He said you were the best cop he knew." Detective Atkin's couldn't help but smirk. "Now I know you have had some serious shit happen to you and you are entitled to fly off the hinge, but if you want to sit back and take it easy, we'll take the composite, we'll do what we have to do and we'll catch the fucker. When we get his face out there to everybody, he'll pop up, you can count on that." Detective Atkins flicked away his half finished cigarette. "I appreciate that Chief, but when he pops up, I want to be right there on his ass." Chief Haim nodded somberly. "That's what I thought."

299

26

The Calm

Daniel and Michelle woke up around eleven thirty from their drunken, coma like slumber. Daniel didn't beat around   the bush by holding back the horrid news and told Michelle the second he saw she was awake. She was shocked by the news and couldn't seem to say anything. Michelle burst into tears at once and as she tried to regain her composure, she remembered what she had done last night and sobbed even harder. Daniel held her then and her tears soaked the shoulder of his shirt. After Michelle had finally stopped, she tried to call Becky but got no answer, she shook her head sorrowfully. Moments later Daniel and Michelle headed downstairs to fix themselves some kind of breakfast/brunch. Michelle was beginning to feel some denial now and if it wasn't quite hitting her then, it certainly did when Daniel turned on the TV. The story was on every local news station and had been since it broke at six am that morning. Almost every reporter covering the story started off by saying something incorporating the fact that it was Christmas Eve. Creative little tag lines like, "Horror on the Holiday" and the particularly cold hearted "Murder under the Christmas tree." To Daniel and Michelle every time they said something about it being Christmas Eve, it

made them feel like the world was backwards. It did not feel like Christmas
Eve now, it felt more like Halloween on acid. As one of the news reporters
began to go into grave detail on what had happened to Eric and Rachel,
Daniel shut the TV.

Paulie popped into the kitchen not five seconds later, Daniel and
Michelle both gasped and jittered at his unexpected greeting. "Good
Morning." Paulie looked confused by their reaction but quickly remembered
what he did last night and why they were so jumpy. "Sorry guys, I know
everybody's a little shaken up." Daniel closed his eyes and sighed. "No easy
way to take it, we knew that kid since he was a baby." Daniel said matter of
factly. Paulie sat down at the table with Michelle and she immediately got
up. She turned her back to him and began making a pot of coffee, while
trying not to make it too obvious that she was trying to get away from him.
Paulie glanced quickly at her and then turned back towards his brother. "Yea
it's crazy, but it is Christmas and you gotta' make the best of it, even with this
tragedy." Paulie said sternly and Daniel nodded. "Should we go get breakfast
at the diner maybe?" Daniel asked. Paulie shrugged his shoulders and
Michelle turned to her husband. "I don't know, the diner will probably be
really busy this morning. We're better off staying in. I could make pancakes
and eggs." Michelle normally wouldn't have been too anxious to make a

301

continental breakfast after a night of drinking, but since they were having the food catered for dinner, she almost felt obligated. Last year Michelle had spent all of the eve of Christmas Eve and the day itself preparing an elaborate meal. By the time the Lawsons had sat down for dinner, she was exhausted. This year Daniel suggested she give herself a break and Michelle happily concurred.

"That'll do for me honey." Daniel said as he gave Michelle a loving and consoling peck on the cheek. Paulie stared with a smirk that showed a hint of jealousy. "Mmmmm I could go for a nice short stack." Paulie said innocently and Michelle proceeded to prepare the food. "Why don't you go wake Nicole, Daniel?" Michelle asked. Daniel nodded and left the kitchen. Paulie stared at Michelle while she looked through the cabinets in front of her. She could feel the hole Paulie was burning through her back, but tried to ignore it. "How did you sleep?" Paulie asked in a provocative manner. Michelle hesitated to answer the question for a moment but did anyway. "Ok." Michelle kept doing what she was doing and didn't look at him. Paulie got up slowly and came behind her, he put his hands on her arms and began to rub them up and down. Michelle closed her eyes and felt chills run up her body and goose-skin form. She felt sick with herself for enabling him to do this. Before Michelle could say a word to stop him, she heard rapid foot steps coming down from above.

Paulie backed off and opened the fridge with hopes to look casual, Michelle sighed and continued her cooking. Daniel burst into the kitchen with a frantic look on his face. "I don't now where Nicole is!" He tried his best to speak calmly but didn't, Michelle turned around toward her husband instantly. "What do you mean?" "She's not in her room or anywhere upstairs."

Daniel picked up the phone and began to dial his daughter's cell phone number. Michelle and Paulie stared silently at him as he waited for an answer. After another moment Daniel hung up the phone. "She's not answering!" Michelle was speechless, with the murders fresh on her mind, she too had began to fear the worst. Paulie walked over to his brother. "Maybe she's with her boyfriend, I'm sure they're fine." Paulie said with a strange kind of certainty. Daniel turned to his wife. "Do you have Jake's number?" Michelle was about to tell her husband "no" when the sound of the front door opening crept into the kitchen. A second later Nicole walked through the doorway. Daniel could feel a weight lift off his shoulders, but still felt shaken. "Good morning." Nicole said dully "Where were you?" Daniel said sternly. "I was with Jake, I wanted to see how he was doing." Both Michelle and Daniel looked satisfied by the answer. Michelle turned to her daughter, "Did you eat?" Nicole shook her head. "I'm making pancakes and eggs." Michelle said with a gentle smile. "How are you doing honey?"

303

Daniel asked his daughter. "I'm alright, I guess." "And Jake, How is he? I know him and Eric were close." "He's seems ok but he doesn't usually show his feelings too much, so who knows."

Moments later, Nicole took a seat at the table next to her uncle. Daniel sat as well and Michelle brought over the finished eggs before continuing to make the pancakes. There was a moment of silence between everyone while Michelle finished up on the stove. The only sound was that of the pancakes cooking. When Michelle finished, she filled a tall stack up on a plate and walked them over to the table, where she took a seat. Daniel was the first to dig in and Paulie quickly followed, Michelle and Nicole gave into their appetites shortly after. "It's just so horrible, you know...Who would do something like that and why?" Michelle said while she reached across the table for the maple syrup. Daniel and Paulie shook their heads simultaneously, each of them hoping the subject of the conversation would change. Daniel felt that double homicide and eggs wouldn't mix well and Paulie had his own reasons. "I think I saw him." Nicole said suddenly. Michelle, Daniel and Paulie all turned to her with the same look of confusion. "What?" Daniel spoke before his brother and wife could. Nicole let out a sigh to prepare herself for what she was about to say. "I wasn't going to say anything but last night when I went outside to throw out the garbage at the hall; I saw this old black sports car driving down the road slowly. The guy was so creepy and there was just something about him and his car, it made me feel wrong." "What time was it?" Michelle asked.

Nicole shook her head. "I don't know maybe twelve thirty, it was right before we left. Anyway Jake and I went over to the police station this morning to talk to the chief of police. The man's license plate was from New Hampshire and Jake did some research and found that there is this wanted serial killer out there. He thinks he might have migrated here to start killing some place knew. "My god." Michelle spoke in a distressed tone. Daniel turned to his brother. "Paulie have you ever heard of a serial killer in Mesapeena?" Paulie shook his head. "No not that I know of but then again I'm not an avid news watcher." He grinned and let out a small somewhat nervous chuckle. Nicole thought about mentioning that Jake had done this research based upon thinking Paulie was the killer but decided not to. "So what happened at the police station?" Paulie asked curiously. "Well the chief was out on a call, so we waited a little and then Jake just ended up leaving his number with another officer. He told him it was very important that the chief got back to him and said it was a life and death matter." Paulie nodded, relief filled his bones. He didn't know why, but Jake had stopped thinking he was the killer. He pondered for a moment at the possible reason and finally

305

assumed that his quickness last night had worked out to his benefit. Nicole and Jake hadn't noticed he had even left when he went to kill Eric and his fuck friend. As far as they knew, he was at that party all night and that meant he could have never committed the murders.

"Where is Jake now?" Daniel asked. "He had to go home and get ready, he's going to his aunt's house on the other side of town for dinner." "Well maybe that's better off. I don't feel safe with you guys being out there while this psychopath's running around." Nicole nodded silently in agreement. "Now it is Christmas and we're gonna' make the best of it." Daniel finished. "I just hope they catch him soon, I feel so scared." Nicole added with a frown. "Don't be scared there's nowhere as safe than in the company of family." Daniel said sternly. Paulie grinned at the irony of his brother's words. Michelle got up from the table and turned the TV back on, she saw that the chubby weather man was now on and sighed in relief. She thought that the murders would be the only thing on TV all day. Michelle sat back down and they all continued to eat their breakfast while the weather man started his forecast. "Now everyone's probably asking, what happened with this big old scary storm that was supposed to hit us? Was that modest amount of snowfall all of it? Well folks we're not quite out of this yet. It seems that last night's snowfall was merely a preview of what's to come.

There are gonna' be storm clouds forming around Darnite by two or let's say three o'clock and you know what that means? That's right a white Christmas! The snow is going to continue into the early morning hours of Christmas day and it should come to a halt at around nine or ten tomorrow. So get where you need to get and enjoy the festivities of the holiday but be wary of the heavy snowfall coming in. Back to you Ernie." The weatherman gave one more great smile before being cut away. "I don't think anyone will be running around tonight, not even that psychopath." Michelle quipped.

Detective Atkins and Chief Haim headed back into the station at ten after twelve. "We'll talk about this in my office." The chief said as they headed pass the other officers, the same officers who earlier, had seen Atkins assault one of their own without getting so much as a slap on the wrist. They watched their chief and the detective walk towards the office. Some stared with looks of concern, others with curiosity and a select few with envy. Officer Stevens was one of the latter. He stared at his chief and attacker with a red rage that felt like popping, instead he took a deep breath and spoke. "Chief, a couple of kids stopped here looking for you, they said it was important, left a number." Officer Stevens held out the number which was written on a piece of crumply paper, Chief Haim grabbed the paper and stared at it for a moment. "What isn't important these days?" Chief Haim said in an annoyed tone. "He said it was life and death stuff." "Really? Well I guess we'll have to give him a call then." The chief said a bit sarcastically. He placed the piece of paper into his pocket and continued to walk to his office. As Atkins walked passed Stevens, he felt the large man staring at him, he turned his head toward him to see the damage he had done. A broken nose and two black eyes to boot, Detective Atkins couldn't help but grin at his handy work. This made Officer Stevens red rage show on his face and if he had been a cartoon character, smoke would have surely come out of his ears. Neither man said a thing and the detective continued to follow the chief.

The two men walked into the office and the chief signaled Atkins to close the door behind him, he did. "Have a seat Detective." Chief Haim said in a welcoming tone and Atkins sat. "But please don't smoke in here, it's not very ventilated." Detective Atkins grinned sinisterly. "So what's the plan Chief?" "Well we're gonna' have to get that composite you have copied. I'll have some of my men start posting it around town." Atkins nodded. "Thing is Chief, it's Christmas Eve, there's not going to be too many people around town to see them. You'll get a few people here and there who are heading to the stores for last minute shopping or even some soda and ice, but it won't get us the exposure we want. At least not today." Chief Haim stared in Atkins' direction with a slight look of distress. "You're right." "What's a local news station here?" Atkins asked. "The most popular, channel one." Chief Haim said. "How about I get the composite, we print them up and have your men start putting them out there anyway. Then you and I contact channel one and tell them what's what. We'll tell them that we need to make an announcement on the air. We could do it around five, that's the time that most people will be sitting down for dinner. I'm sure everyone in town will either be watching TV or will at least have one on in the vicinity. We'll go on, say what we need to say and show the composite. Then we'll tell the station to keep rebroadcasting the composite. Somebody had to see this guy, he'll turn up." Chief Haim nodded. "It sounds good Atkins, but what if these people are watching Frosty The Snowman instead of the news?" "Then we'll tell them to notify all their sister stations, maybe we could even cut in on the others, the president does it whenever he wants."

Chief Haim smirked at the detective's remark and Atkins did as well. "So I'll go grab the composite at my room and we could get started." Atkins stood up and headed for the door. "Ok, I'll see what was so life and death about this." Chief Haim said as he held up Jake's number. Atkins nodded and then was gone. Chief Haim sighed and fixed himself in his chair before dialing the number into the telephone. The phone began to ring and Chief Haim waited patiently as it did. Jake was in the middle of getting dressed to

309

leave for his aunt's house when he heard his phone ring, he stopped what he was doing and ran to it. Chief Haim heard the young voice on the other line speak. "Hello." "Is this Jake Vanucci?" "Yes." Jake spoke rather cautiously. "This is Chief Haim from the Darnite police department returning your call." "How are you Chief?" Jake said nervously and Chief Haim cut to the point immediately. "I'm good, listen I'm curious to what kind of life and death situation you happen to be in." "Well I'm not in any immediate danger, not that I know of at least. It's just about the murders." "What about them?" "Well I have an idea of who the killer is..." Chief suddenly seemed much more interested in the conversation. "Go on." "Well it's nobody I know personally although I did have thoughts it was my girlfriend's uncle at one point." Jake accompanied that with a nervous laugh and Chief Haim was not amused. "Anyway I did some research a few days ago and there seems to be a serial killer in New Hampshire. Now I don't know why he's here but I think he might be hiding out or something..." Chief Haim smiled to himself as Jake continued.

"Now I'm not positive but last night at around the same time the murders had reportedly happened, my girlfriend saw a man in a car with New Hampshire plates." The smile on Chief Haim's face turned to a somber expression. "What is the make of the car and what are the numbers?" Chief

310

Haim now had a pen out and was ready to write the information on the same piece of paper as Jake's number. "Well I don't know the make or model or even the numbers. She said it was an old black sports car, that's all." Chief Haim jotted down the minimal details. "Now she really didn't get a good look at his face, but..." Chief Haim interrupted Jake before he could finish. "Now listen Jake, I appreciate the information and anything will help. We already have a major lead on the murders and it just might be the serial killer from Mesapeena you are talking about. What we also have is a composite sketch of the man that we're going to stat posting around town." Jake didn't have any idea what to say, so he just kept listening. "Now at around five o'clock we're going to have a special news bulletin, where another detective and I will announce our findings and show the composite, so tell everyone you know too look out for that, ok?" "Sure." Jake said. "In the meantime Jake the only thing I ask is that you, your family and your girlfriend enjoy your holiday. Try not to worry yourself with the idea and know that it's in our hands and we'll have it under control soon. Do you think you can manage that?" Jake sighed. "I guess I could try." Chief Haim smiled. "Good kid, that's what I like to hear, now if you need to say anything else feel free to call but like I said don't make yourself crazy." "Ok Chief Haim, thank you." The two hung up.

After Jake hung up the phone, he continued to get ready for his aunt's.

311

He threw on an olive green sweater that his aunt had bought him the year before (His mother had suggested he wear it) and began to gel his hair back, when a knocking came at the door. "Come in." Mrs. Vanucci walked in and couldn't help but smile at her son. "You look so handsome, I told you that was a nice color." Jake forced a smirk. "Yea I guess so." He finished up his hair and walked over to where his mother was. "How are you doing Jake?" Mrs Vanucci asked. "I'm ok." Jake's words were almost emotionless. "Listen I know it's not easy and if you need to talk, I'm here." Jake cut her off with some attitude. "I'm fine." Mrs. Vanucci stared at her son with a helpless look. Jake sighed and softened up his tone. "I am mom, I promise." Mrs. Vanucci smiled, her son was strong. She kissed him on the cheek and headed out of the room. "I'll be waiting downstairs with your father and brother when you're ready." Jake nodded. "Ok, I'll be down in a minute." Mrs. Vanucci left the room and Jake finished getting himself together.

Jake suddenly felt the urge to cry but fought it and called Nicole instead. Nicole was at the supermarket with her mother, they had taken a ride there to get some last minute dinner supplies. A list that consisted of soft drinks, eggnog and rum. "Hey babe, how are you?" Nicole asked. Jake was getting a little sick of everyone asking that but chose not to lash out. "I'm alright, I talked to the chief. He said they have a suspect and that it could possibly be the guy from New Hampshire." "Really?" Jake took a glace at himself in the mirror. "Yea, he also said there was going to be a broadcast at around five that was going to show a sketch composite. You haven't seen any composites around town, have you?" Jake asked. "No, why?" "They said they were going to put some up, but make sure you watch the broadcast, make sure everyone in your house does, maybe somebody has seen him." "I will." Nicole said firmly. "I'm going to leave for my aunt's now, I'll give you a call later." Jake added. "I love you." Jake hesitated before replying. "I love you too." The two hung up. Jake couldn't help but realize that in all this madness, the couple had become closer. Telling Nicole the truth about his lies had only made them stronger. The thought crossed his mind that when this was all over, the worst would be behind them.

27

The Storm

By mid afternoon, the real snow had finally began to fall and was coming down rather heavily. Regardless of this, Detective Atkins and Chief Haim were fully focused into their plans. The chief had contacted channel one and told them the situation. The man in charge, president of the station Peter Cobes was reluctant to have two cops go on TV and announce a serial killer on the loose, but quickly realized he had no choice in the matter. Instead of arguing, Mr. Cobes humbly obliged and even said that with the storm getting worse, more people would probably be watching the news at the time of their announcement. Haim agreed and Mr. Cobes added that they could come down at around four forty to start getting ready for the broadcast. The town's hall of records building was directly across the street from the news station headquarters and Mr. Cobes suggested that be the backdrop of the announcement. Chief Haim responded by saying he didn't give a damn if it was filmed in a back alley, as long as it went on when they wanted it to. Mr. Cobes laughed unenthusiastically and told the chief he'd see him soon. Meanwhile, Detective Atkins was getting frustrated at the copy machine in the station. It was almost as old as him and had been on the fritz all afternoon. Finally when it started to work, it would print ten copies and then restart. The restarting process would take six full minutes. After a while he began to wonder what would happen if he put a bullet in it, perhaps it would work better, Atkins thought. Finally he called a few officers over and gave them each a copy of the composite. "Each one of you find a copy machine around this town that actually works and make as many as you can before the fucking thing jams." The officers reluctantly nodded and went on their separate ways.

The annoyed and envious stares that Atkins had been getting all day had stopped on the account of an announcement Chief Haim had made. He had told all the officers including Stevens, that until further notice Detective Atkins was second in command and that whatever he wanted, he would get. The first order of business Atkins took was sending the bruised and beaten officer Stevens home. Detective Atkins felt slightly regretful at what he had done earlier and knew taking orders from him was the last thing Stevens would want to do. So he took pity on him and sent him on his way to enjoy the holiday. The remaining officers were ordered to try and call each resident they could in Darnite and announce that there would be a special report at five on channel one regarding the three murders. The officers fought their anger at Detective Atkins and at the fact that they were all stuck working on

Christmas Eve and did their jobs accordingly.

The Lawson's household telephone rang at a quarter after four, while Nicole and Michelle were setting the table and awaiting the food catering delivery. Michelle ran to answer the phone. "Hello." She said to the unknown caller. Nicole paid her mother's conversation no mind and continued to set the table. Meanwhile in the guest room, Paulie finished getting ready for what would be his first social Christmas Eve dinner in what felt like forever. In the few months after Paulie had gotten out of prison, before he took his new found hobby to the streets, he had spent his holidays the same way, alone. In preparation of the last Christmas season he stocked up on lots of food and beer so he could shelter himself far away from civilization. He felt the less he saw of decorations and festivities, the better. He spent the eve and day eating and drinking his old self away, the old self that at one time had partially enjoyed all of the holiday nonsense. Though Paulie was trying to ignore the festivities, he couldn't help but indulge a little. He had some eggnog and even watched holiday classics like "It's A Wonderful Life." Not so much because he enjoyed them, but because he was fascinated by his new found perspective on them. When you've killed as much as Paulie had, things changed. Emotions you used to have fade away and certain things that used to trigger those emotions brought on different, more appropriate feelings.

316

Obvious thoughts along the lines of "This movie is nothing like real life" and deeper thoughts like "If Jimmy Stewart was still alive, I'd kill him right now."

Though he would have liked nothing more than to be back at his place examining his feelings over "March Of The Wooden Soldiers" (and some spiked eggnog). He couldn't help but feel the urge to remind himself just what it was like on the other side, the side of normality. Paulie slid into a dark pair of beige khakis he had ironed an hour earlier and slipped into an old but clean looking pair of brown loafers he had brought from Mesapeena. He looked around his bag amongst the minimal shirts he had brought and saw nothing in the wrinkled cluster that caught his eye. Suddenly when he felt he had no choice but to ask Daniel for one, right before the anger began to brew, he remembered the fixed sweater. Paulie threw on a white undershirt and headed for his car. He stepped outside without anyone else realizing and walked through the front door. It was freezing out but from the looks of Paulie you wouldn't know that, as he didn't so much as shiver. The ground was covered in white now and the sky was equally as blinding. Paulie shielded his eyes with his arm as a heavy gust of wind blew the thick snow flakes into his face. The wind whistled and moaned and Paulie had instantly regretted coming outside in just a t-shirt. He shuffled through the snow

rapidly with a soft crunching sound following him. Paulie grabbed the bag
with the sweater out of his back seat and jogged back into the house.

Paulie's face was wet from the snow when he got back into the house.
He wiped it quickly and felt his body shiver as it adjusted back to the warmth
of the house. Paulie pulled the cold sweater out of the bag and could
immediately smell the laundry detergent. He unfolded it and pulled it over
his head, when it was on, he brushed a few pieces of lint off of it and pushed
his hair back into neat order. Paulie took a quick look at himself in a nearby
mirror, before proceeding to go to the rest of the family. Michelle, Nicole
and Daniel were talking in the living room when Paulie walked in. "That
snow outside is really coming down, we could have a blizzard on our hands."
Paulie said drearily. All three faces turned up to him to acknowledge what he
had said before getting back into their own conversation. "I hope everyone
manages to get a look at it." Daniel said to Michelle. "Well that's why they
called. Did you hear anything on when Eric's funeral is going to be?"
Michelle asked her husband and he simply shook his head. "Boy am I
starved, I can't wait for this food to get here." Paulie added and Daniel broke
his grimace with a light smile "I hear you." Nicole and Daniel's minds were
way to consumed to even notice the sweater Paulie was wearing. Michelle on
the other hand had noticed it instantly, when she did she casually made her

318

way back to the kitchen without a word. "What were you guys just talking about?" Paulie asked genuinely curious. "Turns out, the cops have a suspect for the murders." Daniel said. "They think he's from New Hampshire after all." Nicole added. Paulie began to feel a tingle begin in his stomach. "Really?" Daniel nodded. "Yep, they say that they have a sketch composite made up from where he's from. The cops are calling everyone in town and telling them to tune into the channel one news at around five for a special report and a shot of the composite. Michelle just got off the phone with them."

At that moment Paulie felt his skin tighten, it was the first time since that day in prison, when he was cornered by the men in the library. The men who threatened him with a knife, the men who if not for otherwise, would have taken his manhood and then maybe his life. It was the first time since that day, that sort of "rebirth", that Paulie felt panic. The good old human quality that Paulie had thought he'd given up, had just crept back into his spine. Just as those prisoners had once closed in on him, he felt the world begin to do the same. Everything was about to come down on him and there was nothing he could do about it. Though prison had made him who he was today, the last thing he wanted to do was return to those enclosed torture grounds. He immediately thought of fleeing but knew there could be check

points set up on every corner by now, random stops with his handsome face
in each of the awaiting officer's hands. Paulie then thought of the inevitable.
If he wasted more time waiting here, the news broadcast would show his face
and he would surely have to act then. If he was still here at the moment of the
unveiling, the only option he'd have left, would be to kill his way out.
Anyway Paulie thought about it, killing seemed unavoidable. So be it, he
thought, if it came to that, he'd have to do what was necessary.

Back at the police station, Detective Atkins and Chief Haim were
finishing up and getting ready to head down to the news building, to make
their announcement to the people of Darnite. Outside the chief's office,
several officers hanging out by a lone window began talking amongst
themselves and starting a slight commotion. Chief Haim's door was wide
open and he spotted more officers heading over to the window in a childish
scurry. The chief sighed in annoyance and headed over to the window.
"Alright girls, what's the big idea? Santa Clause and his eight reindeer
outside or what?" The chief's words were playful but anger could be heard in
them as well. One of the officers turned around with a large mocking smirk
on his face. "Actually Chief, it's frosty the snowman." As Chief Haim got
closer he could see what the officer's pun was about. Outside the snow was
falling vigorously and seemed to have come from out of nowhere. The light

320

dust that had been left on the floor from the previous night's flurries was growing rapidly and soon there would be almost a foot out there. "Holy shit, it's really coming down." The chief said aloud, although he would have preferred keeping it to himself. A young rookie cop with a badge that read Martinson turned around towards his superior. "I'm dreaming of a white Christmas!" He sang with a big stupid grin on his face. "Alright, I think you guys have seen enough snow for one year." The chief said as he began to push the officer's back towards their stations. They split apart like kids heading back into school after recess and there were even a few let down "Oh's" and sighs of disappointment as they did.

A moment later, Detective Atkins walked over to the window. "There's our storm." He said with a grin. Chief Haim rubbed each side of his temples as the two continued to look out the window. "As if this man hunt wasn't already hard enough." chief added. Detective Atkins looked up at a clock that hung on the wall. "No time to worry about the weather, we gotta' get going." Chief Haim nodded with agreement and headed back to his office to grab his coat. When he came back out, Detective Atkins was back in his trench coat waiting by the empty desk where Officer Stevens had been earlier. The chief turned towards the officers. "Now listen up, we're heading down to channel one. I want you to keep making those phone calls, if no one answers, leave a message. If you get in touch with them after the broadcast, tell them to keep their TV's locked on the channel and wait for an encore of the report." The officers abided and the detective and the chief headed out. Looking out the window may have prepared them for how much snow was out there but nothing prepared them for how windy it was. As they opened the door to leave the station, the wind whistled rapidly into the building. Both men gave each other a look of intrigue and proceeded outside. They could feel their bodies shift from the blow of the chilly wind as they headed to the parking lot. "Fucking wind...you riding with me?" The chief spoke in distress. Detective Atkins shook his head. "I'll follow you, just in case something comes up." Chief Haim nodded is agreement. As he got behind his wheel, Chief Haim didn't take any particular notice to the detective's car, which was now partially covered in snow. Even if he did, it wouldn't have mattered, by then he had forgotten all about Jake's mentioning of the car.

In the Lawson house, Nicole, Daniel and Paulie sat in the living room watching an airing of the classic film "Miracle on 34th Street." Paulie knew the film well and knew that it would be over in about a half hour. Next, the news would start and then shortly after that, a rough sketch of his face would be on this screen, along with the hundreds of screens in town. Though the composite wasn't perfect, it was good enough to know it was Paulie, beard or not. He'd have to kill them all, well maybe not all of them. Maybe he could spare Michelle, for her he felt something that was actually worth keeping alive. Maybe she'd go with him, yea sure he thought to himself sarcastically. Kill her family and then ask her to flee with you, that would work. As Paulie continued to wonder about how the walls were closing in, Michelle was searching out the window frantically looking for the delivery man. She could barely see pass the white that had taken over the town and felt her head begin to hurt from the frustration. Suddenly just as Michelle walked away from the window, the door bell rang, she looked outside and saw the van that read Conti Catering. She sighed in relief and headed towards the door. Paulie heard the front door open and thought for a moment that the police had surely found him, they'd burst in now and if he tried to run, they'd blow his brains all over the Christmas tree. "I guess the foods here." Daniel said as he rose from the couch. The words halted Paulie's rapid imagination and he felt a slight relief. As he noticed the clock above the fire place which now read four forty, he couldn't help but wonder what position he'd be in an hour from now.

28

Fate vs Luck

Chief Haim pulled up to the channel one building with Detective Atkins trailing behind. Both men had been driving cautiously and the five minute ride had taken them ten minutes. The snow coming down was thicker now and when Atkins stepped out of his car, he could feel the wind had gained some more momentum as well. Atkins parked in the building's parking lot and walked over to Haim, the chief had stopped his car in front of the building. The driver's side door was open but the chief was still sitting in the car talking to someone on his radio. As Detective Atkins walked over he could hear the officer on the other line, the static from the radio hid his nervousness. "Chief, this weather is killing us. I don't know if we should even bother with the rest of the composites until the snow stops." The chief closed his eyes in frustration. "How many did you get up so far?" "We got up about twenty, but in this weather they might get ruined." The chief let out an angry sigh and shot a look to Detective Atkins, who was now standing at the driver's side. The detective shrugged his shoulders, not sure of what to do. The two men could see the snow was getting worse with every passing moment. Anyone who was on the streets now wouldn't even notice the

324

composites in the horrid weather. "Go back to the station, keep an eye open and be careful in this God damn weather." The chief's words were stern but reluctant. "Ok Chief, anything else?" The officer asked. "No, I'll call there in an hour or so and let you guy's know if there's anything else to be done." Chief Haim clicked his radio off and got out of his car. He and Detective Atkins made their way towards the channel one building through the friction of the snowy wonderland.

The president of the station Peter Cobes greeted them cautiously, as they entered the door with snow and wind sneaking in behind them. "Chief..." Mr. Cobes noticed Atkins and continued. "Sir. You guys are a little behind schedule..." "Detective." Atkins interrupted him with a partly annoyed tone. "Right, Detective. I was trying to call you guy's at the station, I don't know if we should shoot in front of the hall of records with the weather and all." Detective Atkins cut the man off again. "We don't care where we shoot, we just gotta' shoot." Mr. Cobes swallowed his throat in nervousness and nodded in agreement. "Of course, of course." He was a short, shady looking man. How he ever got in control of a TV station was beyond both Haim and Atkins. Mr. Cobes looked at his watch in an urgent fashion. "Ok, we've got a movie finishing now, so why don't you guys come up with what your going to say and we'll get you on there a quarter after five, five twenty, the latest.

Daniel, Michelle, Nicole and Paulie sat around the table and prepared for their holiday feast. There were three large trays of food that the caterer had brought sitting in the middle of the table. There were smaller more convenient containers all around the table, each with a different kind of side dish. Michelle couldn't have been more relieved. She didn't have to stay up cooking all night and they had more than enough food. Nicole was about to scoop some food into her plate when her mother gave her hand a gentle push. "Someone needs to say grace." She said as she turned to Daniel. "Your right honey, Paulie why don't you say grace." Paulie turned to his brother with a blank look. "Sure." He said passively. Let the murderer who fucked your wife say a prayer, Paulie thought to himself. Michelle stared at Paulie for a moment with a look that could have been disgust, before closing her eyes and putting her palms together as the rest of the table did the same. Paulie closed his eyes, crossed his fingers and began. "Dear God, thank you for blessing us with this hearty meal, and loving family. Watch over us as we assume our lives and let us have many more happy Christmases in the years that come." "Maybe you should add a prayer for the Bernards." Nicole said without opening her eyes. Before Paulie could say anything Daniel spoke. "That would be nice."

Paulie took a breath and began again. "And please bless the Bernards with the strength to get through the tragedy they have just endured." Paulie hesitated for a moment, thinking maybe he should throw in a few prayers for himself. Perhaps God could get him out of his current predicament. "Amen." He finished without another thought. Everyone opened their eyes and began to scoop some food, everyone except for Paulie. "Don't be shy Paul, dig in." Daniel said with a smile. Paulie glanced at him with a smirk and began to do just that. Although he seemed to be in the same mind frame as everyone else, he was far from it. Paulie's mind was in a frenzy and his ears were fixated on the sounds coming from the television in the living room directly behind him. As the family ate, Paulie began to believe that maybe if he was lucky, the rest of the household would forget to pay attention to the TV. Just as he found some hope in this idea, Daniel spoke. "Nicole go shut that TV in the living room and we'll turn the one in the kitchen on for the news." Nicole nodded and proceeded to the living room and Daniel got up and put on the small white television in the kitchen. Paulie stared in silence as the final sequence of "Miracle on 34th Street" played out.

Detective Atkins and Chief Haim were sitting in one of the empty offices preparing for their announcement. Chief Haim was jotting down notes to use as a guideline for what he was going to say, while Detective Atkins was on his fifth cigarette taking a load off. Ironically he was underneath a sign that read no smoking, but that didn't seem to faze him. The chief had never been on television before and part of him had felt a little anxiety coming. After another moment the chief finally put down his pen and stared at the broken scribbles. "I think that's everything. I hope I got it all." Detective Atkins reached across the table and grabbed the piece of paper. He skimmed through it with his eyes while   mumbling some incoherent words to himself in the process. After a moment of silence he nodded. "That seems to be a nice little summary of his unpleasant career." Detective Atkins put his cigarette out in a glass of ice water he had been drinking. "Anything else, you want to add in there?" Chief Haim asked. "I'll add what I need when we're on the air." Atkins spoke confidently. The chief nodded and proceeded to put the pen he had used back into his pocket, as he did, he felt a piece of paper scrunch in his finger tips.

Chief Haim immediately pulled out the piece of paper and looked at it in curiosity. The second he read the name, he immediately remembered what it was. Jake's number, the boy who had come with information about the suspect. As he continued to look at the paper, he noticed the other words written. The description of the car, the chief couldn't believe he had forgotten. Detective Atkins stared curious from his seat. "What's that?" "That kid that came to the station before, I called him back, said he thinks his girlfriend saw the killer. Said he was driving a black car." The detective sat up in interest. "What kind of car?" The chief shook his head. "They didn't know for sure, she said it was a sports car, but it was old looking." The detective immediately sat back in disappointment, Chief Haim unknowingly continued. "Girl told the kid, he was driving around real slow, creep like." Detective Atkins let out an annoyed grunt. "It was me." Haim turned to Atkins with a look of confusion. "What?" "I drive a '65 Challenger, black. I was patrolling around yesterday. With the murders in town, it's no wonder I would scare someone." "Damn it, thought we had something." The chief said with light frustration in his voice. "It makes no difference, once that sketch airs we'll have something. Probably a whole lot of something." Chief Haim nodded with a grimace. "But you should probably call that kid and let him know who I am. I don't need any one trying to protect themselves by hurting me or anything like that." The chief grinned at that and began to dial Jake's number into his phone.

Jake and his family had just settled down to eat and he was nowhere near his phone when Chief Haim called it. The chief continued to hold the phone to his ear as the robot woman picked up. "The kid's not answering, I'll leave a message. I'm sure you'll be fine." Detective Atkins stared at the Chief

with a look that seemed as if he didn't care very much. The beep sounded and
Chief Haim began. "Hi Jake this is Chief Haim from the police department. I
looked into that car and well this is kind of funny. I'm afraid your girlfriend
saw a detective, he's from Mesapeena so that would explain the out of state
plates. Ok well, enjoy your holiday and like I said keep the TV tuned to
channel one." The chief hung up the phone and just as he did, a twenty
something pretty female technical assistant came through the door. "You
guys could follow me to studio four." The detective and the chief got up and
did just that.

Along with Jake's aunt's house and most of the other houses in town,
the Lawson television showed the main titles of the channel one news at five.
The Lawsons who were still sitting at the dining room table enjoying their
Christmas meal, turned accordingly in their chairs to face the kitchen TV.
The heat may have been a little to high in the house and Paulie was wearing a
thick handmade sweater, but neither of those two factors were the reasons
why he was sweating as profusely as he was. Paulie turned his chair around
and began to watch, while his mind wandered around for a way out. The
news anchor came on the screen and immediately wished everyone a happy
holiday before diving into the juicy stuff. "The town's police department has
asked us to present a special announcement regarding the murders that have

occurred in the last few days. We urge you to keep your televisions locked, as we expect this announcement to air at five fifteen." Minor relief fell over Paulie, he had some time. Perhaps enough to run for the hills. Without another second of hesitation, Paulie excused himself from the table and casually walked towards the guest room he'd been staying in. No one at the table took any particular notice to his abrupt actions.

As the Lawsons continued to watch the news, (which was prolonging the inevitable with light hearted, holiday themed stories and events) they couldn't help but turn toward the kitchen window. The snow was heavier than ever and all that could be seen outside was white. A loud gust of wind could be heard knocking against the glass. The Lawsons all had the same look of startled amusement on their faces. "It's really bad out there." Nicole said while she continued to stare in awe. Michelle nodded "I feel bad for people that traveled, those roads are not safe to be driving on." Meanwhile in the guest room, Paulie had pulled his bag out of the closet and was throwing in whatever clothes and other junk he had. He would have to make a break, it was the only way and there was no time to do anything else.

Detective Atkins and Chief Haim stood at a makeshift podium that had been grabbed from a high school auditorium in a last resort to make

studio four look professional. A stylish young man with a television make up
kit walked up to Detective Atkins. "I'm just going to apply some touch up for
the camera's." Detective Atkins swayed out of the way and grabbed the man's
wrist. "You touch me with that and they'll be touching your body up at the
morgue. Ok?" The young man had a horrified look on his face, he
surrendered his hands up and turned towards Chief Haim. "And you?" "What
is this for?" "It's just to liven you up, if you don't, you'll look very pale, like a
corpse." Chief Haim thought for a second and then signaled the man to do his
worst. The young man smiled enthusiastically and proceeded to put some
make up on the chief's face. Atkins grimaced at both men before speaking.
"When are we on bud?" The young man quickly looked at his watch. "About
ten minutes." Detective Atkins took a breath and sat down in a nearby chair.

Jake and his family were halfway through dinner when he decided to
excuse himself from the table. No one objected, as they all knew what he had
been through. Jake went into the living room and sat on the couch that faced
a large window, he stared out the window at the heavy snowfall as it blew
around. He couldn't believe how bad it was outside, it looked as if he was
staring into an oversized snow globe. The TV in the living room was still
locked on channel one but they were now taking a commercial break. As
Jake continued to sit quietly he couldn't help but reflect on the last few days.

From thinking Nicole's uncle was the killer to having his best friend murdered, it was all too surreal to believe. As he glanced at the television waiting for the advertisements to come to an end, he had a strange feeling. Though he had ruled Nicole's uncle out as a murderer. There was another part of his mind, buried deep underneath the surface, that was expecting the sketch to be none other than Paulie. He felt chills as the end of the advertising drew near.

Outside the window the winds whipped around, making trees bend past their normal capacity. The snow covered everything and all was white. Not a single soul was in view and that was for the best. The trees continued to bend and sway as if they were dancing, some began to crack. Large branches fell off trees around town, crushing parked cars and leaving "little mother nature surprises" for Christmas morning. Trees weren't the only thing of that stature that were beginning to shake. The large electrical polls that sat on the corners of select streets were also shaking vigorously due to flawed construction work. At five ten, an electrical pole came down on Stratton Street. Jake's aunt's house was one of the first along with twenty other homes that continued down Stratton Street to lose electricity. That would be the first and last electrical pole that would fall in town today, but it would be far from the last of electrical mishaps. Unbeknownst to anyone in town, Darnite's main electrical grid was about to reach its maximum capacity and have its first major failure in twenty one years.

29

Trouble On The Way

When the Christmas tree lights and the television had gone off in his aunt's house, Jake's first thought was that his little brother had been trying to annoy him. When he heard the rest of the reactions coming from the dining room, he knew there was no way it was his brother's handy work. Jake got up and walked toward the dining room, he and his family exchanged the same looks of confusion. Jake's father looked out the window in the living room and noticed that no other house he could see had lights on. "Maybe it's an electrical shortage." If the family had been as close to the electrical pole as some folks on Stratton Street were, they would have heard or even seen the pole fall, ending their assumptions. Jake turned to the now black TV and immediately knew they were going to miss the special report on the killer. He hurried towards the closet where he had hung his coat and reached into the pocket where he had put his cell phone. He had to call Nicole and see if the power was out by her, if it wasn't at least she would get to see the report. When Jake looked down at his phone, he saw a voice message had been left from a number he didn't recognize. Curiosity got the best of him and he pressed a button on the dial to play back the message.

Paulie took one last look around the guest room to see if there was anything he'd forgotten. Nothing caught his eye, nothing except the clock on the wall that read five thirteen. He swallowed his throat knowing that the news broadcast would be playing any minute. He didn't bother looking around again and headed out the guest room and crept slowly to the front door. As he put his hand on the cold metal door knob, he could hear the news coming from the living room. He gave it a brief listen, before turning the knob as slowly and as quietly as he could. As if turning the knob had somehow triggered it, the lights in the house went out, as did the sound of the TV. Paulie stopped dead in his tracks as he heard the confused sounds coming from the Lawsons' mouths Paulie let go of the door knob and headed back to the guest room just as quietly as he had left it. He placed his bag onto the bed and proceeded to see what had happened. Paulie came back into the living room a moment later. "What's going on?" Daniel shook his head. "Some kind of black out, I'm gonna' see if the Mathesons are having the same problem." Daniel walked to the door and put on his jacket as he stepped outside.

The black out had hit the channel one building just about the same time it had hit the Lawsons' part of town. Detective Atkins turned to the young man who had just finished Chief Haim's TV make up. "What the hell is going on?" The young man looked as confused as the detective. "I don't know, let me go find out what the deal is." The young man headed out the room, Atkins turned to Chief Haim. "You think this is from the storm?" Chief Haim nodded in agreement. "It's definitely possible, last time we had a black out was 'eighty nine. I was just an officer back then, Chief Manning was my boss." The Chief had a smile on his face, the kind you see when an older man speaks of his glorious high school years. A happy smile that seems to be filled with a longing to get back. "Well speaking of that boss, maybe you should call your men and see how they're doing with the electric over there, maybe it's not town wide." Atkins said. The chief nodded and began to dial the station's number into his phone, he put it to his ear and waited for an answer. After a minute, nothing, not even so much as a ring. Detective Atkins stared at the chief, waiting for something. Finally after another moment of silence, Chief Haim hung up the phone. "Oh boy." The chief said mostly to himself. "What, what is it?" "The phone lines seem to be down." "What does that mean?" "Well it most likely means it's town wide alright. Considering the phone lines are down, it could mean the power grid is out." Chief Haim said almost cautiously. "How long could something like that take to fix?" Atkins asked in a concerned tone. "Depending on the damage, best case scenario, a day or two." "Damn it." Atkins fumbled through his pocket,

337

pulled out his pack of smokes and lit one up.

Jake had listened to the message left by the chief and was now sitting on the couch thinking to himself, there was something eating at him. If the man in the old black sports car was a detective from out of state, who was the killer? Jake realized that perhaps he and Nicole had jumped to conclusions. There was nothing else to tie the mysterious man in the black car to Eric's murder other than the fact that he was in the area. Suddenly the unsettling thought of Uncle Paulie crept back into his mind. Jake remembered why he had thought it was Paulie in the first place. Paulie had been outside that house on Stapleton drive the night the man was murdered. That was obviously more solid than just seeing a man in a car drive around slowly. It began to hit Jake that perhaps the other suspect was easier to swallow. When Nicole had told him about the man she'd seen, he liked the idea, hell, he loved the idea that it didn't have to do with Paulie. When she told him that Paulie was at the party all night, a relief had come over him. Deep down Jake never wanted the killer to be Paulie. Now a terror came over Jake as he sat in the gloomy living room, which was now semi-lit by candle light.

Something Nicole had said that morning while the two of them waited at the station for the chief to come back. While they talked amongst themselves, while that doofy officer sat at his elevated desk staring at them every chance he got. Something about her mother being sick at the party. Then it came back to Jake, Nicole's mother had drank too much at the party and she had been in the bathroom with her for what she said felt like forever. Maybe Jake was too tired to grasp what she had said that morning, or maybe it was just that he wasn't looking for a reason to point his finger back at Paulie after finding someone else to blame. If the two were in the bathroom for what felt like forever, then it was possible that Paulie could have slipped away and killed both Eric and Rachel before Nicole even realized he was gone. Jake swallowed his throat as he felt an uncomfortable turn in his stomach with another thought. He had told Nicole about her uncle in the basement of the hall, he had said that Eric was the only other person that knew. Jake began to think the worst, if Paulie had somehow heard them talking, it would have been his fault Eric was murdered. He couldn't think anymore, he had to call Nicole. He had to tell her the man she saw was a cop and that Paulie must have somehow heard them and must have somehow slipped away to kill. He pulled his phone from his pocket and began to dial and then nothing. In the two minute window he had checked his voice mail, the phone lines had still been up. Now they were as silent as could be. Jake turned to the window where the snow fall was still coming down in the masses.

Daniel had returned from the neighbor's house with news that the black out was in fact widespread and wasn't just in their house. Daniel also said that the Mathesons' phones weren't getting dial tones. Michelle picked up the house phone and put it to her ear, immediately realizing their phone was no different. "What are we going to do?" Nicole asked with some concern. "Nothing we can do honey, just hang tight and make the best of it." Daniel spoke passively. Paulie couldn't have been more ecstatic. Not only was there a black out in this house, but in the whole God damn town. Fuck the one on thirty fourth street, this was a real Christmas miracle. He let out an obvious sigh of relief and scooped himself some spiked eggnog which sat in a large glass bowl. "Well we better make the best of it." Paulie said and Daniel smirked. "I hear you there." Daniel walked over and did the same. They clinked their glasses together like old chums and began to drink. Daniel turned to Michelle. "You want some Michelle?" Knowing the monumental mistake she had made the night earlier, she declined. Daniel shot a look to his daughter. "You want some, it is Christmas." Nicole smiled. "No I'm fine." Daniel shrugged his shoulders and took a sip of his eggnog.

After waiting for a follow up from the young man for almost ten minutes, Detective Atkins and Chief Haim decided to head to the source.

They burst into Peter Cobes's office (without knocking) moments later. Mr. Cobes, who was pouring himself a nice holiday glass of Scotch jumped back as the door swung open. "Jesus, don't you know how to knock." The room was dim but not completely dark, as Mr. Cobes had a battery powered lamp on his desk. "What's the deal?" Atkins said without even contemplating the question asked. "The deal is, the whole town's power is out, I can't help you guys anymore." Mr. Cobes said, as he drank his glass of scotch. "You don't have a back up power supply? I mean this is a TV station for Christ's sake." Chief Haim added with disbelief. "This station has been around for sixty years. Unfortunately so has the building. An emergency power supply was never installed. We didn't have one when the last big black out occurred and we don't now." Detective Atkins sighed angrily to himself. "I'm sorry gentlemen, if we're able to get the power back up we'll give you a..." Before he could finish, the detective and chief were gone. Atkins and Haim made their way out the front door and came to the chief's squad car. The snow was still coming down heavily. "What now Detective?" Atkins looked around and spotted his car, which from a distance seemed to be buried in snow. "Well I'm going to have to ride with you, my car's shit in the snow." The chief nodded. "Probably better off." Haim added. The two men got into the patrol car and Chief Haim pulled away from the channel one building.

341

Dominick Tartamella

Jake was jittering in his seat as he continued to make unsuccessful calls to Nicole. He needed to do something, after what happened to Eric and Rachel, he wasn't about to lose someone else he cared for. He took a look out the window and saw that the snow was still coming down just as bad as it was earlier. He could hear his mother and father talking to his aunt and uncle and figured his brother was busy playing his gameboy. He decided this was probably his only chance to slip away. He opened the closet and this time went into his father's coat, he pulled out his mini van keys, put his coat on and took one last careful glance towards the dining room before slipping out the front door. Jake's father said something funny and everyone started laughing hysterically, it was enough sound to cover the light slam of the front door. Before the last of the giggles were finished, Jake was already gone.

30

Shelter From The Storm

Jake was now driving slowly down Cavern Avenue. The windshield wipers were going back and forth hastily, but this didn't help in the least. It seemed as if he was driving through a cloud, with the occasional street sign or street light adding some contrast into the mix. Once again Jake started thinking about Eric, how Paulie had smothered him with a pillow, probably without any regret. Fear filled his mind and then the thought of Nicole being hurt came again. Before he knew it, all he felt was anger, he looked at the time and noticed it was almost six o' clock. He sighed and pressed his foot up against the gas with a bit more force. The speed limit on the streets on a normal day was thirty. On a snowy day like this, (if you were crazy enough to be on the road that is) you should be going no more than fifteen while proceeding with extreme caution. At five fifty six Jake began going fifty five miles an hour. Two minutes after six, Jake lost control of the minivan. The same car he learned to drive in, the car he had passed his road test with and the car he had been in during each and every family outing. That same minivan was now spinning rapidly out of control. Jake could barely realize what was happening, but one thing did cross his mind and that was insignificant relief that he had clicked his seat belt in. This relief didn't last long however, as he spotted thick tree branch (which had been blown out of place from the winds) hanging directly on his probable point of impact. Before he could even begin to panic, the car had come to a crashing stop and the branch crashed through the windshield and poked it's way through Jake's abdomen with disturbing precision.

Detective Atkins and Chief Haim were slowly but surely making their way back to the station. Detective Atkins stared out the passenger side window with a look of distress. "This fucking snow, he could be anywhere you know." The chief nodded as he continued down the snowy road with caution. Suddenly the chief's radio began to speak through static. "Chief Haim.. Chief Haim.. Come in Chief!" Detective Atkins stared at the Chief with a look of concern as he picked up the radio. "This is Chief Haim, what's the problem?" "Chief this is Officer Izzo, I got a bit of a situation here. I was patrolling around Hester place and turned down Cavern Avenue. There's a kid here, crashed his car." There was a deep pause. "He's in really bad shape." Chief Haim closed his eyes in horror. "Jesus, Izzo have you called an ambulance for him?" "I have sir they're on their way. But thing is Chief... he's asking for you." The chief and the detective exchanged a look of confusion. "Me, what does he want with me?" "He said you and him spoke, said to tell you it's Jake. He said he knows who the killer is, guy named Paulie." The detective and the chief exchanged another look, this time a more stern one. "You're on Cavern now?" "Yes Sir." "Ok, Stay there, keep the kid going, tell him I'm coming, I'm five minutes away." "Ok Chief." Chief Haim clicked his radio off, made a U-turn and reluctantly sped his vehicle up.

The drunken escapade didn't last long for Daniel. After five glasses of eggnog, he crawled onto the couch and fell asleep almost immediately. Nicole headed upstairs to the sanctuary of her room, she tried to call Jake a few times but still the phone didn't even ring. As she laid in bed reading the new issue of Cosmopolitan, she dozed into a dreamless sleep. Paulie sat in the living room next to his unconscious brother, he finished what was his eighth glass of eggnog and headed into the kitchen for perhaps one more. Michelle was washing some dishes in the candle lit kitchen when Paulie came in holding his empty glass. Paulie wiped his mouth and realized that the two were alone. "Anymore eggnog?" Paulie said. "No, you guys finished it all." Michelle spoke without turning around to face him. Paulie smirked. "Did we, I didn't even realize." He slowly walked over to the sink and reached his glass over Michelle's shoulder and placed it into the sink. Michelle tried to pretend that he wasn't there and hoped he would just walk away. Unfortunately her hopes didn't come true, as Paulie began to massage her shoulders sensually.

Michelle could smell the alcohol and felt the urge to cry but fought it off. Instead of doing anything, she stood there frozen unsure of what to do. Paulie's face reached around and he kissed her on the cheek softly. He began to slide his hands down to her hips and once he did she felt an uncomfortable chill run down her spine. The tears had now began to fall out of her eyes, Paulie was clueless to this as he continued. She took a deep breath which Paulie probably thought was a good thing, but his suspicions were proved false within the same moment. Michelle turned around rapidly and pushed Paulie's hands away in the process. She wiped her eyes, grabbed a lit candle off the counter and walked out of the kitchen quickly without looking back. Michelle walked into the laundry room and closed the door behind her, she put her hands over her eyes and began to cry to herself. Not even forty seconds later, Paulie opened the door and came in, he also closed the door behind leaving nothing but the glow of the candle between them.

Michelle wiped the tears away. "You have to get out!" She spoke with anger but was sure to keep her voice low. "What are you talking about?" Paulie asked. "This isn't right now and it wasn't right then, I should have never did this. You should have never came back." Michelle exclaimed sternly "Don't talk like that, we'll figure out a way..." Michelle cut off Paulie before he could finish. "There is no way, this is a mistake. You were a mistake. I don't have the feelings I once had for you. I love Daniel, I want to be with my husband." Paulie stared emotionless as a sudden burst of anger took over his body, he could barely think. Part of him began to feel like there was something left to say "I..." Michelle interrupted what ever was supposed to come out, as tears poured down her face. "No Paulie, no more. I want you out, I want you out of my life!" The anger surged through Paulie's body like an electrical charge and he felt himself jump toward her. Both of his hands wrapped around her throat and he began to squeeze her thin neck with every force in his body. She tried to scream but nothing came out, nothing but the light breath of air leaving her throat. Michelle began to squirm and knocked down the lone candle, it smashed on the floor but stayed lit. Tears continued to leak out of her now pink eyes. Paulie grunted in anger as he squeezed tighter and tighter and Michelle's face turned a faint purple. She began to make choking noises and at the same instant, her eyes rolled back in her head. By the time Paulie felt her neck crunch she was already dead.

Paulie let go of her throat and Michelle's lifeless body fell to the ground without hesitation. He looked around the dark laundry room and felt the anger and the need still beating along with his heart. He grabbed the broken candle from the floor and headed out of room, closing the door behind him. He snuck back into the living room and saw that his brother was still asleep, snoring loudly. At this point, killing his brother wasn't even a question, the question was how would he do it. Daniel would put up more of a struggle than Michelle and he wasn't in the mood to get into a fist fight, he simply wanted him dead.

Chief Haim and Detective Atkins pulled up to the corner of Cavern Avenue, parked and jumped out in all what seemed to be the same moment. Officer Izzo stood next to the smashed up minivan and next to what was left of Jake. Chief Haim and Detective Atkins exchanged a look and nod with Officer Izzo and the young officer walked away from the minivan. When they came to the smashed car van, Haim's first impression was that the boy was dead. The thick branch was through his stomach and it looked like something out of some horror movie. Light blood was also leaking out of his mouth and nostrils. Jake was shaking uncontrollably and stuttered as he spoke. "Chiiieff, the killer, the slasher." The color left Haim's face, he knew the kid was close to being gone. Detective Atkins stood over the chief with an emotionless stare. "Who is it kid?" Chief Haim spoke in a caring tone, the kind you would speak to a little kid with. "Nicolee's uuuncle.." Detective Atkins got in front of Jake now and spoke in the same tone. "Where is he Jake? Where is he?" "Paulieee... he's staying with herr familyyy...four eighty one Lange Streeeet. Tell Nicole I'm sorry for..." before Jake could finish he was dead. Chief Haim stared for another moment in horror before Detective Atkins put his arms on him. There's nothing you could have done, we have to go now." The chief reluctantly nodded and the two men headed back into the squad car and drove on toward Lange Street.

Paulie quietly searched around the kitchen for something to kill his brother with, but found nothing quite up to par with something that could do the job quickly. Instead of continuing his search in the pantry, he decided to head to the garage with hopes of finding something more suitable than a kitchen knife. Paulie carried the fragment of lit candle into the garage and skimmed around through a few tools, one in which he thought might be useable was a hammer. Paulie disregarded it rather quickly as he knew it would take more than a lot of swings to do the deed. Suddenly something with a slight shine caught his eyes from the corner of the garage. It was mixed in with what seemed to be a pile of Christmas gifts. As he pulled it up from the pile, he realized it was just that. The shiny new axe had a big red bow on it and had a name tag that read "To Paulie" "From Daniel & Michelle" Paulie grinned sinisterly at the axe and felt irony at the fact that the axe was probably the best gift Daniel had ever gotten him. It was something, he would actually use.

Uncle Sweet Uncle   Dominick Tartamella

Paulie crept back into the house and began to tip toe towards his
brother cautiously. When he got to the living room he found his brother just
as he had expected to find him, sound asleep. Daniel had always been a
heavy sleeper and remembering this Paulie stopped the tip toeing and began
to walk casually. When he came up to his brother, he stared at him for a
moment. Wondering what he was dreaming about, or if he was dreaming at
all. Paulie looked down at the axe and realized this was going to be messy
but didn't seem to mind. Paulie lifted the axe over his shoulder, the bow and
tag still in place and took a deep breath. "Goodbye Danny boy." Paulie
swung the axe into the corner of Daniel's head and it burst open immediately.
Red sprayed onto Paulie's face and sweater but he didn't even flinch. He
cocked the axe back again and this time it landed into his shoulder spewing
out more blood. Paulie put the axe back a third time and then proceeded to
beat the axe in and out of his dead brother's body over and over again, in
rapid succession. Finally he came to a halt and sighed in relief, he looked
down at what used to be his brother and saw something that resembled a
crushed dummy that had been covered in red paint, but that was no dummy
and that wasn't paint. Daniel was dead and had been since the first fatal
swing to the head. Paulie wiped his face, walked towards the backyard door,
opened it and stepped outside for some fresh air.

The thuds of the axe sinking into her fathers bones hadn't woken Nicole up completely but they had played a part. She woke up after the fact and sat up in her bed. The first thing she tried to do was call Jake again but even if the phone had worked, she wouldn't have been able to get in touch with him now. Nicole clicked the phone off and sighed in frustration. She got up from her bed, grabbed a candle and began walking down the dark staircase. As she came to the bottom, she called for her mother. "Mom, are you down here?" She peeked into the living room and saw the silhouette of what appeared to be her father sleeping on the couch, in what she thought was a weird position. Nicole then walked into the kitchen and was surprised that her mother and uncle were nowhere to be found. "Mom, Uncle Paulie. Is anybody home?" Nicole saw the laundry room door and immediately had a hunch that her mother might be in there. She opened the door and held the candle out in front of her as she walked. "Mom?" There was no answer but Nicole could feel that she had stepped on something. She looked down and moved the candle down with her as she did. Suddenly she saw the terrifying horror that lay before her. Her mother, with open eyes laying on the floor, she had not one ounce of life left in her body.

Nicole jumped back and screamed a horrific scream that echoed throughout the house. She fumbled the candle in her hand, but didn't drop it as she ran back into the kitchen. In her chaotic state of mind, she remembered her father was still in the living room and ran in without a moment of hesitation. When she came to the couch she put her hand on what she thought was her father and began to shake him. "Daddy Wake up! Mom's dea..." She stopped dead in her tracks as she felt warm blood all over her hands and saw under the candle light that her father was now in a few separate pieces. She was immediately reminded of the time Jake had shown her some old JFK autopsy pictures on the computer and felt her stomach spin. Nicole could barely scream at that moment and simply fell back onto the floor, this time dropping the candle. It went out as it split in two. Nicole got back to her feet and immediately spotted the back door. She ran out of it and slipped in the snow, busting her nose on the covered concrete, it began to gush red. She managed to get to her feet and could see a bloody axe with a bow sitting in the middle of the snowy wasteland that was her backyard. There were also footprints in the snow that had drops of blood all around them. Nicole looked around the backyard for signs of the killer but saw no one.

Suddenly she heard footsteps in the snow coming around the side of the house. As they got closer, Nicole's heart began to race frantically. When the figure came around, Nicole immediately recognized the face in the shadows. It was the same face she had seen in the black sports car outside of the Knights of Columbus hall. And even though it was just as shadowy as it was that day, she knew it was him. Nicole screamed off the top of her lungs. "Someone help me! He's gonna' kill me!" She ran towards her back door and got back into the house, slamming and locking the door behind her. The man screamed something as she did, but she was too frightened to process it. "I'm hear to help you!" Atkins screamed but he knew she was probably well into the house by now. Nicole slipped in the living room and continued towards the stairs before coming into a pair of unknown arms. She screamed instantly but was relieved when she heard her uncle's voice in the darkness. "Are you ok?" Paulie asked gently. "Mom and dad are dead, the killers outside, don't let him kill me. Please I'm so scared!"

Tears ran down her face as she wined to her uncle. "It's ok, your Uncle Paulie's here now, I got you." As Nicole wiped her tears on her uncles sweater she noticed something that disturbed her greatly. Her uncles hands were as cold as ice, she lowered one of her hands and felt his shoe, she could feel the snow still sitting on the surface. She backed away from him immediately and grabbed a lit candle that sat on a glass table beside her and held it up to his face. Blood spatter sat on her uncles face and hands, with this realization, Nicole let out a thick gasp of horror. "Don't be scared, Uncle Paulie's gonna' help you...just like I helped your cunt of a mother!" Paulie reached for Nicole's throat and began choking her on the floor. Atkins pulled his gun from his holster and aimed it at the back doors glass frame. With a single shot, the entire door disintegrated into nothing. Atkins didn't want to risk shooting Nicole, so he put his gun back into his holster, ran into the house and tackled Paulie off of her. The two men rolled around on the floor punching and choking each other.

Paulie managed to get to his feet and Atkins did as well. Paulie then lifted Atkins up and slammed him through the glass table that sat in the living room. Atkins could feel the back of his head split in two and felt a concussion coming on. He laid on the floor in a daze and in a pile of glass, he felt dizzy and helpless. Paulie got to his feet and grabbed the fireplace poker from it's case, blood was now leaking out of his eye. Paulie heard something at the front door and looked down at the detective and then back up at the door. He cocked his poker back and focused on the door. At that moment, Chief Haim kicked in the front door and was immediately greeted with a fire place poker to the face. He fell to the ground and screamed out in agony, dropping his gun as he did. Paulie laughed loudly. "Darnite's finest! What a fucking joke!"

Paulie stared down at the wounded Chief and cocked back his fireplace poker once again. Detective Atkins began to come to his senses and saw what was about to happen, he reached down to his holster for his gun. Paulie began to swing the poker down and was stopped as a bullet from Atkins gun ripped through his knee and sent him to a wobble. Paulie dropped the poker and fell down to one knee. He screamed in agony and turned toward the detective. "Your dead!" Paulie screamed. Detective Atkins sat up slowly and pointed the gun at Paulie again. "No you!" Atkins said before firing. Paulie threw up his arms in a lousy defense and a bullet ripped through his right hand, he fell back with a thud and another awful scream. Detective Atkins got to his feet slowly and began toward his impaired enemy. Atkins stood over him for a moment staring at the slasher deep in the eyes, Paulie stared back with an even deeper gaze. Neither man showed any fear. Atkins pointed the gun at the head of the man who had ruined his life. The man who was now defenseless like a turtle on his back. The detective pulled the trigger and nothing but a click. The gun was empty, Atkins looked at it for a second. "Looks like your going to have to take me in pal, the honorable way." Paulie laughed and then coughed. "Take you in." Detective Atkins said as he stared at Paulie apathetically. "The honorable way huh? No, I think I'll treat you the same way you treated my wife and daughter. With no

355

remorse." Paulie instantly realized who this man was, the man from the television report in Mesapeena. "Detective, I didn't recognize you without the cameras." Paulie grinned and Atkins did as well and that was the last thing Paulie said.

Detective Atkins jumped on top of the man, pulled him up by the sweater and began to beat him with his now empty gun. He beat and beat and beat while the blood sprayed up into his face. He could feel every bone in Paulie's face smashing and it filled him with a thrill that he had never felt before, similar to the way Paulie had felt when he killed someone. Relief took over Atkins' body as he felt life leave Paulie's. This didn't stop him however and he continued to bash Paulie's lifeless skull in. When Chief Haim finally stopped the detective, Paulie's face was almost unrecognizable and completely different from the sketch composite the detective was now familiar with. "It's over he's dead, come on, the girl's here." The chief said as he held his own battered face. Detective Atkins dropped the gun and let out a huge sigh. Nicole was in the corner of the dark living room watching emotionless, if she felt anything at that moment it was relief.

Epilogue

After the events of that hellish Christmas Eve, Detective Atkins was held by authorities and was to be questioned on what he was doing in town. There were several articles being reported in the papers that said the Mesapeena detective could face charges in relation to a "planned" killing of serial killer Paulie J Aldo. Atkins tried to tell the authorities that he was passing through town and simply fell into what had happened. The authorities didn't believe this and tried to say that the murder of Paulie was premeditated, based upon the fact that Atkins' family was killed by the man. Detective Brodie contacted Atkins and said that he wanted to help but Atkins shut him down and said he didn't want him getting mixed in with bull shit. It wasn't until three days before New Years that Chief Haim realized what the system was trying to do to the detective and intervened. He told his superiors that Detective Atkins was in fact passing through, after taking some time off from his department. The chief claimed that he received a tip that the murders in town were possibly related to the New Hampshire killings from the unlikely source, the recently deceased Jake Vanucci.

After finding out about this possibility, the chief claimed he found and

357

contacted Atkins himself to accompany him to where the slasher was supposedly staying. Atkins selflessly obliged with the plan and accompanied the chief. The chief later said that when Paulie had subdued him with a fire poker, Atkins had bravely risked his life to stop the slasher from finishing the job. Atkins concurred with these statements and added that the slasher was too dangerous to be left alive and that he only did what he was taught to do in the situation, which was to eliminate the threat. Chief Haim swore to his words and by New Years day, Detective Atkins was free to go back to New Hampshire. The only condition was that when he got home, he would have to take an anger management course specifically designed for officers who had to kill in the line of duty and see a department psychiatrist. Both of these would last a mandatory of three months and after that it was on Atkins if he wanted to continue them.

Nicole Lawson didn't have much to say after the whole ordeal. Both of her parents were dead and her uncle was the guy who did it. The local newspapers ate up the story and seemed to post something new regarding her every other day. On Christmas day, when Chief Haim finally found the guts to tell Nicole about Jake she didn't cry. She couldn't, she had nothing left inside, she simply nodded and laid back on the stiffened hospital mattress. There was a pain inside of her, a dark burning pain and she wondered if that pain would ever leave her. On the advice of several doctors and psychologists who had interacted with Nicole after the horrible events of Christmas, Nicole went away to a mental rehabilitation center. She did not fight it and she did not throw a shit fit or anything like that, she merely accepted it. Nicole had no grandparents and had no guardian or relative that she wanted to stay with. So she took the road less traveled, she took the road to help.

Detective Atkins attended his therapy and anger management sessions as he promised he would. Detective Brodie got together with him during these three months as much as he could and the two rarely talked about what had happened in Darnite. They instead talked about sports, movies, women and the same old bull shit that two guys would talk about any day of the week. Through it all there was something different about Atkins, Brodie thought. Something calmer. He had surely stopped drinking and he was almost completely off the cigarettes, knocking his old habit down to three a day. But there was something else, something Brodie couldn't believe, Atkins was happier. The man had finally closed an ugly chapter in his life and the weight was lifted. Looking at his partner, Brodie thought for the first time that maybe life does go on, Atkins thought the same.

On a rainy day in April, Detective Atkins walked into the Mesapeena police station. He hadn't been there since before he left for Darnite and when he walked in, a strange feeling hit him. Atkins was soaked with rain and the first thing Detective Brodie noticed about him was that he was wearing Jeans and a sweat shirt. Brodie couldn't help but smile. He hadn't seen the detective dressed like that in at least five years, casual and comfortable. Then as Detective Atkins locked eyes with him, Brodie suddenly knew what he was there for. Atkins knocked lightly on the chief's door and walked in. He spent seven minutes in there or maybe ten the most but when he came out he was smiling, Jesus, Brodie thought, he looked ten years younger. Atkins waved into the chief's office and said the words that turned Brodie's suspicion into a fact. "I'll see ya around Chief. Take care." Detective Atkins turned back to look at Brodie and smirked before proceeding to his desk.

When Atkins arrived at Brodie's desk, the detective was standing with a painful smirk on his face. "I think I know what this is." Brodie said drearily. Atkins threw his hands up. "What can I say partner, sometimes you just gotta' walk away." Brodie nodded. "I guess everybody's gotta' retire sometime." "And start some place new." Atkins added with a smirk and Brodie's expression saddened. "Where?" Atkins shook his head "I don't know yet, maybe somewhere a bit warmer, I never wanna' come into contact with

360

snow again." Brodie smiled. "When are you leaving?" "I have to take care of a few things but right after that." "Is this?" Brodie asked cautiously. "Goodbye." Atkins said before nodding. "I'm afraid it is, you're one of the few things I have to take care of." Brodie smiled and extended his hand. "Don't be a stranger when you get where you're going." Atkins grabbed Detective Brodie's hand and shook it firmly. "I won't." Atkins walked away and was gone a moment later.

Twelve hours later Atkins pulled up to his destination and stared at a sign that he never thought he'd see again. "The Great Palace" The building looked just as shitty as it did when he had last seen it and that was no surprise. Atkins pulled his car up to the side, got out and stopped at another smaller sign that read "Good Beer and Good Food." He smiled and walked into the sports bar. Atkins looked around quickly trying to spot that familiar pony tail and just as he thought that his luck was up, he did. There she sat, alone at the bar with a beer at her side and a cigarette in her mouth, he walked up to her. "Cheryl." Atkins called and Cheryl turned around immediately. "Well look who decided to come back."

Two weeks later Cheryl and Atkins found a nice cottage in Orlando, Florida. They flew out to see it and made an offer. Three days after, as they woke in Cheryl's apartment at ten in the morning they got the call that it was theirs. The two celebrated with a a bottle of champagne and a breakfast at the local diner spot "Hot Grits!" After their filling breakfast Atkins headed into a nearby store to get a pack of his newly found cigarette substitution, Trident gum. As the cashier rang up the pack of gum Atkins eyes spotted a local Newspaper that read "After five months tragedy stricken teenager finally ready to start a new life. Atkins picked up the newspaper in a daze and instantly recognized the teenager in the accompanying photograph was Nicole Lawson. He smiled and added the newspaper to his purchase.

That afternoon Atkins and Cheryl found themselves waiting in the lobby of the Woodrow Mental Rehabilitation clinic. Minutes later Atkins sat on a chair across from Nicole Lawson. Nicole thanked Atkins for coming and found herself thanking him for what he had done for her on that terrible day. Atkins couldn't help but notice how bright the girl looked and how much color was in her face. She seemed a little nervous of course but was hardly anything like he thought she would be. Atkins told her that he read that she was doing well and was looking to start her life over. He started off by telling her how he had had a wife and a daughter around her age and that Paulie was responsible for taking their lives. Atkins then asked what Nicole planned on doing after she left here. Nicole said that she wasn't sure and that she would

362

likely finish up what ever high schooling she had left before going about any college plans. She also added, sadly,that she didn't know where she would live. If she moved back into Darnite, she knew her past would follow her and she didn't like the idea of students looking at her different. This is when Atkins cut in. He told her about Orlando and Cheryl and instead of beating around the bush more simply said "I want you to come with us."

Nicole didn't know what to say. "That's a long ways away." She said finally with a smile. "That's exactly what you want, isn't it?" Nicole sat silent thinking to herself. "You get out of here whenever you say you're ready, and we'll leave as soon as you are. I know you don't know me well but you can trust me. I know you know that much." Nicole nodded but was still thinking. "If you don't like it you could leave, no one will keep you, I just think it's the best thing for you. The best thing for all of us." Nicole looked up at the man who saved her life with sad eyes. "Why do you want to help me?" Nicole asked. "Because I know how you must feel. Because I've been through it all already, hell I'm still going through it. And I know it doesn't get any easier unless you got somebody there to help you through. I want to be there for you Nicole and you could be there for me." "I wont force you, you can make your own..." "Ok." Nicole interrupted and Atkins stared at her in silence. "I'll come." She added and Atkins smiled gratefully.

Acknowledgements

Thank you to all my family and friends who believed in me while I was writing this, Without your support I would have never been able to finish this story. Special Thanks to Krystie for being the first to read about Uncle Paulie and for having a close eye on my sloppy writing. I hope whoever reads this book enjoys it and I hope that number will exceed my wildest dreams. More stories to come...

About The Author

Dominick Tartamella lives with his family in Staten Island, New York. When not writing, he makes his living as a baker.

Uncle Sweet Uncle   Dominick Tartamella